The

GOLEM

Also translated by Joachim Neugroschel

No Star Too Beautiful: A Treasury of Yiddish Stories

Radiant Days, Haunted Nights:
Great Tales from the Treasury of Yiddish Folk Literature

Great Tales of Jewish Fantasy and the Occult

The Dybbuk and the Yiddish Imagination:
A Haunted Reader

The

GOLEM

Edited and translated by

JOACHIM NEUGROSCHEL

W. W. Norton & Company

New York   London

For information about permission to reproduce selections from this book, write to Permissions, W. W. Norton & Company, Inc., 500 Fifth Avenue, New York, NY 10110

Manufacturing by The Haddon Craftsmen, Inc.
Book design by Rhea Braunstein
Production manager: Amanda Morrison

Library of Congress Cataloging-in-Publication Data

The Golem / edited and translated by Joachim Neugroschel. — 1st ed.
    p. cm.
  ISBN-13: 978-0-393-05088-2 (hardcover)
  ISBN-10: 0-393-05088-2 (hardcover)
  1. Golem—Literary collections. 2. Jews—Czech Republic—Prague—Folklore.
  3. Judah Loew ben Bezalel, ca. 1525-1609—Legends.
  4. Yiddish literature—Translations into English.
  I. Neugroschel, Joachim.
  PN6071.G6G65 2006
  378.761'84—dc22

                                    2006017195

W. W. Norton & Company, Inc.
500 Fifth Avenue, New York, N.Y. 10110
www.wwnorton.com

W. W. Norton & Company Ltd.
Castle House, 75/76 Wells Street, London W1T 3QT

1 2 3 4 5 6 7 8 9 0

I am grateful to Edna Nahshon for her help

And to Yeshaye Metal (YIVO)

And Aaron Rubinstein (National Yiddish Book Center)

And Rabbi Dov Taylor

And especially to Amy Cherry for her fabulous editing.

Contents

Introduction   ix

Yudl Rosenberg
The Golem or The Miraculous Deeds of Rabbi Leyb   1

S. Bastomski
Yiddish Folktales and Legends of Old Prague (*Selections*)   77

Dovid Frishman
The Golem   87

H. Leivick
The Golem   111

Introduction

Golems, robots, androids, humanoids, automatons—these partly over-lapping terms identify human creations, which, especially golems, can be helpful or monstrous. These man-made human-looking creatures, which recur throughout Jewish culture and ultimately in the modern era, present a split personality.

The golem first appeared in Psalm 139:15: "Your eyes saw my unformed substance," the word root for *substance* being *GLM* in Hebrew. After that, the idea of a golem was reiterated in the Baby-lonian Talmud (the compilation of rabbinical commentaries set down in the fifth and sixth centuries C.E.) and by later mystical writ-ers. However, it was only a long time after that that the golem, a fig-ure produced from dust and clay, became magical.

In the sixteenth century, two rabbinical masters were linked more closely to the creation of a golem: Eliahu Ba'al Shem of Chelm (d. 1583) and Reb Judah Leyb ben Bezalel, the Maharal of Prague (d. 1609). (*MaHaRaL* is a Hebrew acronym meaning "Our Teacher Rabbi Leyb.") Legends about golems now flourished, as did debates about the status of a golem, his functions within the Jewish community, his overall lack of intelligence, and his inability to speak. As in Franz Kafka's ape ("A Report to an Academy"), the power to speak is what makes us human.

The rabbi, being on good terms with Emperor Rudolf, was vir-tually a go-between, linking imperial culture with Jewish culture. As a result, he became an admired hero in both Czech and Jewish folklore. Christian notions of the golem's destructive force permeated the German Romantics of the nineteenth century: Achim von Arnim, Jacob Grimm, and Heinrich Heine (a Jewish convert to Christianity).

Meanwhile, starting in the mid-nineteenth century, Rabbi Leyb, the traditional maker of the golem, moved into first place in the folk stories. He began to play a far greater role, with stories proliferating about him without any golems present. This is true of both folk arts and modern media. In Yudl Rosenberg's Yiddish/Hebrew chapbook (1909), Rabbi Leyb's travails are the main subject, that is, the resistance to anti-Semitism and genocide and especially to the blood libel. The blood libel was the persistent belief among certain gentiles that Jews killed Christians in order to have blood for baking their matzoth. It served to justify the anti-Jewish riots and killings around Passover. Of course, there were countless pogroms in Russia during the late nineteenth and early twentieth centuries not necessarily instigated by the blood libel. In the 1920s, S. Bastomski, an anthropologist, issued two chapbooks of Yiddish legends about old Prague. While both collections contain a number of stories about Rabbi Leyb, the golem is mentioned only once in one of them and not at all in the other.

Still, the figure of the golem remains resonant. According to the legends, Rabbi Leyb fashioned a golem to fight the enemies of the Jews. His work, however, was twofold. The golem was both a domestic servant and a resistance fighter. And the domestic side could be humorous. Once, for instance, the rabbi, hurrying to the synagogue, forgot to switch off the golem, who then kept hauling bucket after bucket of water, causing a flood. Using this motif, Goethe wrote a narrative poem, "The Sorcerer's Apprentice," which was set to music by Paul Dukas. This story was so famous that Walt Disney imitated it in his cartoon *The*

Sorcerer's Apprentice (in *Fantasia* starring Mickey Mouse in a rather grim retelling).

It was the twentieth century that witnessed an explosion of the golem material in both the high arts, such as operas, and in the low arts, such as movies. There were several screen versions, including Julien Duvivier's French-Czech coproduction *Le Golem*. One of the sound tracks of this sumptuous version offered an intriguing experiment: The gentile characters speak French; the Jewish characters speak Yiddish.

The most famous treatment of the golem legend is H. Leivick's verse drama *The Golem, Dramatic Poem in Eight Scenes*. After spending several years in Siberia for political crimes, Leivick arrived in New York in 1913. His entire life, hence his corpus, was marked by violence, from the pogroms of the late nineteenth to the early twentieth centuries, from World War I to the carnage of the interwar period, the persecutions of Jews in Russia and Germany, World War II, and the postwar failure to deal with so much horror. Even though Leivick wrote *The Golem* and all his subsequent work, mainly plays and verse, in the United States, his oeuvre was largely European in its sensibilities, particularly in its adherence to modern expressionism.

Leivick's play was first published in 1921 and first performed in 1923—in Hebrew, not Yiddish—by the Habimah Theater in Moscow. The first Yiddish production occurred in 1931 in New York. After that, the play was translated into several languages and staged in a variety of places despite the problems of mounting what is virtually a chamber drama made more difficult by its blank verse. While blank verse had been thriving for centuries in European literature, it came into Yiddish only as a modern device to ensure a Yiddish poet's acceptance as a "modern European."

In my translation, I have stuck to mostly blank verse, making it more pungent by infusing it with a great deal of alliteration. This alliteration echoes the Anglo-Saxon stave rhyme, a meter that evokes the mystical origins of poetry and, in this case, is meant to draw us back to primal magic.

I wish there were more Yiddish stories about the golem. These few will have to suffice. I could have used a very brief sketch by Y. L. Peretz, but his text is too flimsy. The golem requires strength.

New York, 2005

The

GOLEM

Yudl Rosenberg (1860–1935)

The Golem or The
Miraculous Deeds of Rabbi Leyb

1904

Rosenberg brought out this folk book in 1904, passing it off as a translation from Hebrew. He actually wrote it himself in Yiddish, following the tradition of Hasidic hagiography, i.e., stories extolling the wondrous souls and feats of the great rabbis. Drawing on the old legend of a man-made humanoid, which tradition had somehow connected with the historical Rabbi Leyb of Prague, Rosenberg produced a journalistic chronicle of adventures, primitive, schematic, and tendentious. His work was a striking example of Jewish pulp writing for the masses, yet it inspired Leivick's renowned drama The Golem and was adapted into an episodic German novel by Chaim Bloch (who never gave Rosenberg credit for supplying him with the contents of his book). The blood libels against Jews, accusing them of murdering Christians and using their blood to bake unleavened bread for Passover, were growing in force during the 1890s. It was this disastrous trend that Rosenberg attacked in his vita of Rabbi Leyb. The one-dimensional pop quality of the writings, the intrusive journalese and the linear optimism contrast with more complex literary treatments of Jewish life in Eastern Europe. Conventions of pop and pulp tend to be ignored by historians and

literati, yet such grade-B gothic is always widely disseminated and cap-
tures a much-greater segment of the popular imagination.

A historical description of the great wonders that the world-renowned
gaon Rabbi Leyb of Prague performed with the golem, which he created to
wage war against the blood libel.

Foreword

Dear readers! I am giving you a rare and precious treasure, which has hitherto been lying in a library for three hundred years. Jews have always been thinking and talking about this treasure, and some have actually come to deny the whole story, claiming that Rabbi Leyb never even created a golem, that the tale is fictitious, a mere legend. The truth of the matter is that when the great scholar Rabbi Ezekiel Landau was rabbi of Prague, he did, in fact, confirm that the golem was lying in the attic of the old great synagogue. The day he found the golem, the rabbi fasted and took his ablutions in the ritual bath. Then, donning his prayer shawl and phylacteries, he asked ten of his disciples to recite psalms for him in the synagogue, whereupon he mounted to the attic of the old great synagogue.

The rabbi lingered there for a long while and then returned in great terror, saying that from now on he would reinforce Rabbi Leyb's decree forbidding anyone from venturing to go up there. Thus it once again became known that the story of the golem is true.

But then several decades went by, and a number of people once again began saying that the story is merely a legend. This happens, of course, because there is no precise account of the whole story in Jewish history books. But truth will out. And thus you see that the entire story was written down by Rabbi Leyb's son-in-law, that great scholar Rabbi Isaac (a true priest, blessed be the memory of that righteous man). However, the manuscript lay hidden for so many years in the great library of Mainz, where so many of Rabbi Leyb's writings can be found. I had to devote a great deal of labor and expense to having this manuscript printed. And thus I hope that every intelligent person will be grateful to me for my work, and I am certain that every Jew will soon give this valuable treasure a place on his bookshelf.

—YUDL ROSENBERG

The Birth of Rabbi Leyb

Rabbi Leyb was born in the city of Worms, Germany, in the year 5273 [or, according to the Christian calendar, 1513], on Passover evening during the seder. His father, Rabbi Bezalel (blessed be the memory of that righteous man), was a great saint.

Right after Leyb's birth, the Jews were saved from a great disaster. Christians were persecuting the Jews, claiming they used Christian blood to bake unleavened bread at Passover. And almost no Passover went by in the lands of Moravia, Bohemia, Hungary, and Spain without someone's smuggling a dead Christian into the home of a wealthy Jew so that he might be falsely accused of committing murder for religious reasons. And thus, for that Passover in Worms, a blood libel had been prepared.

A Christian put a dead Christian child into a sack and set out with it, intending to plant the corpse in Rabbi Bezalel's home by throwing it through a basement window. Bezalel's wife was in her seventh month. Sitting at the seder that first night of Passover, she suddenly felt sharp pangs. The others in the house began shrieking, and they dashed out to find a midwife.

At this point the Christian with the dead child in his sack wasn't very far away, and when he saw all those people running toward him with a yell, he was convinced they were after him, and he turned and took to his heels. He was so terrified that he dashed toward the Jewish district, past a police station. The police, seeing a man race by with a sack over his shoulders and a crowd running after him, thought he was a thief being chased. They stopped him and found the dead child in the sack. The Christian had to confess and name the people who had hired him to plant the corpse for a blood libel.

Rabbi Leyb was born that very same moment, and his father prophesied: "This child will comfort us and ward off the blood libel." And he was named Judah Leyb, the Lion, for he would be like a lion who does not permit his cubs to be mangled.

The Wondrous Story of Rabbi Leyb's Betrothal

In the city of Worms there lived a Jew named Shmelke Reich, a wealthy and honored man from a fine family. When Rabbi Leyb was fifteen, Shmelke Reich took him as a prospective bridegroom for his daughter Pearl. The future father-in-law sent the youth to the yeshiva of Przemysl to study with a gaon.

But then Shmelke Reich lost all his wealth and was unable to provide a wedding or a dowry for his daughter.

When Rabbi Leyb turned eighteen, Shmelke Reich wrote him a letter saying that the sages maintain eighteen is the right time to marry but since he, Shmelke Reich, had lost all his wealth and was in no position to keep his promises, he didn't want to hold the youth to the engagement contract. They were willing to release him so that he might find another bride, whomever he wished.

Rabbi Leyb sent back the following answer to his future father-in-law. He, for his part, was unwilling to break his word; he agreed to wait and look forward to help from the Lord God. So if Shmelke Reich wanted to cancel the contract, he ought first to find another match for his daughter, and then he, Leyb, would know that he was released from his vows.

But unfortunately, Shmelke Reich's business affairs didn't get any better; on the contrary, he kept losing more and more money.

When Pearl, the bride-to-be, saw how unhappy her father was because of his livelihood, she rented a tiny store and began selling bread and baked goods to help out her parents. She thus burdened her youth for some ten years. And Leyb also didn't want any other betrothal, and he spent those ten years studying the Torah and the Talmud, day and night. And because he was a bachelor, people nicknamed him Leyb the Bachelor. And the gaon used to say that a verse from the Psalms had come true with Leyb the Bachelor. For Leyb's soul had a spark of King David.

Now this is what happened with the betrothal:

At that time the country was in a state of war, and many soldiers were passing through Worms. These soldiers were followed by a cavalryman, and as he rode past the little store where Pearl was sitting with her baked goods, he speared a large loaf of bread on the end of his pike and then seized the bread.

The young girl ran out to the horseman and tearfully begged him not to rob her, for she was just a poor girl trying to support her old, weak parents. The horseman shouted: "How can I help you? I don't have any money to pay you, but I'm famished for a piece of bread. There's only one thing I can do for you. Since I'm sitting on a double saddle, I'll give you one saddle for the bread."

And with these words, he pulled out a saddle from under himself, hurled it into the store, and then galloped away.

When the young bride went to have a look at the saddle, she was terribly frightened at seeing that the saddle had burst on one side and several golden ducats had fallen out. She realized that the saddle was stuffed with ducats. With a great effort she managed to lift up the saddle and hide it. Then she hurried to tell the news to her parents. Her father wrote to Rabbi Leyb, asking him to come for the wedding, for the Good Lord had miraculously helped him, and now he was in a position to pay for everything and to give the wedding in great honor, as was fitting for him.

Rabbi Leyb used to tell this story whenever he had to settle a case concerning a prospective father-in-law who was unable to pay in accordance with a betrothal contract. The rabbi never liked to get involved in such cases. But if it happened that the rabbi couldn't get the two parties to agree on the marriage, he would send them to his assistant judges, so that they could settle the case in their homes but not in Rabbi Leyb's house.

Rabbi Leyb's Struggle against the Blood Libel

Rabbi Leyb moved from Posen to Prague in the year 5333 [1572, by Christian reckoning]. He was famous throughout the world for being wise and learned in all branches of knowledge and for speaking many languages. Because of this, he was very popular among gentiles too, and greatly respected by King Rudolf of Hapsburg. He was thus able to fight against the enemies of the Jews, who besmirched Jewish honor with the blood libel. He finally conquered them, and King Rudolf promised him he would permit no more blood libels against Jews in his lands.

When Rabbi Leyb first arrived in Prague, the blood libel was making life very difficult for the Jews, and much innocent Jewish blood had already been shed because of that foul accusation. Rabbi Leyb proclaimed he would struggle with all his might against the blood libel and rid the Jews forever of that dreadful lie.

Rabbi Leyb Engages in a Disputation with the Catholic Priests

Rabbi Leyb immediately wrote a petition to Jan Cardinal Sylvester, requesting that he be summoned for a disputation to prove the falsity of the blood libel against Jews. The cardinal did not wait to be asked twice. He called together three hundred great priests for the debate. The rabbi informed him that he could not possibly debate with three hundred priests at one time. He asked that the debate last for thirty days and that ten new priests every day submit their arguments and questions in writing to the cardinal. He, Rabbi Leyb, would then come to the cardinal to examine their submissions and reply to them in writing.

The cardinal agreed. At every dawn of those thirty days and in every synagogue, the Jews of Prague recited the entire Book of Psalms, and they fasted on Mondays and Thursdays, the traditional Jewish days for fasting.

The Disputation

The disputation produced so many questions about Judaism and Christianity that they filled an entire history book. The major controversy turned around the following five questions:

1. Is it true that Jews need Christian blood for Passover?
2. Are the Jews guilty of the murder of "Christ"?
3. Does Jewish law require Jews to hate Christians because it regards Christianity as idol worship?
4. Why do Jews hate a person who converts from Judaism and why do they strive to wipe him off the face of the earth?
5. Why do Jews consider themselves greater than other nations because of their Torah? After all, other nations can be even prouder of being honest and decent, since they haven't been urged to be so with a great and difficult Torah.

In reply to the first question, Rabbi Leyb quoted the Bible and the Talmud to demonstrate how strongly Jews regard blood as an unclean thing. Jews are strictly commanded to avoid blood even more lard, for the Torah calls blood an abomination.

In reply to the second question, Rabbi Leyb demonstrated: "Firstly, the only Jews guilty of the murder of Christ were the priests in league with King Herod and the Roman government, who ruled Jerusalem at that time and deeply hated Christ because they feared he wanted to liberate the Jews from the Roman yoke by means of an uprising and have himself crowned king of the Jews. But most of the Jews, particularly the Pharisees and the Essenes, who all despised the priests and Herod, refused to have any part in the judgment against Christ.

"Secondly," Rabbi Leyb went on, "any man who wishes to take over for God and accuse the Jews of murdering Christ is a true heretic and has no belief whatsoever in God. Let me tell you a parable. An emperor had only one son, and that son was condemned to death for rebelling against his father, and his father knew that the accusation was a lie. Now, they were about to carry out the sentence and execute the son before his father's very eyes, and the father only needed to say a single word to have his son set free. But the father refused to interfere and watched them kill his only beloved son gratuitously, merely for his own glory. Who, then, is more guilty of the murder? The emperor who clearly knew that the accusation was a lie or the judges who, by virtue of their discernment, felt they had to act for the emperor's glory. Certainly, everyone realizes that more than anyone else, the emperor was at fault.

"Now, let us examine the story. Christianity says that Christ was God's only beloved son. And the judges falsely accused him of rebellion against his father, the God of all the universe, and gratuitously condemned him to death, only for the glory of God. How could the Father allow them to kill his only beloved child gratuitously, before his very eyes, for his glory? Let us assume further that the Father, God, did not have the power to prevent the execution or else did not know about it. One could only conclude that this Father was not God. Thus anyone pursuing that course would have to be a complete heretic. But what else can you Christians assume except what Christianity tells you, namely, that Christ had to be killed. His death was to atone for the sin of Adam so that anyone accepting Christianity would not suffer in hell but go straight to heaven. One would therefore have to conclude that those who carried out the sentence of death on Christ did the finest of deeds for Christians, and according to the Christian viewpoint, this was certainly in fulfillment of God's decree and Christ's goodwill. So how can anyone accuse the Jews?"

As for the last three questions, Rabbi Leyb replied with an ingenious parable:

"Let us closely examine the way an emperor deals with his armed forces. An emperor has, serving under him, generals, colonels, majors, lower officers, and the rank and file. The rank and file have to obey the officers, the officers the majors, the majors the colonels, and so on, but only when the emperor is not present. When the emperor himself visits the army, then everyone, from the bottom to the top, has to show due honor to the emperor alone. And any request that a man may have must be submitted to the emperor personally. If a simple soldier directs his request to an officer before the emperor's eyes, paying tribute to the officer instead of to the emperor, he will be regarded as rebelling against the state and handed over for a court-martial.

"The same is true of the nations. According to Jewish law, we regard as pagans only those nations who do not pray to the One Creator of the universe, who worship and serve the stars and the constellations. Such nations are despised in the Talmud. But those nations who address their prayers to the One Creator of the universe cannot be counted among the pagans, and they are not discussed in the Talmud.

"And as for converts, the Talmud heaps scorn only on Jews who become pagans and no longer believe in the Sole Creator of the entire universe. But a Jew who converts to Christianity isn't even mentioned in the Talmud. However, today, Jews do despise a convert to Christianity, just like an emperor who rules in this world and passes judgment on his armies. His armies consist of different branches. There is an infantry, a cavalry, an artillery, a corps of guards, and a navy. Furthermore, in the great kingdoms, there are various kinds of soldiers who serve from the day they are born. For example, in Russia, the Cossacks or the Circassians. Now, what happens when a soldier runs away from his company and joins some other branch of the armed forces, serving the same emperor? Isn't he regarded as a criminal? Isn't he punished? And isn't this even more true of the born soldier who tears himself away from his roots, his sources, and joins another branch of the army under the same emperor? He is certainly punished even harder and despised by his brothers.

"The same is true of converts, even if they become Christians rather than idol worshipers. As a born Jew, who tears himself loose from his roots, he brings shame upon his own brethren, which is why he is hated by Jews and regarded as despicable. And any intelligent man will understand that such hatred is a natural thing, like all natural things. But this is not the same hatred and the same laws that the Talmud directs against the Jew who converts to paganism and denies the existence of the One Creator of the entire universe.

"Now, as for the question of why Jews consider themselves greater than any other nations because of their great Torah and why they say, 'Thou hast chosen us among all the nations.' There is no reason for other nations to feel resentment or envy or to attack the Jews.

"Let us assume that in an imperial residence there are two regiments of soldiers and the emperor has assigned a great task to one of those regiments, physical labor and mental labor, to keep the soldiers occupied all day long with serving their emperor. The other regiment has been given greater freedom and assigned only light tasks.

"Now, one day the two regiments began arguing. The soldiers with the greater task claimed that they were superior, that the emperor loved them more, and that they were the emperor's guard. A proof of this was that he was willing to entrust his teachings only to them and not to the other regiment. And that was why he gave the other soldiers more freedom because he did not consider them suitable for and capable of his service and his teachings.

"However, the soldiers in the regiment with greater liberty shouted that the very opposite was true: The emperor loved them more, and they were the emperor's guard. A proof of this was that the emperor was considerate of them and unwilling to overtask them, for he also regarded them as decent and orderly men. But he imposed such enormous work on the other soldiers because he realized that if they were to become better men, decent and orderly soldiers, they would have to devote their entire days to service and study. The judgment reached the minister of war, and he in turn issued an order that this judgment should not be the cause of any discord and rivalry among the soldiers. Each regiment had the right to be proud of its service and to proclaim that the emperor loved it more than the other. In fact, that would make their service more enjoyable. As for the question of which regiment was more beloved by the emperor and was considered the emperor's guard, they could only determine that later, on the basis of two pieces of evidence:

"First, they would see which soldiers the emperor would reward more generously at the end of their service. Second, when the emperor went out into the world, they would see which regiment would have the honor of escorting and surrounding him wherever he went. These soldiers would then certainly be recognized as the emperor's guard.

"Now, it is obvious how that parable applies to Jews and the other nations."

That is a summary of Rabbi Leyb's answers to the five questions. And then came twenty-five more questions, Rabbi Leyb had a fine answer for each one, and they were all set down in a special tome.

The cardinal was very pleased with the rabbi's answers to the thirty questions, and he heaped great honors upon him. But Tadeush, the renowned priest of Prague, who was a great anti-Semite, still had his heart set on disputing against Rabbi Leyb. He argued that there were still a lot of fanatics among Jews who were uneducated and thought that a Jew needed Christian blood for the unleavened bread at Passover. How, then, could Rabbi Leyb assume responsibility for all the lower classes of Jews?

Afterward the entire disputation was presented to King Rudolf. The king was very pleased with the rabbi's responses and issued an order to have Rabbi Leyb come to court.

Rabbi Leyb Is Presented at the Court of King Rudolf

In Shebat [January], at the new moon, the king sent a carriage to Rabbi Leyb, summoning him to court. The rabbi left immediately and was received there with great honor. The audience lasted a full hour, and no one knows what they spoke there. Rabbi Leyb came home in a fine mood and said:

"I've managed to destroy more than half of the blood libel, and with God's help I hope to remove this foul lie fully from the Jews."

Ten days later a royal decree was issued: In a trial concerning a blood accusation, the tribunal was not to prosecute any outside person, but only those parties whose culpability in the murder could be adduced by proper evidence.

And the king issued a second decree. The rabbi of the city was to be present at any trial concerning a blood accusation. And the tribunal's judgment was subsequently to be submitted to the king for his signature.

Jews now began living a bit more freely. But their troubles were not completely over. Whenever a Christian felt any hatred of a Jew, he could plant a dead child in his home. How could the Jew be left free if the corpse were found on his premises? But most of all, Rabbi Leyb feared the priest Tadeush, who was a terrible anti-Semite and a magician as well and who was bent on waging war against Rabbi Leyb and driving him out of Prague altogether. The rabbi told his pupils that he would not ordinarily have been so afraid of the priest. But he, the rabbi, had a spark of King David, and the priest had a spark of the Philistine in Nob, who so relentlessly persecuted King David. The rabbi decided to put all his efforts into battling against the priest, his antagonist.

How Rabbi Leyb Created the Golem

Rabbi Leyb directed a dream question to determine how to wage war against the priest, his antagonist. And the answer came out alphabetically in Hebrew: "Ah, By Clay Destroy Evil Forces, Golem, Help Israel: Justice!" The rabbi said that the ten words formed such a combination that it had the power to create a golem at any time. He then revealed the secret to me, his son-in-law, Isaac ben Sampson Ha-Cohen, and to his foremost pupil, Jacob ben Khaim-Sassoon Ha-Levi. It was the secret of what he had to do, and he told us he would need our help because I was born under the sign of fire, and the pupil, Jacob ben Khaim-Sassoon Ha-Levi, was born under the sign of water, and Rabbi Leyb himself was born under the sign of air, and the creation of the golem would require all four elements: fire, air, water, and earth. He also told us to keep the matter secret and informed us seven days ahead of time how we were to act.

In the Jewish year 5340, in the month of Adar [corresponding to February 1580 in the Christian calendar], all three of us walked out of the city early one morning until we reached the shores of the Moldau River.

There, on a clay bank, we measured out a man three cubits long, and we drew his face in the earth, and his arms and legs, the way a man lies on his back. Then all three of us stood at the feet of the reclining golem, with our faces to his face, and the rabbi commanded me to circle the golem seven times from the right side to the head, from the head to the left side, and then back to the feet, and he told me the formula to speak as I circled the golem seven times. And when I had done the rabbi's bidding, the golem turned as red as fire. Next, the rabbi commanded his pupil, Jacob Sassoon, to do the same as I had done, but he revealed different formulas to him. This time the fiery redness was extinguished, and a vapor arose from the supine figure, which had grown nails and hair. Now the rabbi walked around the golem seven times with the Torah scrolls, like the circular procession in synagogue at New Year's, and then, in conclusion, all three of us together recited the verse "And the Lord God formed man of the dust of the ground, and breathed into his nostrils the breath of life; and man became a living soul."

And now the golem opened his eyes and peered at us in amazement.

Rabbi Leyb shouted in Hebrew: "Stand on your feet!"

The golem stood up, and we dressed him in the garments that we had brought along, the clothes befitting a beadle in a rabbinical household. And at six o'clock in the morning, we started home, four men. On the way, Rabbi Leyb said to the golem: "You have to know that we created you so that you would protect the Jews from harm. Your name is Joseph, and you will be my beadle. You must do everything I command, even if it means jumping into fire or water, until you've carried out my orders precisely."

The golem was unable to speak. But he could hear very well, even from far away.

The rabbi then told us he had named the golem Joseph because he had given him the spirit of Joseph Sheday, who was half man and half demon, and who had helped the Talmudic sages in times of great trouble.

Back home the rabbi told the household, in regard to the golem, that he had met a mute pauper in the street, a great simpleton, and that he had felt sorry for him and taken him home to help out the beadles. But the rabbi strictly forbade anyone else from ever giving him any orders.

The golem always sat in a corner of the rabbi's courtroom, with his hands folded behind his head, just like a golem, who thinks about nothing at all, and so people started calling him Joseph the Golem, and a few nicknamed him Joseph the Mute.

The Golem Carries Water at Passover

Rabbi Leyb's wife, Pearl, may she rest in peace, was unable to contain herself, and on the day before Passover Eve, she broke her husband's prohibition against giving orders to the golem. She asked him to bring some water from the river and fill up the two kegs standing in a special, festive room. Joseph promptly grabbed the two buckets and hurried down to the banks. But no one watched as he poured the water into the kegs. Joseph the Golem kept bringing back more and more water until the room was flooded up to the threshold. And when the water began pouring into the other rooms through chinks and cracks, the people saw what was happening and raised such a hue and cry that the rabbi, upon hearing it, came running in terror. He now saw what was going on, and he smiled at his wife.

"Dear me! You've certainly got yourself a fine water carrier for Passover!"

Then he hurried over to the golem, took the two buckets away from him, and led him back to his place.

From then on, the rabbi's wife took care not to give the golem any orders. The whole incident gave rise to a proverb in Prague: "You know as much about watchmaking as Joseph the Golem does about carrying water."

Joseph the Golem Goes Fishing at New Year's

The kind of help that Pearl, the rabbi's wife, got from Joseph the Golem's water carrying for Passover was the kind that the rabbi got himself when he sent Joseph fishing at Rosh Hashanah [New Year's]. The incident took place several years after the golem was created.

There was a shortage of fish for Rosh Hashanah because of great winds and a cold wave. It was the morning of the day before New Year's, and there wasn't even a minnow in all Prague. Since it is a good deed to have fish on Rosh Hashanah, Rabbi Leyb was extremely upset, and so he made up his mind to order the golem to go fishing.

Rabbi Leyb told him to bring a net and then go to the river outside the town and catch fish. Since the rabbi's wife didn't have a small bag to give him, she handed him a large sack instead, for holding the fish he would catch. Joseph the Golem paid no heed to the bad weather. He grabbed the equipment and dashed over to the river to catch fish.

Meanwhile someone brought the rabbi a present, one scant fish from a village near Prague. As a result, they were less concerned about Joseph and his fishing, and they forgot all about him, because on New Year's Eve Jews are usually busy with other matters. Twilight was setting, and it was time to go to the synagogue for evening prayers. The rabbi needed Joseph for something and asked where he was. He was told that the golem hadn't returned from the river yet, and everyone assumed that he still hadn't caught anything and didn't want to come back empty-handed. But since Rabbi Leyb needed him urgently, he sent out the other beadle, Abraham-Khaim, to call him home. And in case he hadn't caught any fish and refused to come back, then Abraham-Khaim was to tell him that the rabbi said to forget about the fish and just come home right away.

Abraham-Khaim, the beadle, left for the river immediately. He arrived at the top of the riverbank and shouted down to Joseph the Golem that it was time to go home. Joseph held up the sack and pointed out that he had to net only a few more fish to fill it up. He motioned that he couldn't start back until the sack was full. Abraham-Khaim shouted down that the rabbi had ordered him to forget about the fish and just return home right away because the rabbi needed him. The golem, upon hearing these words, grabbed the sack and dumped all the fish back into the river. He slung the net and the sack over his shoulders and ran home. When Abraham-Khaim, the beadle, returned, he told them what a fine thing Joseph had done! Everyone had a good laugh and Rabbi Leyb told us in secret that he now realized the golem was good only for saving Jews from misfortune but not for helping them with good deeds.

What Rabbi Leyb Used the Golem For

Rabbi Leyb used the golem only for saving Jews from misfortune, and with his help he performed a number of miracles. Most of all, he used him to fight against the blood libel, which hung over Jews in those times and caused them great difficulties. Whenever the rabbi had to send him to a dangerous place and didn't want him to be seen, he gave him an amulet to make him invisible.

Around Passover the rabbi would have Joseph the Golem put on a disguise. He gave him Christian clothing to wear and a rope around his waist. He looked just like the Christian porters.

Rabbi Leyb told him to spend each night, wandering up and down the streets of the Jewish quarter, and if he saw anyone carrying something or transporting it in a wagon, he should hurry over and see what it was. And if he saw that it was something for bringing a blood accusation against the Jews, he was to tie up the man and the object and lug them over to the police at city hall to have the man arrested.

Rabbi Leyb's First Miracle with the Golem

There was a wealthy Jew living in Prague, a community leader named Mordecai Mayzel, who lent money on interest. A Christian butcher owed him five thousand crowns, and Mordecai Mayzel was dunning him to repay the debt.

The slaughterhouse was outside the city, and the butcher always drove the meat into town through the Jewish section. Being unable to pay back the money, he decided to bring a blood accusation against Mr. Mayzel, which would keep the moneylender so busy he would forget about the butcher. A few days before Passover one of the butcher's neighbors lost a child, and it was buried in the Christian graveyard. That same night the butcher dug up the dead child and killed a hog, taking out its innards. Next, he cut the child's throat to make it look as if the poor thing had been slaughtered, stuffed the corpse into the dead hog, and then drove to town in the middle of the night to plant it somewhere in Mordecai Mayzel's home. He was driving down the street, and just as he stopped not far from Mr. Mayzel's house, along came Joseph the Golem. He ran up to the wagon and, upon seeing what it was, he took his rope and tied the butcher and the hog to the wagon. The butcher was a strong man; he fought and struggled with the golem and tried to break loose. But Joseph wounded him several times and finally overpowered him, for the golem's strength was greater than natural force. Joseph climbed into the wagon and drove off to city hall.

Upon his arrival, a great hubbub began in the courtyard, policemen came, and other people, but meanwhile Joseph the Golem slipped out of the crowd and returned unmolested to patrol the Jewish streets.

In the courtyard of city hall they lit torches and saw before them the butcher, bloody and maimed. Upon seeking further, they found the dead child in the belly of the hog. Since it was wrapped in a Jewish prayer shawl, the butcher couldn't worm his way out; he had to confess everything he had planned to do to Mordecai Mayzel. When they asked him who had brought him here against his will, he replied that it had been a mute Christian, who was more like a devil than a human being. The butcher was locked up and sentenced to several years in prison. No one in town knew who that mute Christian could be, and the enemies of the Jews were stricken with fear.

But Tadeush, the renowned priest, knew very well who was behind it, and he began spreading a story that Rabbi Leyb was a magician. He hated the rabbi more than ever and bent his entire heart and soul on a war against Rabbi Leyb and all the Jews of Prague.

The Wondrous Tale of the Healer's Daughter

There lived in Prague a Jewish healer named Moritsy. And even though he had strayed far from Judaism, he nevertheless considered himself a Jew. The healer had a daughter, fifteen years old, who became rather licentious and allowed herself to be talked into converting to Christianity. During Passover Week she ran away from home and took refuge with Tadeush, the infamous priest, who was known far and wide as an anti-Semite. This incident was connected with another.

There also lived in Prague a Christian woman from the country who lit the fires in Jewish homes on the Sabbath, and thus she was known to all the Jews in the city. Before Passover, the servant girl had an argument with her employer and ran away that same night, so that no one knew what had become of her. Her employers did not make a big to-do about it; they assumed she had gone back to the country, but they didn't know for sure where she was from.

Tadeush, the priest, took advantage of this opportunity. He knew that Rabbi Leyb had a strange beadle, Joseph the Mute, who helped him shield the Jews from the blood libel. Now the priest was intent on capturing both of Rabbi Leyb's beadles, for it would then be easy to get his hands on the rabbi himself.

When the healer's daughter came to his closed church, he made her promise that when the cardinal asked her why she wanted to convert, she would say it was because she couldn't comprehend the ferocious customs of the Jews, who had to kill a Christian soul every Passover and use the blood to bake their unleavened bread. The priest instructed her to bear witness that prior to Passover she had personally seen both of Rabbi Leyb's beadles, one of them an old man with a gray beard, and the other a young mute with a black beard. They had come to her father at night and had given him a small flask of blood, and he had paid them well and then used the blood in his unleavened bread. She had been disgusted at the very thought of eating the matzoth and simply had to run away from home and totally renounce the Jewish faith. The priest also instructed her to say that according to what she had heard, the victim was the heating woman who had vanished around Purim.

At the baptism, the cardinal did ask the expected question, and the girl answered just as the priest had instructed her. However, she requested them not to bring charges against her father because he had been forced to act upon the wishes of Rabbi Leyb, who was highly respected among Jews, and every Jew was afraid to go against his orders.

The things the healer's daughter said made the rounds of the city lightning fast, and the cardinal had to take down her testimony, even though at heart he cared little for her denunciation. But he could not hush it up because of Father Tadeush. He promptly sent word to Rabbi Leyb about the matter so that he might hit upon some way of proving the truth.

Meanwhile Father Tadeush wrote down the girl's testimony, but in a dreadful way: She claimed that she had witnessed Jews putting blood in the unleavened bread for Passover, that the blood had come from the Christian woman who used to light the stoves for Jews on the Sabbath, and that the men behind it were Rabbi Leyb and his two assistants.

When Rabbi Leyb heard about this testimony, he realized they would come for his two beadles in the middle of the night, which was the way they usually did it. He hit upon a plan. It was clear to him that the convert wasn't really acquainted personally with Joseph the Golem. Now, there was no lack of mutes among the vagabonds in Prague, so the rabbi secretly sent for one who was about the same height as Joseph and had a black beard like his.

As soon as they brought back a man of that description, they concealed Joseph the Golem so that he wouldn't sleep by the stove in the rabbi's courtroom. They put the other mute in his place, dressed him in Joseph's clothing, and served him a good glass of spirits and a decent supper. He was very satisfied and fell sound asleep in Joseph's bed.

In the middle of the night, the police surrounded the home of the old beadle, Abraham-Khaim, took him out of his bed, and led him off to jail. At the same time, other policemen surrounded Rabbi Leyb's house and woke up the groggy mute, who had been sound asleep on the golem's bed and didn't grasp what was happening. They helped him throw on the golem's clothes and took him off to jail. The next morning the town was in a turmoil over the dreadful news that there was a new blood accusation against the Jews, but no one could think of any solution except to weep, wail, and recite psalms. The trial was to take place in another month. Rabbi Leyb was called to the trial, in accordance with King Rudolf's new law. Meanwhile, never resting for a moment, he labored with might and main. He had several intelligent men out, thoroughly investigating the house where the heating woman had stayed, in order to determine exactly where she came from since she might have gone back there. They also investigated the intrigues against her since presumably those intrigues had made her so angry that she ran away. Rabbi Leyb finally narrowed down the search to two villages and two towns, which were several miles from Prague. He then secretly sent out eight men, two for each place, to wander about and try to locate the Christian girl.

Twelve days elapsed, and all eight messengers came back empty-handed.

The rabbi went about with an aching heart. Three days later Rabbi Leyb sent for Joseph the Golem late at night and asked him if he was personally acquainted with the Christian heating woman, who was supposed to be the victim in the blood accusation because she had disappeared. Joseph nodded that he knew her very well and would be able to recognize her among a thousand people. Then the rabbi wrote a letter in German on behalf of the head of the house where the girl had been staying. He said he was deeply sorry about the intrigues and the injuries done to her in his home. He begged her forgiveness and was sending a special messenger, a mute assistant, with money for her to rent a wagon and return to Prague. He earnestly beseeched her, upon receipt of the letter with the money, to rent a wagon immediately and return to Prague with the mute messenger. And he assured her that she would have a decent life in his home.

Rabbi Leyb put the necessary sum into the letter and sealed it. He explained to Joseph the Golem that the Christian woman was in one of those four places, and he gave him strict orders to start out that same night and spend several days in those places, hunting carefully until he found her. He was then to give her the letter and come back to Prague with her immediately. He also commanded him to be sure to return within the two weeks remaining until the trial.

Next, he dressed Joseph in gentile clothing and gave him provisions, and just before dawn the golem left Prague.

The two weeks flew by, the day of the judgment came closer and closer, and Joseph the Golem still wasn't back. The rabbi was in the throes of despair. On the day before the trial, Rabbi Leyb ordered the Jews of Prague to observe a fast. And at dawn of the day of the trial, Jews were reciting the entire Book of Psalms in all the synagogues of the city.

A huge mob, mostly Christians, began collecting at the gates of the enormous stone building of the court. The judges assembled. Father Tadeush and the convert arrived in a closed carriage. The two beadles, in chains, were brought from the prison, escorted by a strong guard. Next, Rabbi Leyb drove up, accompanied by Mordecai Mayzel, a leader of the Jewish community in Prague.

The trial got under way.

The presiding magistrate asked the old beadle, Abraham-Khaim, whether he owned up to the crime of distributing Christian blood for Passover among the Jews of Prague.

The beadle replied that he had no idea what they were talking about.

Next, they questioned the mute by means of sign language. The presiding magistrate showed him several vials filled with red water. He made signs with his hands and his head, asking the mute whether he knew anything about the matter. The mute thought they were offering him little bottles of sweet brandy. He smiled and nodded his head, pointing at his mouth.

There was an uproar in the courtroom. Father Tadeush got to his feet and said that the mute was an honest witness; he had admitted in sign language that the Jews had indeed made use of such bottles of blood for their Passover food. But others understood what the mute really meant, and they burst out laughing.

The defense attorney walked over to the mute, took a small knife out of his pocket, and drew it across his throat the way one man kills another. He pointed at Rabbi Leyb and asked the mute whether he knew anything of such a matter. The mute turned deathly pale and shook his head violently.

Father Tadeush stood up again and said the mute thought they were asking him whether he wanted to kill the rabbi. That was why he had gotten so pale and shaken his head. The defense attorney began arguing with the priest, but then the judge asked for order in the courtroom and told the convert to reveal what she knew about the case. The convert quietly began telling the very same story that had already been taken down: A few days before Passover the two beadles, whom she was personally well acquainted with, had come to her father at night. There was no one else in the house but her and her father, and the old beadle had said to her father that the rabbi of Prague was sending him a bottle of Christian blood for the unleavened bread and asking him to pay a good price for it. Her father handed the money to the old beadle, who then made a sign to the second beadle, the same mute, and he took a small bottle of blood out of his pocket.

"My father called me over and quietly told me to take the bottle from the mute and hide it well. So I took the bottle from the mute's hand, and I hid it. And when they were leaving, the old beadle said good-bye to my father and spoke the following words to him: "Don't worry, Mr. Moritsy, by the time it gets cold, the Good Lord will send us another victim, a heating woman."

The defense attorney went over to the convert and asked her whether she recognized the two beadles.

She replied with a laugh: "I would recognize them in the dark."

The defense attorney now asked that her father be summoned. The presiding magistrate answered that they had already sent out word to the father to appear at the trial, but a note had come back, saying that the healer had moved away from Prague two weeks earlier, and no one knew where he was. However, that wasn't sufficient reason to delay the trial.

No sooner had the presiding magistrate spoken than a loud noise and a yelling could be heard from the mob in front of the court building. All the people in the courtroom jumped to their feet, shouting: "What's that? What happened?"

It was truly miraculous. Joseph the Golem had suddenly driven up in a wagon with the Christian woman, the one who heated ovens on the Sabbath. He had found her with her family in a village.

When the wagon had gone down the street where Rabbi Leyb resided, Joseph had halted, jumped down, and gone into the rabbi's study. He had thrown off his peasant clothes, put on his Sabbath garments, and run to announce that he had brought back the Christian woman—only to discover that the rabbi wasn't home. He had been told to hurry to the big court building, and there he would find Rabbi Leyb.

Joseph the Golem dashed back out, leaped on the wagon, and drove the horses in a wild rush to the court. The mob had burst into screams. Some of the people were fearful of being run over; others were shouting: "Hooray! Hooray!" For they quickly recognized the real Joseph and the Christian woman. They were aghast and wondered where the two of them had come from, and they immediately realized that a great miracle had happened to the Jews. The people were so overjoyed that they yelled and clapped their hands. It didn't take long for those inside the courtroom to grasp what was happening outside. The real Joseph the Golem and the Christian woman were brought in, and the golem bounded over to the rabbi and informed him with his bizarre gestures that he had found the woman and brought her back.

Father Tadeush and the convert were terror-stricken. The convert was so frightened that she fainted. But she was promptly revived.

Now the presiding magistrate summoned Rabbi Leyb and asked him to explain what was going on. The rabbi submitted to the judges the work he had done to prove the truth. Heaven had assisted him in revealing the truth so that no innocent blood would be shed. The judges called over the Christian woman and also the man for whom she had worked, and they established that she was indeed the same woman.

The presiding judge kissed Rabbi Leyb on the forehead and thanked him for his energetic labor and great wisdom, which had prevented the judges from falsely convicting pure souls.

The defendants were instantly released. But the convert was sentenced to six years' imprisonment for bearing false witness. Father Tadeush drove home in a fury, like Haman, with his head downcast. And like Shushan in ancient Persia when Queen Esther saved the Jews, the city of Prague "rejoiced and was glad."

The Wondrous Tale That Was Widely Known As the Sorrows of a Daughter

There lived in Prague a very wealthy wine merchant named Mikhel Berger. You could get the choicest wines only from him. All the priests and all the officers would buy their wine only from Mikhel Berger.

This rich wine dealer had a daughter who was sixteen years old and very beautiful and learned. She spoke several languages and was a perfect merchant because she could talk to people of any class.

Father Tadeush, who was infamous for his hatred of the Jews, would also come to the wineshop to buy wine. The priest cast an evil eye upon the daughter; he wanted to get her to his home and talk her into converting to Christianity. He had already ruined a number of Jewish girls in this way. But this time there was no way of getting to her. She was a decent girl with pious parents and a fine lineage. She never even went for a stroll.

The priest hit upon a plan. He began taking wine on credit and then always paid in full, reckoning that at some point there would be a conflict so that the girl would have to come to his home.

And Tadeush's plan really worked.

Usually the servant would bring the bill to the priest, and the priest paid punctually. But one day, when the servant presented the bill, Father Tadeush claimed that he was being overcharged for ten bottles of wine, and he angrily accused the servant of trying to get too much money out of him. He demanded that the wine merchant's daughter accompany the servant in presenting the account. She was to bring the ledger, and he would prove to her that he was in the right.

The girl didn't even think twice about it because the servant was escorting her. When they arrived at the priest's home, the priest demanded that the girl write out a correct bill from the ledger. But the bill copied from the book tallied with the figure that the servant had presented. The priest cried out! He remembered now what the mistake was: He hadn't noted down ten bottles they had sent him a few weeks earlier because he hadn't wanted to accept the wine; it was as sour as vinegar. He added that it wasn't right for such a large business to try to cheat him.

The girl exclaimed that it just couldn't be; she was certain that they had always sent him the choicest wines. So the priest told his butler to bring up from the cellar the ten bottles, which were in a basket.

When the butler brought up the basket, the priest asked the servant to open any bottle he wanted to; the girl could taste it, and she would see that he was right: They must have made a mistake and sent him vinegar instead of wine. The servant uncorked a bottle and poured out a glass for the girl to taste.

The girl was so wrought up she didn't stop to think that she mustn't even taste the wine. After a few sips she saw that the wine was perfectly good. She told the priest there was nothing wrong with the wine. The priest had a taste for himself and then said that the girl was right: There was nothing wrong with the wine; he must have been mistaken.

With these words, he offered the girl his hand, asking her to shake hands with him and forgive him for offending her. Even though the girl was always careful not to give any strange man her hand, she didn't want to be impudent to the priest, and so she gave him her hand, saying there were no hard feelings, and that they were still friends.

The priest paid her the full sum, and now he began speaking more and more familiarly with her. The girl, for her part, had drunk some of the priest's wine, which was a pagan liquor forbidden to Jews, and when she had given him her hand, she had been virtually poisoned with a lewd venom.

Her character changed. She entered into a long conversation with the priest and felt more and more drawn to him. And when she left his house to go back home, she shook hands of her own accord and very amicably said good-bye to him, giving the priest the opportunity of asking her to visit him more often.

And that was indeed what happened. She began secretly corresponding with the priest and would sometimes visit him alone late at night, until one night she didn't even come home to sleep. She vanished like a stone in water. Her parents wept and wailed; the girl was their only child, all they had. They questioned lots of people until they finally had a clue: That night the girl had gone into the street where Father Tadeush's church was located. The miserable parents ran weeping to the priest, but he was furious and told them he didn't know what they were talking about. Weeping and broken-hearted, they returned to their home, and at the mere sight of them everyone joined in their tears.

Father Tadeush had locked up the girl in the courtyard of the church, in a place where no one could possibly get to her. He made sure that she lacked nothing in the way of pleasure, and he kept telling her that she ought to accept baptism. Each time he visited her, he would study something of the Christian religion with her.

But one day the priest saw that she wasn't very cheerful sitting all cooped up like that. He realized he couldn't make her happy until he got her a proper bridegroom. The priest assured her that he would find someone, and thus he became a matchmaker.

Not far from Prague there lived an old, rich duke, and he had an only son, who was eighteen years of age, handsome and educated. Father Tadeush was friendly with the duke, and it occurred to the priest that the duke's son would be a fitting husband for the girl.

The priest went out to visit the duke and presented the idea to him, heaping praises upon the girl. His words made a strong impression on the old duke and his young son. It was decided that the two of them would come to the church in Prague that Sunday and have lunch with the priest, and the priest would present the girl to them.

On Sunday they came to Prague, and Father Tadeush prepared a huge lunch for them. When they were drinking wine, the priest sent for the girl. She had already been informed of the visit, and so she had made herself very beautiful for the presentation. The young man was greatly taken with her, and he and his father spent the night in the priest's home.

The next day the priest threw a grand ball, and from the very start of the evening the girl sat next to the duke's son. She was in high spirits as though they were already engaged.

At a later ball, it was decided that the cardinal himself should baptize her in two months and that her marriage to the young duke would take place on the same day, right after the christening.

The duke and his son drove home, and the bridegroom gave the bride a going-away present, a valuable ring with his name engraved in it.

The girl's parents meanwhile hadn't slept all that time. They did all they could to get their child back from the priest, but to no avail. Next, they went to a close relative, the great scholar Jacob Gintzberg, who was the rabbi of Friedburg, and they asked for his help. The great scholar replied that the rabbi of Prague, Rabbi Leyb, was in a better position to help than he, and he gave them a letter to Rabbi Leyb, asking him to do everything in his power to rescue the girl because it was a blow to his family honor.

The parents drove back to Prague and delivered the letter to Rabbi Leyb. The rabbi was deeply upset by the letter because he had preferred to keep clear of this matter rather than battle with Father Tadeush. But he had to be hospitable for the sake of the great scholar Jacob Gintzberg. There were a number of people present when the parents gave him the letter, and the rabbi said out loud that he couldn't help the parents and that he didn't want to get involved in the matter.

But that night Rabbi Leyb secretly sent the old beadle, Abraham-Khaim, to summon the parents, and they came immediately. The rabbi told them he intended to do something about the whole business, but nobody was to know about his participation. He also told them that as of the next day they were to have a carriage with a pair of good horses in their courtyard, along with a good driver and two strong men, all in secret, and to be ready to escape with the girl as soon as he succeeded in getting her home. And he asked the parents if they had some distant place where they might take their daughter. The father answered that he had a brother, who owned the largest wine business in Amsterdam, and he was very wealthy and learned. His name was Khaim Berger. His home would be a good place to bring the girl. The rabbi agreed, and he ordained that the father and mother should fast for three days, starting tomorrow, and read the entire Book of Psalms with tears every single day, and eat only at night. He told them to go home and not let anyone know that they had been to see him. The parents went home and did everything exactly as the rabbi had ordained.

During those three days the girl began to feel a deep longing for her parents, and she looked wretched. The priest asked her why she looked so wretched. She said she felt a bit under the weather, but it didn't matter.

At the same time, many priests were gathering in Cracow for a conference, and they summoned Father Tadeush. Before he left, the priest ordered his servants not to allow anyone into the courtyard of the church.

When Rabbi Leyb discovered that Tadeush was also going to the conference, he summoned Joseph the Golem secretly at night and gave him the amulet of invisibility so that no one could see him. Next, he wrote the following words on a slip of paper: "I, your grandfather, have come down from the other world to rescue you. Get into this sack, and I will carry you home."

Rabbi Leyb took a large sack and handed it to Joseph along with the note. He ordered him to leave at the crack of dawn and go to the church. There he was to wait at the small iron door, and as soon as someone opened the door to go in or out, he was to slip through quietly. Then he was to go around the courtyard all day long, find out exactly how to open the door from the inside, and figure out where the girl was. As soon as he knew these things, he was to creep into her room and hide there until late at night, when all the servants and guards were asleep. Now he was to wake up the girl and place the sack and the note in front of her. When she had given sufficient thought to the message, he was to open the sack, let the girl climb in, and take her home to her parents.

Rabbi Leyb knew that the small iron door leading to the courtyard of the church could be opened from the inside, but not from the outside, yet not everyone knew how to work it.

Joseph the Golem took the difficult task upon himself, and he succeeded in doing everything exactly as the rabbi had ordered. By two o'clock in the morning Joseph the Golem was already back with the girl in her parents' home.

One can scarcely imagine the joy and weeping when the parents saw their only child again. The daughter fell at their feet and tearfully kissed them and begged their forgiveness. But then the father recalled the rabbi's instructions. He ordered his servants to prepare the carriage, got into it with his daughter and the two men, and hurriedly left Prague for Amsterdam.

When they asked the daughter who had rescued her, she showed them the note; her grandfather had come down from the other world and brought her here. And the parents likewise believed that this was what had happened.

The next morning, in the courtyard of the church, the lackey let out a yell when he saw that the girl had run off. He was terrified that the priest would accuse him of helping her to escape. We would never have known what the lackey did, but a later story, which can be found after this story, tells us that he went down into the cellar of the church, took some human bones, and put them on the girl's bed. Then he started a fire, and by the time the firemen arrived, the whole room was destroyed, and they found the charred remains of a human being.

The police reported that a stranger who happened to be spending the night there had been burned up, and the name was supplied by the lackey and the priest.

The lackey informed the authorities that the priest had violently forced a girl surnamed Berger to accept baptism, and she felt so wretched that she set fire to the room in which she was imprisoned.

Naturally, when the priest came back from Cracow, he had to keep silent. But he really assumed that the lackey had let the girl go for money, and Father Tadeush took revenge on the lackey, which is described in the story that follows.

When the priest saw the duke, he told him that while he had been at the conference in Cracow, the room in which the girl was sleeping had caught fire at night and she had been burned up, and all they had found of her was her bones.

When the young duke heard the terrible news that his beloved fiancée had been burned up, he was overcome with grief and fell into a deep melancholy. He couldn't eat or sleep, and he looked wretched. His father tried to put his mind at ease with all kinds of pleasures and asked marriage brokers to find him a fitting bride. But the young duke didn't care for any of the proposals after the beauty and nobility he had seen in the Jewish girl. He decided he would take only a Jewish wife, and since he realized it would be difficult to get a Jewish girl to accept baptism for him, he resolved to go to another country and convert to Judaism without his father's knowledge. However, he understood that he would need a lot of money for this, and so he suggested to his father that since it was so hard for him to forget his fiancée here and he felt he might lose his mind, the best thing for him would be to go and study in Venice for a few years. By the time he finished the university, he would forget his sorrows and come home and marry. The old duke had to consent. He gave his son all the money he asked for, and the young duke left for Venice.

When he got to Venice, he rented himself a private room and registered as a traveling merchant. The room was to be constantly vacant and ready for him so that he could use it at any time, even though he might come only a few times a year. He also gave instructions that if any letter were to arrive for him, it was to be placed promptly in his room, because he knew his father would write him in Venice, and in this way he could come there anytime to get the letters and write back.

Now at this time, the great gaon Jacob Gintzberg of Friedburg was renowned through the world and was regarded as second only to Rabbi Leyb of Prague. So the young duke made up his mind to go and ask the gaon to initiate him into Judaism.

The young man went to him and made a very favorable impression on the gaon, and before long the gaon converted him and began studying the Torah with him, and he changed the young man's first name to Abraham and gave him the last name of Yeshurun, which is the poetic name of Israel.

Now, Abraham Yeshurun had a very able mind, and he quickly absorbed everything he studied with the gaon. But the gaon being the rabbi of the city, was extremely busy and couldn't give up that much time to him. So he sent the young man to the great yeshiva of Amsterdam with a letter to the head of the school, saying that Abraham was a relative of his and asking the head of the yeshiva to welcome him and take special care of him.

Abraham Yeshurun tearfully took leave of the gaon, and the gaon gave him his blessing and assured him he would find his destined bride in Amsterdam. And by way of proof he told him that if the marriage they proposed to him would be with a member of Rabbi Gintzberg's family, he was to agree. The gaon also instructed him not to reveal who he was, but to say that his name was Abraham Yeshurun, and that he came from the city of Bucharest and was a relative of the gaon, all of which could be checked with the rabbi of Friedburg.

Abraham Yeshurun journeyed to Amsterdam, and there he called upon the head of the yeshiva. He told him who he was and showed him the letter from the rabbi of Friedburg. The headmaster welcomed him as a friend and began studying the Torah with him. Abraham Yeshurun worked hard and became a great scholar. His fame spread, and he was known as the young prodigy of Bucharest.

Meanwhile he kept going to Venice to get his father's letters and to answer them, so that his father would think he was studying there and not worry about him.

Abraham Yeshurun studied in the yeshiva for two years, and then the headmaster told him to return home and get married. Abraham replied that he preferred to remain in Amsterdam because it was a more pious city than Bucharest, and he would rather marry a girl from Amsterdam. He added that money was no problem; he could get all the money he needed from his father, who was a very wealthy man and had no other child but him.

It soon became known throughout the city that there was a rich yeshiva student here who wanted to marry a girl from Amsterdam. And the marriage brokers started visiting him. He turned down many offers until one marriage broker suggested the girl who was staying with her wealthy uncle, Khaim Berger, and who was kith and kin with the great gaon Jacob Gintzberg, and as for her family, the matchmaker explained that according to her reputation in Amsterdam, she was an orphan from a distant city and her inheritance was very large.

As soon as Abraham Yeshurun heard that she was related to the gaon Jacob Gintzberg, he realized she must be his destined bride, and he agreed to the match. The betrothal was carried out in great dignity. The bridegroom deceived the bride in regard to his background because he didn't want anyone to find out that he was a convert to Judaism. The bride in turn deceived the bridegroom, as well as the whole city of Amsterdam, in regard to her background because she was afraid the people might find out about her bad reputation in Prague, where she had very nearly converted to Christianity. The girl did look familiar to the boy, but it never occurred to him that this was the same girl who had been burned to death in the courtyard of Father Tadeush's church two years before.

A few weeks after the official engagement the bridegroom bought some costly presents for the bride, among them two diamond rings. When she tried on the diamond rings, she had to remove the gold ring she had been wearing ever since her arrival from Prague, the one she had gotten at the ball from that very same bridegroom, the young duke. The moment she put the gold ring on the table the bridegroom began inspecting it, and he promptly recognized it as his own ring, for his name was still engraved on it. The young man was so startled and upset that he fell into a swoon. They revived him, but he was unwilling to explain why he had fainted. Now he came to realize that the bride was the same as the girl in Prague.

The bridegroom could no longer control himself, and he asked the girl in secret to tell him the whole truth as to who she was and where she had gotten the ring, and that she needn't be afraid to tell him everything. The bride was so frightened that she too fainted. He revived her, but now she was unable to keep her secret anymore. In short, they revealed themselves to each other, and both of them burst into tears of joy.

The young man went out and told the entire story to the head of the yeshiva and to the bride's uncle, and he also repeated the blessing and the parting words of the gaon of Friedburg. The headmaster was overjoyed and said: "It is obvious that this marriage was made in heaven and that something which was nearly unlawful has been done in a lawful manner."

A short time later the wedding took place in Amsterdam with great honor. And not long after that, the old duke died, Abraham Yeshurun and his wife inherited all his property, and they decided to settle near Prague.

When the young couple arrived at their estates, Father Tadeush was no longer in Prague. He had been sent away after a great trial, as we shall hear in the next story.

A few days later Abraham and his bride gave a grand ball and invited her parents, Mikhel Berger and his wife, as well as Rabbi Leyb and other prominent Jews of the city.

At the ball the entire story was told from beginning to end, and now they saw that it wasn't the grandfather from the other world who had carried off the girl inside a sack. It really was Rabbi Leyb, who had gotten Joseph the Golem to do the trick.

A few years later old Mikhel Berger died, and soon his wife followed him. And Abraham Yeshurun donated his father-in-law's house to be used as a synagogue. And it was named the Yeshurun Synagogue. The couple did many charitable deeds in Prague and lived very happily.

A Very Wondrous Tale about a Blood Libel That Spelled Final Defeat for Father Tadeush

This wondrous tale took place in the year 5345 [or 1585 according to the Christian reckoning].

In Prague, not far from the great synagogue of the city, there stood a large old mansion that looked like an ancient royal palace. The old building was known as the five-sided palace because it had five walls facing the streets. In front of each wall there were five columns, and in between the columns there were five windows. On top of the mansion there were five large towers with ancient figures, which were obviously from the days when men worshiped the sun. Now because there was no owner and the mansion belonged to the government, it fell into greater and greater disrepair, and only beggars lived in it.

Underneath the building there was a large cellar, but the tenants were afraid to go down into it. They said the cellar had been defiled by demons who had settled there and constantly terrorized the beggars, and it was rumored that a number of people had already been harmed down there. That was why there were so few tenants in the Five-Sided Palace, which looked like an ancient ruin.

Now, one day, during preparations for Passover, after the ceremonial search for unleavened dough in Jewish homes, Rabbi Leyb was in the synagogue to pronounce the annulment of leaven for this

Feast of Deliverance. He was about to begin when the candle went out. Since it was the rabbi's custom to read from the prayer book rather than recite from memory, he motioned to the beadle to relight the candle. The beadle lit it over and over, but it merely went out again each time.

The rabbi turned deathly pale, and the worshipers were likewise terrified. Rabbi Leyb had to interrupt the service. He asked the old beadle, Abraham-Khaim, to take the prayer book over to the candle burning in the sconce and to read the annulment aloud word by word; the rabbi would repeat it from memory word by word.

The beadle did as he was bidden. Terror-stricken, he went over to the candlestick on the wall and began to read: "All the leaven that I have . . ." But when he came to *have*, he thought it said *five*, and that was what he read aloud for Rabbi Leyb.

The rabbi paused and then cried out to the beadle: "Well? Well?"

The beadle was even more terrified and began all over again, and when he came to *have*, he repeated *five*.

Rabbi Leyb snapped his fingers, which he always did when something surprised him, and he exclaimed: "Aha! Now I understand! 'It is a time of trouble unto Jacob, but out of it shall he be saved.' Our enemies want to put out the Jewish light. Now I know the meaning of the dream I had the night of the Great Sabbath, before Passover."

The rabbi hurried over to the candle and climbed up on a chair because the sconce was high on the wall. He read the prayer from the book, and then he told everyone else to go home. No one remained except for his son-in-law, the gaon Jacob Gintzberg (blessed be the memory of that true priest and righteous man), the old beadle, Abraham-Khaim, and Joseph the Golem.

When they were alone, Rabbi Leyb told the others what he had dreamed on Friday night: The Five-Sided Palace was burning furiously, and the flames were leaping into the windows of the great synagogue, which was packed with Jews. Rabbi Leyb screamed in his sleep and woke up in dread.

He realized now what his dream signified. Someone in the Five-Sided Palace was preparing a blood libel, a calamity for the Jews of Prague, and they would have to remove it just as they got rid of all leaven on the eve of Passover.

At this point God had sent those words into the beadle's mouth. They signified that the Jews had to remove and destroy the leaven in the Five-Sided Palace, where someone had prepared a disastrous calumny against the Jews of Prague.

Rabbi Leyb desperately tried to figure out what kind of catastrophe someone could be planning in that building. He asked about all the tenants; but the beadle went through each of them in his mind, and he felt that not one of them could be suspected of any evil. However, one thing that the beadle said came as a great surprise to Rabbi Leyb. The beadle recalled that when he was a child, the little boys used to tell one another stories they had heard at home about the Five-Sided Palace. Their parents had said that once upon a time a king had lived in the palace and he would never show himself to the people of the city. Whenever he wanted to attend church, he would go to the Green Church by way of a cavern running underground from the cellar of the palace to the cellar of the Green Church. And that was the church in which Father Tadeush lived, the priest who was an infamous anti-Semite.

Upon hearing these words, Rabbi Leyb realized that Tadeush had prepared a great blood libel in the cellar, something he could easily do because of the underground cavern that ran from the cellar in the church to the cellar of the palace. The rabbi knew quite well that the priest was stealthily waiting for a chance to take revenge on him because the rabbi prevented any blood libel from succeeding in Prague. And the priest was even angrier because he was fully aware that Rabbi Leyb had somehow helped to ruin his plans for baptizing Mikhel Berger's daughter. Afterward, in the courtroom, it turned out that the priest had assumed that his lackey had given the girl back to her parents for a sum of money while he, the priest, was in Cracow and that the rabbi had been behind it all, and that the fire had merely been a decoy. That was why the priest had made up his mind to settle accounts with the lackey and also with Rabbi Leyb.

And the truth of the matter was that a dreadful blood libel had indeed been prepared in the cellar. This is what happened:

The priest's lackey had a wife and several little children. The priest's house stood in the courtyard of the church, and on the other side there was a large orchard surrounded by a wall. Inside the wall there was an iron gate that opened on to a path outside the city.

Two weeks before Passover, when the weather was turning warm, the lackey and his wife began doing a bit of work in the orchard every day, and their young children ran around in it, each child playing with whatever it could, and while the parents were working in the orchard, they had to open the iron gate and throw out the unnecessary things that had gathered during the winter, and then some or all of the children would dash through the gate and start playing outside.

Father Tadeush knew about this, and he wanted to take this opportunity to carry out his revenge against the servant and start a blood libel against Rabbi Leyb. The priest waited until the lackey and his wife were busy with their work in the orchard while some of their children were scattered around the orchard and others were running around outside the gate. When no one was looking, the priest lured one of the children to come along, and he then killed the child. He poured his blood into several small vials, on which there were labels with Jewish names, the names of Rabbi Leyb, his children, and his sons-in-law and the names of three leaders of the Jewish community and some of the richest and noblest men in Prague.

Then he took the vials from his cellar through the cavern leading to the cellar of the Five-Sided Palace, and he hid them there so that on the eve of Passover he could invade the Jewish quarter, launch an investigation, and then have Rabbi Leyb, his children, and all the leading Jews of the city put in prison.

The priest made his preparations on Friday, the eve of the Great Sabbath before Passover. And that night Rabbi Leyb had the terrible dream described above.

With darkness coming on, the lackey and his wife wanted to stop work in the orchard and go home. They started calling their children together, and then they saw that one was missing. They hunted for a long time, but in vain. The child was gone. At the crack of dawn they went to the priest and told him what had happened.

The priest said that it seemed to him the child must have run out through the iron gate and wandered off somewhere. He added that they had reason to worry because it was close to the Jewish Passover, and the Jews were on the lookout for Christian blood to use in their matzoth. For all they knew, the child might have fallen into Jewish hands by now. There was little they could do except notify the police. And the priest instructed the mother to say that last night, when they were about to go home and she was closing the iron gate, she had seen a Jew in the distance, carrying something in a sack on his shoulders, and the sack had been shaking. Tadeush told her to weep and wail and plead with the police to make a thorough search of the Jewish quarter. And she was also to ask the police to take Father Tadeush along on the investigation.

Hearing these words, the mother began to weep and wail, and then she hurried to the city hall and notified the police just as Tadeush had instructed her to do. The police in turn told her not to worry. The next day, which was the eve of Passover, they would start out early in the morning and make a thorough investigation everywhere in the Jewish quarter, together with Father Tadeush.

However, it is written in the Psalms: "Behold, he that keepeth Israel shall neither slumber nor sleep." This means that the Good Lord never sleeps. He watches over his nation, the Jews.

Rabbi Leyb had gotten the tiding from heaven that a disaster was threatening the Jews, and he wasted no time. He said it was certainly dangerous to go down into the cellar, but he girded himself with the Talmudic saying that "a man sent on a pious mission shall meet with no evil."

This was the night of the inspection for leaven. And after midnight prayers Rabbi Leyb set out with the old beadle, Abraham-Khaim, and Joseph the Golem. They took along a tinderbox and three of the twisted candles used in the ceremony closing the Sabbath, and then they stole over to the Five-Sided Palace, very quietly so that no one would notice them.

When they were about to go down the steps into the cellar, they kindled a fire and lit all three candles. Then they opened the door and stepped inside, and at once a wind arose and dust whirled about, and they heard the barking of dogs as the wind tried to blow out the candles. But the rabbi told his beadles to recite "He who dwelleth in secret . . ." three times, and then everything began quieting down and grew perfectly still. The three men kept going.

But now stones began dropping from the vault of the cellar, and they were afraid that the vault would cave in upon them. Rabbi Leyb and the old beadle, Abraham-Khaim, stopped, but the rabbi ordered Joseph the Golem to go on alone with the candle in his hand and to inspect the cellar carefully, and if he found any suspicious object, he was to bring it back and show it to the rabbi. Joseph the Golem set about his task.

It wasn't long before he came back to the rabbi with the murdered child wrapped in a prayer shawl and a small basket containing some thirty vials of blood, and on the vials there were labels with Hebrew characters, the names of all the leading Jews in Prague.

Rabbi Leyb ordered Joseph the Golem to take the dead child through the cavern leading to the cellar of Father Tadeush's home and to hide the body carefully among the kegs of wine that the priest had standing there, and then Joseph was to come right back.

Joseph the Golem did as he was told and carried out the rabbi's instructions precisely. A half hour went by, and Joseph the Golem was back again.

Now the rabbi ordered him to take stones and smash the vials and then dig a hole in the cellar and bury everything in it. When it was done, they all went home in high spirits. Rabbi Leyb told them to keep it all a secret. No one was to say anything about it.

At ten in the morning, on the day before Passover, the police suddenly appeared in the Jewish quarter with many soldiers, accompanied by Father Tadeush. The soldiers dashed into the Jewish homes, two to a house, and searched them thoroughly. First they went into the great synagogue, then Rabbi Leyb's home, and then the homes of all the community leaders and many prominent men.

When they came past the Five-Sided Palace, the priest cried out that they ought to search the palace as well. Naturally, they searched it thoroughly, taking longer than anywhere else, but as it is written in Exodus, "If he come in by himself, he shall go out by himself." They went home empty-handed.

Meanwhile, alas, a deathly fear took hold of all the Jews in Prague. However, Rabbi Leyb said to pass the word that the Jews had nothing to fear; they were to have a happy holiday because the Lord God had worked secret miracles to rescue the Jews from false accusations.

The dead body lay well concealed among the wine kegs in the cellar, and after a few days it began to smell. The Catholic holiday of Easter was approaching, and the priest ordered his lackey to put the cellar in order and to see how much wine there was so that they would know how much more to buy for Easter. The lackey went down into the cellar, and as usual his dog followed him everywhere. But then the dog smelled the stench of the dead body and ran over to where it was hidden, and there he began barking and pawing the ground. The lackey realized something was wrong, and he hunted carefully until he came upon the dead child, whom he recognized at once.

The lackey ran out of the cellar and brought the police back with him. Everyone understood that this was the priest's doing because he had always been plotting to bring a blood accusation against the Jews. The priest tried to deny the whole story. He said he knew nothing about it. But in the face of so many facts he finally had to confess that it was indeed his work. He had wanted to get even with his servant, who had taken a precious soul away from the Christian faith, a girl who had been staying with him for several weeks and who had been ready to accept baptism. But the servant had helped her go back home in exchange for money. And he, the priest, had also wanted to get even with the Jewish rabbi, who had most surely been behind the escape, and so he had planned a blood accusation against him, using the child, in order to settle accounts with both the rabbi and the lackey.

The lackey, however, said it wasn't so. The priest had tricked Mikhel Berger's daughter into coming to him and had been forcing her to accept baptism. He had done terrible things to her and made her life wretched, and so she had set fire to her room when she was alone.

The priest was arrested at once, and he was tried and banished forever.

In regard to these events, Rabbi Leyb repeated the Hebrew "He wanted to protect the worthy woman," by which he meant that God wanted to protect the holy Shekhinah, the divine emanation, "and her children as well"—the Jews. And the holy Shekhinah had sent the word *five* to his lips so that he would know enough to search the Five-Sided Palace.

This Is the Wonderful and Miraculous Tale of What Rabbi Leyb Did for the Two Beryls Whose Children Were Exchanged by a Midwife

There lived in Prague a man who taught elementary subjects to young Jewish children, and he was known as Tall Jacob. One day two poor little boys, two orphans from Romania, came to him, and the teacher hired them as assistants. Both of them were named Beryl, but one had dark hair and so was known as Black Beryl, and the other had a ruddy face and so was known as Red Beryl.

The two Beryls loved each other. They lived together and shared their food. They were liked by the teacher and also by the people of the city because they did their work with honesty and devotion. And little by little they saved up some money for their marriages. Both of them married women from Prague, and since the two men couldn't live without each other after their weddings, they decided to go into business together.

Their first business as partners was a slaughterhouse and a meat shop. Their business prospered, and little by little they became wealthy. Then they closed up their meat shop and began dealing in cattle. They continued to prosper and became great cattle dealers. Their wealth was renowned throughout Prague.

Now they bought a large mansion in Prague, and the two Beryls lived in it, next door to each other.

But there was one thing in which they were not equals, their children. Red Beryl had both sons and daughters, all of whom survived, while Black Beryl had only daughters, and not all of them survived.

The wives of the two Beryls had the same midwife, and her name was Esther. Black Beryl's wife felt a keen envy of Red Beryl's wife. But because she was a very noble person with a noble character, she did all she could to contain herself and not show any rivalry with the other wife. Esther, the midwife, fully realized what was happening, and she felt a great pity and sympathy for Black Beryl's wife. She began wondering if there was something she could do for her so that she might also boast to her husband that she had given birth to a son.

One night both wives went for a ritual immersion, and the midwife found out. She made up her mind that if both women were to conceive that night, and Black Beryl's wife had another daughter, and the other wife a son, and both children were born at the same time, then she, the midwife, would exchange the babies, with no one the wiser.

And that was exactly what happened. Both wives began moaning at the same time, but Red Beryl's wife had her baby first, and she bore a son. Esther the midwife, wished her joy for her daughter. She thought that even if Black Beryl's wife had a son, she would still exchange them because Red Beryl's children were stronger and hardier than Black Beryl's children, and she would tell Red Beryl that she had wished his wife good luck for a girl in order to ward off the evil eye by not saying aloud that it was a boy.

The next day Black Beryl's wife also had a baby, and it too was a boy! Esther, the midwife, wished Black Beryl all the luck in the world for his son, and the joy was very great. Then Esther, told Red Beryl that his wife had also had a boy, but since Black Beryl's wife was about to give birth herself, the midwife had been afraid of an evil eye, and so, to ward it off, she hadn't wanted to say aloud that the child was a boy. He took her at her word.

A few nights later, when everyone was asleep, Esther, the midwife, switched the two children. No one was the wiser and she told no one what she had done. She did, however, write in her diary that at this time on this day she had taken the two boys that had just been born to the Beryls and exchanged them in secret, for a hidden reason. But whoever looked into her diary? The whole thing remained as secret as a stone in water.

The two boys thus grew up and became adults. Esther, the midwife, died. Her diary passed into the hands of a daughter, who followed in her mother's footsteps and became a midwife too. But since she never had any cause to look into her mother's diary, the book was stored in the cellar along with other useless things.

The two Beryls began marrying off their children, and they found wonderful matches for them. Now since Black Beryl still had two daughters and an only son (the one the midwife had exchanged), and Red Beryl had four sons and two daughters, plus the last son (the one the midwife had exchanged), the two fathers never arranged a match between their own children.

But as the years went by, a number of marriage brokers suggested that Black Beryl's only son should marry Red Beryl's youngest daughter, who was just one year his elder, and everyone agreed it was a fine match.

The marriage contract was drawn up with great rejoicing, as is customary among the wealthy, and then the wedding day arrived. The two Beryls insisted that Rabbi Leyb perform the ceremony, just as he officiated at all the rich weddings in Prague.

But something peculiar happened at the wedding. When Rabbi Leyb took hold of the wineglass to pronounce the first blessing, it tumbled out of his hand. People thought it had been knocked out of his fingers because the synagogue was so crowded. The guests were asked to stand back so that there would be more space, and the glass was filled with more wine. But as soon as Rabbi Leyb said, "Blessed art thou . . ." the glass tumbled out of his hand again. The rabbi turned pale, and all the onlookers were bewildered and frightened.

Meanwhile there was no wine left in the bottle for a third glassful. So the old beadle, Abraham-Khaim, cried out to the mute beadle, Joseph the Golem, to run quickly and bring up another bottle from the rabbi's cellar because the rabbi would never use any other wine for a blessing.

Joseph the Golem dashed over to Rabbi Leyb's home, which wasn't far from the great synagogue, where the wedding was taking place. But just as Joseph the Golem came to the rabbi's door, he halted abruptly, and the people saw that he seemed to be talking to someone. From afar the wedding crowd began shouting at Joseph the Golem to hurry up with the wine. But Joseph the Golem didn't even go down into the cellar. Instead he calmly walked into the rabbi's office and wrote some Hebrew words on a piece of paper:

"THE BRIDE AND GROOM ARE BROTHER AND SISTER." And instead of the wine, he hurried back with the note and handed it to Rabbi Leyb.

The crowd wanted to tear Joseph apart, but they knew better than to fool with him.

When the rabbi read the note, he became very frightened, and he cried out: "Oh, dear God! Brother and sister!"

The other people were also terrified; they realized that something awful was happening.

Rabbi Leyb asked Joseph the Golem: "Who told you the bride and groom are sister and brother?"

Joseph the Golem pointed at the window of the synagogue to show who had said those words to him and told him to repeat them to Rabbi Leyb. The rabbi took a few steps from under the wedding canopy and stood facing the window that Joseph had shown him. The rabbi peered up at the window and then went back to the canopy. The whole crowd peered up at the window, but no one saw anything.

When Rabbi Leyb was back at the canopy, he said that the wedding could not take place today because there would first have to be a thorough investigation. He told them to distribute the entire feast to the poor.

That same night, after midnight, Rabbi Leyb called over Joseph the Golem and said something to him quietly and gave him his staff. Joseph the Golem hurried off and came back an hour later. Afterward people found out he had been sent to the graveyard to tell Esther, the midwife, she was to appear at Leyb's rabbinical court the next day.

Early in the morning the rabbi told his servants to prepare a place for himself and his two assistant judges, a few cubits away from the northeast corner of the synagogue, and to set up a wooden screen forming a triangle with the corner. Next, he asked them to call out that all the men praying in the synagogue should remain after prayers rather than go home and should gather on the other side of the reading desk, toward the western wall.

After the rabbi finished praying, he and his two assistant judges sat down at the table in their prayer shawls and phylacteries. He sent the old beadle, Abraham-Khaim, to summon the families of the bride and groom, the two Beryls with their wives, and the bride and groom themselves.

When they arrived, Rabbi Leyb asked them to stand on the other side of the table, toward the south, and he questioned the two Beryls and their wives about everything concerning them, to the last detail, but it did not come out that the children had been switched, so far as anyone knew.

Next, Rabbi Leyb called over Joseph the Golem and handed him his staff, saying: "Go to the graveyard, Joseph, and bring back the soul of Esther, the midwife, so that she can clear up this matter for us."

The others were terrified, but Rabbi Leyb rose to his feet and said in a loud voice: "Do not be afraid, I beg you, for nothing bad shall come of this."

The people calmed down a bit.

A half hour later Joseph the Golem returned to the synagogue and gave the rabbi back his staff. Then he pointed at the screen to show that the person they were waiting for was on the other side.

There was a deathly hush in the synagogue. No one had the heart to look at anyone else.

Now Rabbi Leyb said: "We, the Earthly Court, decree that thou, Esther, shalt explain in detail why the bride and the groom are brother and sister."

The dead midwife began to tell the whole story.

The crowd in the synagogue only heard a faint voice, but the court, the parents, and the bride and groom clearly heard the dead midwife tell the story of how she had switched the two children. And she added that in the twelve years since her death she had known no rest and would not know any until she righted the wrong she had done. On the wedding day she had been empowered to prevent the marriage of a brother and sister from taking place; otherwise she would be doomed to Gehenna forever.

When she ended her story, she burst into tears, pleading with the court to have mercy on her soul and to set the matter aright and switch back the children, and she begged the families and the children to forgive her. In the end, she added that if they didn't believe her, they could go and find her diary, which was in her daughter's home and which listed all the children she had brought into the world. And if they checked the day and year when the children were born, they would see her entry, which said she had exchanged the two children. And if she had been in her right mind at death, she would have corrected the matter herself before dying. But because she had died of a sudden, severe illness, which had made her lose her mind, she had been unable to set things aright.

With these words, they could hear the sound of weeping.

When Rabbi Leyb had heard the story, he sent both his beadles to the midwife's daughter, asking her to come immediately with her dead mother's diary. It took them a good hour to locate the half-rotted book in the cellar. But they did find it, and they did find the entry in the diary.

The court ruled that first of all, the dead midwife would have to ask forgiveness of the bride and groom for having shamed them. And if they were willing to forgive her with all their heart and soul, then she would be free of her sin.

Now they heard the weeping voice from the other side of the screen: "I, Esther, ask you, brother and sister, for forgiveness."

They answered that they forgave her with all their heart and soul.

Now the rabbi and the two assistant judges got to their feet and spoke: "We, the Earthly Court, exempt you, Esther, from any manner of punishment. Go in peace and rest in peace until all is peace."

Rabbi Leyb then called the entire crowd in the synagogue and said it had been clearly proved that the youngest sons of the two Beryls had been exchanged by the midwife Esther, so that the two children would have to be switched back again, and both the bride and groom would have to be registered as Red Beryl's children. The youngest son of Red Beryl was the only son of Black Beryl.

The rabbi added that if the fathers-in-law agreed, then it would be fitting and proper for the real son of Black Beryl to marry the same bride, and the wedding would take place the following week.

The fathers-in-law and the children promptly agreed to the rabbi's proposal, and a new marriage contract was drawn up in the synagogue. Spirits and cakes were served to everyone, and Rabbi Leyb blessed them all.

The rabbi then asked for the book of records. When it was brought to him, he briefly set down the full story, and the judges all signed their names.

Rabbi Leyb then gave the new couple his best wishes for a happy marriage and told the people that they could go home. He asked his beadles to take a board from the wooden screen and nail it up in the corner as a reminder. The beadles did as he told them.

The following week the proper wedding took place with great merriment. Rabbi Leyb himself performed the ceremony, and he was overjoyed that heaven had stayed his hand from uniting a brother and sister in wedlock. The young couple lived to a ripe old age in Prague, and their life together was very happy.

The Tale of the Torah That Fell to the Ground on Yom Kippur

In the year 5347 [or, by Christian reckoning 1587], on Yom Kippur, when Rabbi Leyb was attending evening prayers at the great synagogue in Prague, someone went to roll up the scroll of the Torah after the reading of the Law, only to drop the Torah on the ground.

Rabbi Leyb was greatly upset and confused by what had happened. The first thing he did was to proclaim that all the worshipers who had seen the Torah fall upon the ground were to fast throughout the day before the eve of the Feast of Tabernacles. The rabbi understood that this was not enough, that something like this did not just happen at random, without cause. But he couldn't find the reason, and he went about very gloomy.

On the day of the fast Rabbi Leyb asked heaven in a dream to reveal why the Scroll of the Law had fallen to the ground. But an unclear answer came from heaven. The Hebrew words were such that the rabbi failed to grasp their meaning.

Rabbi Leyb was at a loss to figure out what these words were hinting, and he made up his mind to use Joseph the Golem once again.

He wrote out each letter of the words on a separate piece of paper and then asked Joseph the Golem to put the letters in the proper order. Joseph, without thinking, laid them out in a certain order, and Rabbi Leyb saw that these letters were the initials of the words in a line of the evening prayers that had been read from the Scroll of the Law for Yom Kippur. These words were: "And thou shalt not lie carnally with thy neighbor's wife to defile thyself with her."

Rabbi Leyb realized that the man who had gone to roll up the Scroll of the Torah had committed adultery with another man's wife. The rabbi sent Joseph the Golem with a note to the sinner, asking him to come immediately. And when Joseph the Golem went for someone, that person knew he had to come, for if not, it had often happened that Joseph the Golem would take the unwilling man and throw him over his back like a sheep and then carry him back to the rabbi through the streets.

The man he sent for left immediately with the golem, and when he came to Rabbi Leyb, the rabbi took him into a private room and asked him in a kindly tone to confess the sin that had caused him to drop the Torah on Yom Kippur. The man saw that no amount of lying would help, and he confessed that for a long time now he had been sinning with his partner's wife.

Rabbi Leyb put a penance upon the man and righted the matter in accordance with the Law.

The Attack on Joseph the Golem

During the years when Rabbi Leyb was rabbi of Prague, the inhabitants of Prague would use a dreadful word to one another if ever they got into a fight. This word was *nadler*, a slanderous accusation that the other man did not have pure Jewish blood flowing in his veins. It came from the expulsions from Spain and Italy when many Jews accepted baptism and then returned to Judaism upon finding refuge in Prague. The slanderous word *nadler* was sometimes hurled at their descendants in a quarrel.

Rabbi Leyb wanted to do away with this slander because it brought a great deal of harm to the Jewish community. So he called together a great number of rabbis, and they decreed with a blast of the ram's horn and with the burning of black candles that any Jew who insulted another Jew with the word *nadler* would be placed under a ban.

The decree worked very well, and the Jews took care never to utter the word. However, there were three porters, impudent fellows, who, only a few weeks after the proclamation of the decree, again began insulting other Jews with the word *nadler*. They were reported to Rabbi Leyb.

The rabbi was very angry and sent for the most impudent of the porters, the first one to flout the decree. But the porter merely laughed at the beadle, Abraham-Khaim, and told him to tell Rabbi Leyb that he didn't have the time, and he would come as soon as he could make the time for himself.

This made the rabbi even angrier. He called in a few strong young men and asked them to prepare a bundle of rods and a rope.

Then he summoned Joseph the Golem and ordered him to go over to the porter right away and bring him back by force on his shoulders. Not losing a moment, Joseph the Golem went over, snatched up the porter by the scruff of his neck, and carried him through the streets like a sheep. The porter was no weakling, everyone was afraid of him, but there was nothing he could do against Joseph the Golem.

As soon as the golem delivered the porter to Rabbi Leyb, the rabbi had his men tie up the culprit and give him a good whipping to bring him to his senses.

The men did as they were told, and Joseph the Golem went to work with a vengeance, like a slaughterer with a bull. When they had carried out the sentence, they ordered the porter to take off his boots and go to Rabbi Leyb in stocking feet to receive his reprimand. He obeyed and then barely dragged himself home, and once there, he had to lie in bed for two weeks until his wounds were healed.

But a fire of vengeance burned in the porter, and he made up his mind to get even, especially with Joseph the Golem, whom he planned to wipe from the face of the earth.

The porter had a secret talk with his cronies to hit upon a way of dealing with Joseph the Golem, and at last they devised a plan of attack that could be carried out easily. And this was their plan:

At the close of every Sabbath, after the blessing, Rabbi Leyb would customarily have someone bring a pitcher of water from a deep well. The water was used for brewing his tea. Normally, other people performed this task, but when it was dark and slippery outside, he would send Joseph the Golem, who brought back the water safe and sound. Little by little he got used to doing it, so that right after the closing of the Sabbath, he would hurry out and bring back the pitcher of water.

The porter and his cronies got ready to carry out their plan.

At the closing of the Hanukkah Sabbath, several powerful young men hid near the well. As soon as Joseph the Golem came by and lowered the pail into the well, bending far over the rim as usual, the men ran up to him, grabbed his legs, and sent him hurtling headfirst into the well. The pole with the bucket sprang back out.

Joseph the Golem got a good dunking, and when he came to the surface, he began to splash about with his arms. The men had planned ahead and prepared some heavy rocks, which they threw in the well to make the golem sink and drown. The rocks crashed upon his head, wounding his eye and his nose. He sank down, and they kept hurling rocks at him. But then he rose to the surface once more and remained floating on the water.

In Rabbi Leyb's home, they were waiting and waiting for the water, until at last the old beadle, Abraham-Khaim, and two other men went out with lanterns to look for the golem. When they arrived at the well, they caught sight of Rabbi Leyb's pitcher nearby. They realized something had happened, so they peered into the well with their lanterns. The moment Joseph the Golem spied them, he began clapping his hands, and they saw it was really Joseph down there. They lowered the bucket into the depth and hauled him out. He was bruised and bloody. They took him home and changed his clothes, and they washed and bandaged his wounds.

Rabbi Leyb examined him and said he would be all right. They put him into his warm bed, and he fell asleep. But it was awhile before he could get up again. By the third day, however, he was up and about.

The rabbi called him in and asked if he knew who had attacked him. Joseph the Golem replied by writing down what had happened, saying he recognized one of the attackers, the porter who had been whipped. The golem asked Rabbi Leyb to allow him to get even with the porter. The rabbi answered he would not allow him to do so, adding that the porter would be struck down by heaven.

Not long after that, the porter fell ill with a black mange, and they had to cut out pieces of his living flesh. The porter now confessed the whole story. He and three friends of his, powerful fellows, had thrown Joseph the Golem into the well and hurled large rocks at him. He sent his wife to plead with Rabbi Leyb for forgiveness. But it was no use.

The porter died a horrible death.

Afterward the other three bullies came to Rabbi Leyb to ask his forgiveness for participating in the attack on the golem. They defended themselves, saying that the porter had incited them and given them money, but now they deeply regretted what they had done, and they wept bitter tears. The rabbi required them to pay a fine, which went to his yeshiva, and to fast forty days throughout that year, and to recite the entire Book of Psalms every Sabbath.

The three men did everything he told them, and they remained alive.

The Dreadful Tale about the Deserted House near Prague

Outside Prague, on a road leading into the city, there stood an old ruin, which at one time had been a factory for gunpowder. And because the building stood on the roadside and had become too old, they moved the factory farther from the town, to the huge barracks of the imperial fort. And thus the building went to ruin, standing there for a long, long time.

It slowly became dirtier and filthier, terrifying anyone who passed it at night. Many claimed they had heard a band playing there in the darkness. And some people said they had seen a pack of several hundred black hounds milling about the walls. One Jew swore that while walking by one night he had sighted a soldier standing on the roof and blasting a trumpet.

All these stories made people wary of going near the ruin at night.

Now one night it happened that a Jewish courier was coming home from a small village near Prague. Unmindful, he walked along the side of the road near the ruin. All at once he saw a huge black hound, which came running out of the building and barked at the wayfarer. The hound ran around him and then dashed back inside. The courier was so terror-stricken he scarcely made it back home. Upon his arrival, he told his family what had happened.

That night the Jew began barking in his sleep like a dog. The rest of the household woke him up in alarm. He was exhausted and drenched with sweat. He told the others he had dreamed he was riding on a black hound along with many other people, like a troop of soldiers, and since all the other hound riders were barking like dogs, they also forced him to bark like a dog. And they warned him that if he didn't bark, then the dogs would devour him alive, and so he barked along with them.

The rest of the household told him not to worry, it was only a dream, he had been thinking about the ruin when he fell asleep, and the best thing for him would be not to think about it.

The next night came, and the same thing happened. And night after night the man kept barking in his sleep. He started growing weak and losing weight.

The man and his wife decided that only Rabbi Leyb could help. They took along their few children and went to the rabbi. They wept bitterly as they told him the whole story. They begged him to take pity and help them in their plight. For the man supported the entire family with his work as a courier, and now they might starve.

First, Rabbi Leyb inspected the fringes on the Jew's undergarment, worn in accordance with God's commandment, and he saw that they were blemished. Next, he examined the man's phylacteries, and he found that the phylactery to be worn on the head was blemished. The rabbi said that this was why the Jew had not been protected and had fallen into an impure mire. For it is written that "Every Jew is accompanied by angels who guard him on every road, and the angels are created by his fulfilling the commandments of the phylacteries and the fringes. As proof, we need merely rearrange the letters of that verse in Hebrew and we get another sentence meaning "Thus the phylacteries and the fringes."

Rabbi Leyb told the courier to fix the phylacteries and the fringes immediately and then go to the ritual bath. Next, he told his scribe to set down a biblical verse on a slip of paper and put it in an amulet: "But against any of the children of Israel shall not a dog move his tongue, against man or beast." The amulet with the verse was tied around the Jew's forehead every night before he went to bed. And for seven nights, at the rabbi's bidding, he slept in the rabbi's home, in Joseph the Golem's bed, while Joseph slept in the courier's bed.

They did everything that Rabbi Leyb told them to do. The Jew slept peacefully in the golem's bed and no longer barked.

On the seventh night the rabbi summoned Joseph the Golem and gave him his staff and told him to go into the ruin at midnight with two bundles of straw and fuel and to kindle the straw, so that the entire building would burn down. Joseph the Golem followed the rabbi's orders, and the entire ruin was burned to the ground.

From that night on, no more evil things were to be seen in that place, and the courier fully recovered.

The Wondrous Tale of Duke Bartholomew

A few leagues east of Prague, in a large village, there once lived a rich duke, who owned ten villages. In the middle of his large park there stood a tiny castle topped with a peaked tower and ringed by a thick wall. Around the wall there lay a deep moat filled with water, and a narrow iron drawbridge spanned it on one side.

The castle is empty now, but there are two headstones marking the graves of a mother and a son. And the story about this mother and her son is indeed wondrous.

Once there was an old duke living here, and his name was Bartholomew. He had only one child, a son.

The old duke was very fond of Jews, and there were many Jews living in his ten villages and taking care of his many businesses. After his wife died, he would take his son and visit the Jews in his village, just to feel at home. Most of all, he liked going to them on the Sabbath. He would have some fish in one house, some pudding in another, and so on.

In the village where the duke resided, there lived a wealthy Jew who leased land from the duke. The Jew had a learned daughter, a beauty, and she was the same age as the duke's son. The son liked her very much and spent long hours talking to her.

One day the old duke said to his Jewish landholder: "Listen to me. If your daughter were willing to become Christian, my son would marry her, and you would never have to pay for the land you lease from me."

The Jew tried to laugh it away and answered that such a marriage wasn't worthy of the duke's son; he could find a far more beautiful wife in a ducal family. The Jew realized, however, that he couldn't take the matter lightly, and he was afraid that the duke's proposal might become an awful truth. So he quickly engaged his daughter to a Jewish scholar from Prague. The bridegroom was an orphan, but he was a fine young man, and the wedding took place soon thereafter. A year later the young wife bore a son.

But soon an epidemic struck that region, claiming many victims, even whole families, and a great number of people fled into other countries, losing complete sight of one another, not knowing who had perished and who had survived. The epidemic raged through the villages of the old duke. And the young wife lost her parents and husband both. She was left alone with the tiny baby and had nowhere to flee.

She finally took refuge in the castle park. The old duke and his son found out she was there and felt great pity for the young wife and her child, so they offered her a private apartment and took care of her every need.

In Prague, as in the ducal villages, people assumed that the entire family of the Jewish landholder had perished. Meanwhile the young widow forgot about her troubles. The duke's son felt a stronger love for her than ever, and so they decided to marry with no one realizing who she was.

They sent her and the child to Venice in secret, and there they gave the child to a wet nurse. Shortly thereafter, the wedding took place in the same city. Back home the duke announced in the village that his son had married the daughter of a Venetian senator and would return with his bride in a year.

Meanwhile the young couple were living happily in Venice and journeying to other lands. It wasn't until a year and a half later that they came back to the old duke's village. No one was aware that the young aristocrat was actually the Jewish landholder's daughter. The young couple announced that they had already had a baby in Venice; they had given him to a wet nurse and would bring him back as soon as he was weaned. It wasn't long before the old duke died, and all his property and his title passed down to the son.

After a time the baby was weaned and brought to the village, and since his Hebrew name was Jacob, he was registered as the duke's son with the name of Jacob Bartholomew.

The young duke led a good life with his Jewish wife, and she bore him two lovely daughters. Now the duke felt that since the son was born of a Jewish woman, he would be strongly drawn to the Jewish religion, for everything is drawn to its own roots. So the duke made an effort to pour a hatred of Jews into the boy's heart, and he hired tutors who despised Jews. Little by little the hatred that the boy felt in his heart for Jews kept growing, so that in the end he wouldn't even speak to a Jew.

The three children grew up in the ducal castle. They were endowed with beauty and learning, and all three made brilliant marriages. The two daughters went off with their husbands, and only the false son and his wife, who was a general's daughter, remained with the duke.

At the age of sixty the duke went to his reward, and all his property and his title passed down to the false son, Jacob Bartholomew, who lived with his mother, the daughter of the Jewish landholder.

As soon as the new duke, Jacob Bartholomew, took over all the property and began to rule in the villages, he set about oppressing the few Jews who lived there and did terrible things to them, making sure they stopped earning their livelihoods. He did all he could to get rid of them. Many Jewish families were left without a crust of bread. When they saw how bad things were, they came to Rabbi Leyb, begging him to help them. The rabbi answered that for the moment he didn't know what to do, but he hoped that heaven might reveal some plan to him. He asked them to come back in a week.

That very night, when Rabbi Leyb was dreaming, the duke's real father came to him from the other world and bitterly lamented what had happened. The dead man told Rabbi Leyb the whole story. Duke Jacob Bartholomew was born a Jew, and he, the dead man, was his father. His name was Isaac ben Aaron Ha-Levi, of Prague, and he was the son-in-law of the Jewish landholder and had died during the epidemic. The duke's mother had been his wife, and after his death she had married the duke. Her Jewish name was Rosa, the daughter of Moses. And when his son, Jacob, known as Jacob Bartholomew, had taken over the title of duke, he had started oppressing all the Jewish inhabitants of his villages, and their tears had flowed up to heaven. These tears had brought him, the dead man, great suffering, and he was not allowed a moment's peace. The dead man added that he had come to his son in dreams to reveal to him that he was a Jew, for he was circumcised after all, and he had asked him not to do any harm to the Jews. But the son paid no attention to dreams!

Thus the dead man lamented bitterly, and he pleaded with Rabbi Leyb to take pity on his soul and lead the duke away from his evil path. The dead man then said to the rabbi that he had heard in the True World that only the rabbi with his wisdom could help him.

The next morning Rabbi Leyb asked his old beadle, Abraham-Khaim to go to the village where the duke resided and find out whether a landholder named Moses had really lived there and had had a daughter named Rosa and whether there had ever been a boy named Isaac ben Aaron Ha-Levi in Prague and whether he had married the landholder's daughter.

Abraham-Khaim, the beadle, found it was all true. Whereupon Rabbi Leyb said: "Well, if all this is true, then what was said in heaven must also be true, that I can be of some help. I'll have to devise a plan."

And this was the plan that Rabbi Leyb carried out:

Rabbi Leyb knew that Duke Jacob Bartholomew drove to Prague every Sunday to attend church. The rabbi wrote the following letter.

My dear child,

You must know that I, Isaac ben Aaron Ha-Levi, of Prague, am your real father. I was the first husband of your mother, Rosa, who lives with you, and she was a daughter of the Jewish landholder Moses, who dwelt in the village of the deceased duke's father. And I and my father-in-law died in the epidemic. The name I gave you was Jacob.

And now I have come from beyond the grave to ask you not to do any harm to the Jews who have lived in these villages for so many years.

I have come into your dreams several times to reveal that you are a Jew by birth, but then I saw that you paid no attention to your dreams. Thus I had to descend myself to give you this letter so that you might realize the truth, for I have had no peace in the next world ever since the tears of the Jewish families began flowing into heaven. You can tell that you are a Jew because you are circumcised, and if you repeat these things to your mother, Rosa, she will surely confirm what I have said. If you wish to know what to do, place your trust in the rabbi of Prague.

Your father, Isaac ben Aaron Ha-Levi

That was the content of the letter. And early in the morning of the day that Duke Jacob Bartholomew was to attend church in Prague, Rabbi Leyb handed the letter to Joseph the Golem as well as the amulet that made him invisible. The road that the duke was to take went uphill as it neared the city. Rabbi Leyb ordered Joseph the Golem to station himself there with the letter and wait for the duke. As soon as the duke came and started driving slowly uphill, Joseph the Golem was to go over to the carriage and drop the letter into the duke's lap.

Joseph the Golem carried out the plan exactly as told. When the duke saw the letter, he turned pale. He peered all around carefully but couldn't see anyone, and so he really believed it had been his dead father.

When the duke arrived home, he questioned his mother thoroughly and showed her the letter. His mother confessed that it was all true and told him not to oppress the Jewish families who were their brothers and sisters.

The next day the duke sent out his carriage for Rabbi Leyb. The rabbi accepted his invitation at once and rode to the castle, where he stayed for a day and a night. Rabbi Leyb never repeated what had taken place. But people did find out that Duke Jacob Bartholomew had given the rabbi a large sum of money, which he used to found the great yeshiva of Prague, and it was named the Yeshiva of the House of Jacob in honor of its patron, Jacob Bartholomew. As for the Jewish families that lived in his villages, they all remained, of course, and were given great concessions.

Sometime later Duke Jacob Bartholomew built the well-known little castle at the center of his park and the two tombs, one for his mother and one for himself, so that in death they could lie apart rather than in the Christian churchyard.

The Last Blood Libel in Prague during Rabbi Leyb's Lifetime

For three years now Prague and the surrounding region had been resting from the hardships caused by a blood libel. And their rest was due to Rabbi Leyb, whom everyone feared for his powerful mind, which revealed all secrets.

But in the year 5349 [1589], a terrible blood libel spread throughout Prague. This is what happened:

There lived in the city a wealthy man named Aaron Ginz. His home was truly Jewish and rich. "Learning and affluence in the same place," as the Talmud says. He had three sons-in-law boarding with him, and they spent their days studying the Torah and the Talmud. He also had three sons and a daughter who weren't married.

Aaron Ginz's business was a leather tannery. The entire household lived in town, in a brick house, but the tannery stood outside the city. There were twenty workers employed there, twelve Jews and eight Christians. And since these men had already been working there a number of years and were always together, the Christian workers came to speak Yiddish as well as the Jews did.

Now, there were three brothers among the Christian workers, and they came from a village some four leagues from Prague. Their father had died long ago, but they still had a poor old mother, who lived in a hut away from the village.

The two older brothers were named Karl Kozlovsky and Hendrikh Kozlovsky. At the tannery, people didn't quite know the name of the youngest brother, but everyone called him Kozilek because when he first came to the tannery, he had been as young and as wild as a *koziol*, a billy goat. His two older brothers were unwilling to tell people his real name. They were ashamed of him and didn't allow him to use their family name because their mother had given birth to him two years after the father's death and without a legal husband. So he was registered as a child born out of wedlock, with the first name of Yan, the son of Yadviga (their mother).

The two older brothers were already married, and they had been living in Prague for some time now. Since the mother was a widow and earned a meager living in wash, she pleaded with her two older sons to take their youngest brother into the tannery as a worker like them. And she asked them to watch out for him. They agreed for her sake and asked the owner.

When the "billy goat" started in the tannery, he was fifteen years old. He worked hard for three years and was already getting good pay.

One day Kozilek, the billy goat, was jumping and playing around. All at once he tumbled into a deep vat full of unclean water where the hides were soaking. He was fished out more dead than alive. And two fingers on his right hand were so badly hurt they had to be amputated. Kozilek was laid up for several weeks. He barely regained his health, and he was no longer able to do the same work as before. For not only had he lost two fingers, but he became very sickly after his accident, and sometimes he spit blood.

The owner wanted to let Kozilek go since he was of no use for the work. The two older brothers wouldn't hear of it; they flatly demanded that he be allowed to remain and receive the same salary as earlier. But if the owner laid him off, he would have to give him a good sum of money. The two brothers had several arguments with the owner about it, and in the end the owner agreed to keep him on. They would use him for hauling and cleaning, but as for pay, he would receive only half as much as before.

From that time on, the two brothers harbored a grudge against the owner, Aaron Ginz, and they started thinking of a way to get even with him, for they saw that Kozilek, the billy goat, was badly treated. He had to sweep and clean everything, and he had to carry and lug the heavy loads. Besides his chores in the tannery, Kozilek had to work for the owner at his home in town. He had to sweep, and clean and scrub, and on the Sabbath he had to heat the stoves. In the end Kozilek became consumptive and constantly spit blood. His life was a living death, and he made up his mind to escape from work even if it cost him his life.

Purim came, and at the banquet in Aaron Ginz's home there were many guests. The company made merry as they always did at Purim, to celebrate the victory of Queen Esther in Persia, who had overcome Haman and prevented him from massacring the Jews. The guests drank a great deal of wine from silver goblets, after which Aaron Ginz and his entire household fell asleep.

Kozilek took advantage of this opportunity. He sneaked into Aaron Ginz's home and took off with ten silver goblets, a dozen silver knives and forks, and Aaron Ginz's watch. That same night he fled with all the booty to his old mother by the village, so that no one knew what had become of him.

In the morning, when they saw that there had been a robbery and that Kozilek was gone, they realized it was his handiwork. Aaron Ginz promptly sent for Kozilek's two brothers and told them what he had done, and he accused them of talking Kozilek into the robbery and hiding him and his booty. The two brothers argued with their employer, saying he had no right to accuse them. They knew nothing about the robbery, and they certainly couldn't know where Kozilek was, because he had no parents.

They didn't want to tell about their old mother because they were sure that Kozilek had fled to her. If they said anything, then Aaron Ginz would certainly go to her hut to look for the booty.

Aaron Ginz reported the robbery to the police and had them make a thorough search in the home of the two brothers. But nothing was found. As a result, the hatred of the two brothers for Aaron Ginz grew even greater, though they worked in his tannery and earned their living from him. All the same, they agreed to get even with him.

On Friday evening the two brothers went out to their mother's hut by the village to see what was going on. When they arrived, they found Kozilek dying. He had fled Prague a few nights earlier and gone out to the country on foot through terrible cold, so that his consumption grew worse. He was losing a good deal of blood, and he lay in bed all through the night. At daybreak he died.

The two brothers decided to bury Kozilek on Sunday in the village graveyard. Now, since they had no money to pay for the funeral and the rites, they took along the watch that Kozilek had stolen from Aaron Ginz, and they brought it to the village priest. They told the priest that their half brother had just died, and since their mother was very poor, they had no money for the funeral and the ceremonies. The only thing they could give him was the watch that the old widow had as a memento of their deceased father. And they asked the priest to accept it and let them bury their brother without rites.

The priest took the watch and carried out their wishes. Kozilek was buried in the village graveyard, quietly and without ceremonies, and no one in the village noticed.

The brothers took the rest of the stolen silver articles and sold them to someone in the village, giving the money to their old, poor mother. And Sunday afternoon they went back home to Prague.

On Monday morning the two brothers didn't come to work until midday, for of course they were tired from their trip. Aaron Ginz was annoyed at this and upbraided them and treated them very harshly. He yelled that they had probably been drinking all day and all night on what they had robbed from him. The two brothers deeply resented this. They were so angry they couldn't reply. But they made up their minds that the time had come to get even with the owner.

The two brothers worked out a plan. No one knew what had become of their brother Kozilek, and even the people in the village where he was buried didn't know he had died. The two brothers wanted to take this chance to organize a blood libel against the owner of the tannery, using the dead body of their Kozilek.

On a certain night the two brothers stole out to the village where Kozilek was buried. They took the corpse out of the grave and then put the empty coffin back and set up the wooden cross again, so that no one could see what had happened. Next, they cut the dead man's throat as in a ritual slaughter, pulled off his clothes, and wrapped him in a blood-strained white sheet.

They then brought the corpse back to Prague, to the Jewish cemetery, and took it to the side near a road that led from Prague to a neighboring village. The road was traveled by many Christians driving their wagons out to the country. The brothers dug out a grave under the wall surrounding the cemetery and waited until some Christians drove by in a wagon, on their way out to the country.

The brothers started burying the corpse and kept laughing and speaking loudly in Yiddish so that the passersby would ask them what was going on. And when the Christians asked them what they were doing, the brothers laughed and answered that they were burying a Jewish gentile, who was neither Jewish nor Christian and thus not worth burying except near the wall in the darkness of night. The Christians who passed by took them at their word and continued driving home.

The two brothers then took Kozilek's clothes and boots, which were well known to all the workers at the tannery, and stuffed them into a sack. They drove home, and as soon as it was night, they smuggled the clothes into the cellar of Aaron Ginz's home in Prague. There they buried the sack in a pile of sand when no one was looking.

The next day, in various parts of the city, the two brothers claimed they had heard that some Christians from the nearby village had seen two Jews at night, burying a Christian under the wall of the Jewish cemetery. The brothers remarked that it could only be a

Christian victim who had fallen into the hands of the Jews before Passover, for they needed Christian blood in their matzoth.

The rumor quickly spread throughout Prague, and there was certainly no lack of anti-Semites spreading it further day by day. Some of them even started going about inquiring whether any Christian had vanished during the past few days.

The two brothers stealthily did their share in spreading the rumor and finally claimed that the victim was no other than the Christian known as Kozilek, who worked in the tannery. During the past few days he had suddenly vanished, like a stone in water, and it must have been because he was sick, and the owner, who wanted to get rid of him, had turned him over as a Passover victim, and to avert any suspicion, he had spread a rumor that Kozilek had robbed him and run away.

The rumor circulated by the two brothers grew and grew from day to day, until at last it reached the ears of the police commissioner. And since so many inquiries were coming to him from so many places, he had no choice but to launch an investigation.

The commissioner and the police went over to the nearby village and summoned the Christians who had witnessed the scene. He then took them back to Prague so that they could show him the exact location of the grave.

As soon as the commissioner came home, he asked the leaders of the Jewish community, and Rabbi Leyb, and the gravediggers to explain whom they had buried there. But they all flatly denied knowing anything about such a burial and said it was a falsehood and slander.

Finally, the commissioner, the police, and several Jews went out to the Jewish cemetery and began to search it until they found the grave. They took the dead body out in front of all the people.

Meanwhile a crowd of people from the city had gathered at the cemetery. Kozilek's two brothers were there, along with several other Christian workers from the tannery. As soon as the corpse was unwrapped, they saw that it was really Kozilek. The best proof was that two fingers were missing from his right hand. At once, the two brothers stepped out of the crowd, weeping and wailing, and they mourned their brother.

Turning to the crowd, they yelled: "See what those damned Jews do to us! See how that Jew from the tannery, Aaron, slaughtered our young brother!"

The whole mob of Christians became all worked up by the shouts. They wanted to tear apart the few Jews who were there, but the police prevented the murders. Still, several of the Jews had stones hurled at them. The Christians were on the verge of starting a pogrom, but Rabbi Leyb hurried over to the city hall and begged the authorities not to let any such dreadful thing happen until the matter was thoroughly investigated. And thus the Jewish quarter was saved from a pogrom.

But the two brothers wouldn't let the matter rest there. They asked the police commissioner to make a thorough search of Aaron Ginz's cellar, for it could well be that they might find their brother's blood in small vials, prepared by the Jews for Passover. The commissioner followed their suggestion, and together with a huge squad of policemen he broke into Aaron's home and undertook a thorough search of the cellar until they found the bundle of Kozilek's clothing, which the two brothers and the rest of the Christian workers from the tannery immediately recognized. The police promptly arrested Aaron Ginz and his two sons-in-law and the women and children and took them all to prison. The house and the tannery were locked and sealed.

The next day they put the clothes back on Kozilek's dead body, and a large crowd of Christians, with many priests, carried the corpse to a church with all possible ceremonies. The priests mourned the deceased and sermonized against the Jews. Then they informed the police commissioner that they couldn't bury Kozilek until the Jew who had killed him confessed at the victim's side and sewed his throat together again. The commissioner had to do as they said, and they brought Aaron Ginz in fetters, guarded by a huge number of soldiers, to the church.

The most important priest said to the Jew: "Your hands shed this pure blood and severed the throat. You must therefore make good your crime. Beg the dead man's forgiveness, and sew his throat together again."

Aaron Ginz, as pale as death, replied: "Since I did not sever the throat, I shall not sew it together again!"

The crowd in the church wanted to pounce upon Aaron Ginz and tear him to shreds. But the soldiers surrounding him held the Christians back.

Again, the priest addressed Aaron Ginz with these words: "You can see that your sin was revealed as clear as day. And you will most surely be judged and sentenced to death. So if you confess your crime to the dead man and sew his throat together again, you shall do much good for your soul. And when your soul comes to the afterlife, it shall not be so sinful if you confess your sin and name the people who incited you to such a crime."

To this, Aaron Ginz retorted: "I do not have to do any good for my soul, for it is innocent of this crime."

When the priests saw they couldn't do anything with him, they told the soldiers to take him back to prison. Then they buried the victim with great honors. A terrible fear and gloom came upon all the Jews of Prague. They were afraid to show themselves in the Christian streets. *And the city of Prague was perplexed.*

Rabbi Leyb himself was horrified at this blood libel. He went about in a state of bewilderment. He had lost the good graces of the rulers, for what could he say in Aaron Ginz's favor? The rabbi realized it was a libel, but it was so cunningly organized that for the moment he had to hold his tongue.

It was the month of Nissan, and the rabbi did not wish to ordain any fasts. However, he issued a decree that the entire city should rise very early each morning and recite the entire Book of Psalms, until after the trial for the blood accusation.

The crisis brought on another crisis. The priests of Prague proclaimed that the Christians were not to purchase anything from Jews, for they were not sure of their lives with the Jews.

When Rabbi Leyb saw that the crisis was worsening and that he still hadn't hit upon a solution, he decided to consult his dreams, and he received seven Hebrew words as a clear answer. They meant: "Investigate, inquire thoroughly, they shall be released." The rabbi felt stronger now, and he comforted his community, saying there was hope and the truth would out.

The day of the trial arrived. It was the new moon of Sivan, in early summer. Rabbi Leyb was present in court. But there was nothing he could offer by way of defense. Aaron Ginz and his three sons-in-law were sentenced to fifteen years at hard labor, the four wives to six years' imprisonment, and only the little children were allowed to go free. The city was shrouded in gloom.

However, Rabbi Leyb was not asleep. He knew very well that Kozilek had suddenly died of consumption where he had taken refuge, that he had been buried there and then dug up again and smuggled in with his clothes. But how could it be proved?

For one thing, they didn't know where he had died because they didn't know where he had sought refuge. And secondly, how could they find out if they didn't even know his real name, which was registered in the book of the deceased, Kozilek being only his nickname?

The first thing Rabbi Leyb did was to bend all his efforts to discovering where Kozilek could have died and been buried. Now, since it made sense that he had sought refuge in his native town, the rabbi began investigating where the three brothers came from. By questioning the workers of the tannery, he managed to ferret out that they came from the large village four miles from Prague.

The rabbi sent capable men to that village, to find out about the

Kozlovsky family. They did discover where the mother lived, but they couldn't get any information out of her. She stuck to the story that she hadn't seen hide nor hair of her youngest son ever since he had joined his two older brothers.

The rabbi's men came back to Prague empty-handed. But when Rabbi Leyb heard there was a Christian cemetery in the village, he said that now there was a way to bring forth the facts, but they would have to depend on a higher power. He explained that during the first year of a person's death, the soul remained by the grave because it was still somewhat attached to the body, but if a body wasn't in the grave, they wouldn't see the soul above it. Now a dead man's soul could be seen only by people on a high level or by cattle, beasts, and birds. And Joseph the Golem could see a soul as well as cattle, beasts, or birds could.

Thus Rabbi Leyb demanded that the authorities allow him to send two men to look upon all the graves of the last three months in the Christian cemetery of that village. They would determine if there was any empty grave from which a dead man had been unlawfully removed. He also demanded that city hall give him two policemen. The commissioner yielded to the rabbi's request and sent him two policemen, together with an order that the gravediggers of that cemetery should show them all the fresh graves of the last three months.

Rabbi Leyb assigned the task to Joseph the Golem and gave him a capable man, and they went to investigate the cemetery. There the golem paused at a grave and motioned that it was empty. They sent word to Prague, and the commissioner came with several policemen, and the rabbi with several intelligent men accompanied them.

They dug up the grave and took out an empty coffin.

The commissioner sent for the priest and had him bring the book of the deceased and tell them who had been buried in that grave. The priest came with the records, and they discovered that just a few days before Purim, the gravediggers had buried a man named Yan, the son of Yadviga. They already knew that this was the name of the old mother of the two brothers.

Now the commissioner realized that Kozilek had actually been buried here and that the body had then been stolen. The commissioner questioned the priest closely to make him remember the men who had asked permission to bury the corpse. The priest recalled that they were the two brothers of the dead man. They had paid him no money but had given him a watch, which he had in his pocket. The priest showed the watch to the police commissioner.

The others remembered that Aaron Ginz had been robbed of a watch, and so the commissioner sent a horseman to town to ask Aaron Ginz whether this was indeed his watch. Aaron Ginz identified the watch as his at a distance and with the help of a hidden sign. The horseman quickly rode back to the village and told the commissioner how Aaron Ginz had identified the watch.

The commissioner and his men broke into the old woman's hut. The old woman kept denying everything, but then, after two hard slaps, she began crying and pleading and said she would tell them the whole story, and she gave them a correct account of what had happened. She even told them where the rest of the stolen articles had been sold in the village.

The police commissioner ordered a narrow search of the village, and they found the rest of the stolen articles. The commissioner promptly arrested the old woman and the man who had bought the valuables, and they were taken back to Prague.

Next, the commissioner entered the home of the two brothers because the man who had bought the stolen articles told the police he had gotten them from Yadviga's two older sons. However, the two brothers were no longer in Prague. They had made their escape. Now the authorities finally realized the truth about how the blood libel had been organized, and they quickly released Aaron Ginz and his two children, and *the city of Prague rejoiced and was glad.*

Rabbi Leyb wrote down a full protocol of exactly what had happened, from start to finish, and sent it to King Rudolf with a request that the king allow him to present himself at court. The king gave Rabbi Leyb permission, and on a certain day the royal palace sent two generals after him in a coach.

When the rabbi appeared before the king, he tearfully begged the ruler to put an end once and for all to the blood libel, so that such a trial would never again be repeated in any court of justice anywhere in the land, for the sin of accusing innocent souls falls upon an entire kingdom.

The king had a long conversation with him. Rabbi Leyb never cared to reveal what was said. But afterward the king issued an order that no more blood accusations were to be made against Jews in his kingdom.

How Rabbi Leyb Removed Joseph the Golem

After King Rudolf's law was put in effect, and another Passover went by with no incidents, Rabbi Leyb summoned his son-in-law Isaac and his pupil Jacob ben Khaim-Sassoon Ha-Levi, who both had participated in the creation of Joseph the Golem. The rabbi said the golem was no longer needed because there would be no more blood libels in this country. This was the night of Lag b'Omer in the year 5350 [or 1590, according to the Christian reckoning].

Rabbi Leyb ordered the golem not to lie down on his bed in the rabbi's home, but rather to take his bed to the attic of the synagogue and to go to sleep up there. Joseph the Golem did as he was told when no one was watching. After midnight Rabbi Leyb, together with the gaon and his pupil Jacob Sassoon, mounted the stairs up to the attic of the great synagogue. Before going, the rabbi had a thorough discussion with his son-in-law to decide whether a Cohen could be in the same room as a corpse like the golem's, since such a thing was forbidden to a descendant of priests. Rabbi Leyb demonstrated that such a corpse is not really a defilement.

Rabbi Leyb had given Abraham-Khaim, the old beadle, his permission to attend, and he told him to stay back a bit with two candles in his hands.

When they reached the attic, the three men stood in positions opposite the ones they had taken when creating the golem. First they stood at the head of the prostrate golem and faced his feet. Next, they began circling him along his left side to his feet and then along his right side to his head, where they stopped and said something. They did the same thing seven times.

After the seven encirclements the golem was dead. He lay there like a piece of hardened clay. The rabbi then called over the beadle Abraham-Khaim and took hold of the two candles and stripped the clothes off the golem, leaving only his shirt on him. Since there was no lack of old prayer shawls in the attic, they wrapped him up in two old prayer shawls and bound him up. Next, they shoved him under the mountain of stray leaves from holy books so that he was fully hidden from sight.

Rabbi Leyb told Abraham-Khaim to take the bed and the clothes downstairs and burn them up slowly without anyone seeing him. Next, they all descended and washed their hands.

The next morning it was announced that the beadle Joseph the Golem had gotten angry and departed that night. The mass of Jews believed it, but some of the community leaders knew the truth.

A week later Rabbi Leyb proclaimed a ban against going up to the attic of the great synagogue. He forbade any further storing of loose pages in the attic. People said the prohibition was due to a fear that someone might start a fire up there by kindling a light. But some of the community leaders knew the real reason:

No one was ever to know that Joseph the Golem is lying up there.

S. Bastomski (1891–1941)

Yiddish Folktales and
Legends of Old Prague (*Selections*)

1923

Jewish folklore about a mystical Prague often centers on the figure of Rabbi Leyb (1525–1609), who is credited with creating the golem. Indeed, S. Bastomski, renowned as an educator and folklorist and for other achievements, issued several Yiddish booklets about the legends of old Prague. Of his two booklets (1923, 1927) about Prague, one mentions the golem only in passing, and the other ignores him totally, whereas both collections offer several tales about the adventures of Rabbi Leyb. This preponderance most likely indicates that the rabbi was believed to be more important and more significant than his most famous creation. For more information regarding the mystical tales about Rabbi Leyb, see my translation of the booklet Yiddish Folktales and Legends of Old Prague *(1927) in* Radiant Days, Haunted Nights.

The Jewish Ghetto

Three hundred years ago a large Jewish community resided in the town of Prague. In those days the Jews of Prague lived in a ghetto, a separate district known as the Old Town. It could be reached only through six gates, which led into and out of the ghetto. At night the gates were locked, so that the ghetto was totally isolated from the surrounding world. During Easter, the Christian Holy Week, the gates were locked both day and night.

The ghetto had a very different appearance from the rest of the town: ancient, mostly wooden houses, built in an old-fashioned style, with bizarre attachments to and above one another and with lots of small porches and small balconies. The courtyards were dark and dirty, as well as narrow, crooked, and twisted, and the streets were unpaved.

The inhabitants of the ghetto also looked different from the gentile population. A Jew mainly wore a yellow fur hat and a cloak with a red patch on its back in accordance with the anti-Jewish laws.

The Jews didn't dare live in the gentile areas of Prague even though the Christians accepted the legend that the persecuted Jews were the original dwellers of Prague. The Jews had established a community there before the famous heroine Lubushe laid the earliest foundations. Indeed, Jews claimed that their old synagogue was even older than the local Christian church. Everyone gazed with great awe at the ancient synagogue with its tiny windows and its lofty roof, which had blackened in the course of time. Like a loyal servant, that strange monument towered over the crooked and constricted lanes, the survivors of edicts and agonies.

Elderly Jews declared that the walls of the Old Synagogue contained stones carried here by angels from the Temple in Jerusalem to the place where the Chosen People had settled. And the angels cautioned our fathers and forefathers that the synagogue would stand solid and that the places where the Temple stones lay would endure and remain forever and ever. And woe unto anyone who tried to alter anything in the synagogue. They either stumbled in their work or else perished quite suddenly.

The earliest synagogue was made entirely of wood. When it grew very old, the congregants gathered together and decided that they would build a new synagogue on a hill not far from the old synagogue. But when they started digging for a new foundation, they unearthed a stone wall. The deeper they dug, the more they realized that this was a wall of an ancient, ancient synagogue. And the situation grew clearer and clearer when they discovered a Torah scroll in the earth.

At that time there were two Jews from Jerusalem living in Prague. And they advised the Prague Jews to build the windows in such a way that they would be wide inside and narrow outside. The synagogue itself should be built in such a way that you would have to climb a staircase, for it is written in the Book of Psalms: "I call upon God from the depths."

And the Jews of Prague actually built their new synagogue in accordance with that advice.

The old-new synagogue is still standing today, and it has hummed with the Torah and with prayers for generations now.

How often has the dark Christian mob vandalized the ancient synagogue! How often has the dark Christian mob charged into the holy building, desecrating and profaning the sacred Jewish instruments, beating and torturing the Jews!

Often the eternal light has been snuffed, and the holy ark has been hurtled to the floor! At first the synagogue had suffered terribly under King Jan, who ordered his underlings to search for the hidden Jewish treasures. And indeed, the underlings unearthed lots of gold and silver—lots of Jewish property. A great deal of Jewish blood was spilled during the reign of King Jan.

The Jews then suffered much more under his grandson King Vyatsheslav IV. One Passover evening the mob slammed into the ghetto, violating it and burning it down. Three thousand Jews were martyred that night. The walls of the synagogue were silent witnesses to the horrendous weeping and wailing. The holy inscriptions that adorned the walls were covered with the blood of the victims. Ever since that time a penitential prayer commemorating that dreadful night and lamenting the fate of the fallen brethren has been read on the Day of Atonement. The author of that prayer was Joseph Caro, who saw the massacre with his own two eyes. The Old Synagogue likewise depicts what it observed. As of that night, no one has cleaned or white-washed the walls. No rabbi has allowed anyone to touch them.

Let the blood of the martyrs serve to remind coming genera-tions that this is the blood of the afflicted.

The old synagogue has suffered many other storms. One day the ghetto was swept up in a horrible fire. It destroyed most of the houses, sparing only the old synagogue, which stood like a fortress in the middle of the fiery sea. On all four sides there were columns of choking black smoke while sparks and embers flew through the air. Not a single spark fell on the synagogue, and not a single roof exploded. . . . Two white doves were perched on the turret, and they stayed there until the fire was put out. The terrible heat, the stench of the smoke didn't drive the doves away. It was only when the dan-ger was passed that one dove soared out, followed by the other dove. They beat their white wings and disappeared in the dense, far-away clouds.

Rabbi Leyb of Prague

In the days of King Rudolf II, the renowned Rabbi Aryeh Leyb lived in the Jewish ghetto of Prague. Rabbi Leyb was a great expert in the Bible, the Talmud, and the rabbinical tradition. He also had immense knowledge of mathematics and astronomy. Furthermore, he solved countless natural mysteries, which were beyond the ken of a normal human being. His brilliance was indescribable, and his fame spread beyond his surroundings.

The Christian scholars also knew about him, as did the famous astronomer Tycho Brahe, his great friend and admirer. Eventually the fame of Rabbi Leyb's wonderful merits reached the royal court. And this is what happened at his first meeting with the king.

One day the king, accompanied by a squad of horsemen, was in his coach, riding from New Town to Old Town. Around that time the king had issued an edict banishing all Jews from Prague.

Rabbi Leyb decided to approach the king and ask him to rescind his edict. But the rabbi was not allowed to enter the royal palace. So he had to find the king somewhere else. He knew that on that day the king would have to cross the Stone Bridge, which linked the two parts of Prague.

The rabbi waited there until that special time when the king would be coming. The rabbi waited and waited.

Finally, the king's coach appeared, hitched to four horses and escorted by a squad of rich horsemen. Now the king was already close to the bridge.

"Make way!" the horsemen shouted in the distance.

But the rabbi stood in the middle of the road as if he didn't hear the shouts.

Upon seeing this, the street mob started yelling and hurling stones at him.

But the rabbi didn't move.

Instead of stones he was pelted with flower blossoms.

And now the coach was drawing very close. It was as if the ardent horses were going to trample the rabbi in another moment. But to everyone's astonishment, the horses came to a halt even though the coachmen didn't intend to stop them.

And now the rabbi moved. He went over to the side of the coach, fell down at the king's feet, and begged for mercy for the Jews.

The king was amazed, and so he invited the rabbi to his castle.

This alone was already a great favor. But the king showed his true mercy the next day, when the rabbi appeared at the castle. The king listened carefully to the rabbi's request, and then he rescinded the horrible edict.

After that incident the rabbi was invited to the royal palace several times. Once the king wanted the rabbi to show him the patriarchs: Abraham, Isaac, and Jacob with Jacob's children. For a long time Rabbi Leyb refused. But the king was so insistent that the rabbi was compelled to fulfill the royal demand. However, the rabbi had one condition: When the holy figures passed by, nobody was to smile.

At the scheduled moment, the king and his courtiers gathered in a special room, where they waited, trembling and shuddering. The tall, proud rabbi stood by the high window. Suddenly he vanished as if into a fog, and out of the fog came the clear shape of the old man Abraham. His figure drifted by and dissolved into the darkness. Abraham was followed by Isaac and Jacob as well as Jacob's sons, each in turn.

Horrified and shivering, the people who were gathered here peered at the patriarchs. All at once Jacob's son Naphtali emerged. He had red hair and freckles. Indeed, his entire figure was so ridiculous that the king couldn't help smiling. The instant a smile crossed the king's face, Naphtali's figure promptly disappeared. A moment later the fog from which the various figures had emerged also disappeared, and the room was filled with dreadful noises.

The courtiers sprang away, and their trembling hands pointed at the ceiling. It hung down and started collapsing. Pale with terror, they all wanted to dash toward the door. But they couldn't move; they were virtually fettered. Now they yelled for the rabbi. After a while the rabbi emerged at the window. He raised his arms, and the ceiling remained suspended. The king and his courtiers swiftly dashed out of the room.

The king ordered his servants to lock that room, and he never entered that room again.

This incident did not alter the good relationship between the king and the rabbi. On the contrary! Within a brief time the king paid the rabbi a great honor. He told the rabbi that he would visit him personally. The ghetto had never been honored in this way. The following legend developed around the royal visit.

Like all the houses in the ghetto, the rabbi's home was old and neglected. But when the king and his retinue crossed the threshold, everything was suddenly transformed. The simple house was changed into a magnificent palace, the wooden steps into clear marble steps, which shone like a mirror. The way was covered with expensive carpets. The king and his retinue couldn't get enough of the surrounding splendor. The guests were brought up to a lofty hall, with the most luxurious wallpaper and the loveliest pictures. Through the wide-open doors they could see a whole series of richly decorated halls. After accompanying the king through all those halls, the rabbi finally led him into a chamber where tables were prepared with the costliest food. The rabbi invited his guests to sit down at the table.

The king and his men sat down, and the rabbi favored them with those delicacies, which the king himself would have liked to enjoy forever. He just couldn't get over those miracles. He spent a long time with the rabbi and then left the rabbi's home with great delight.

After that, the king often showed the great rabbi his mercy and friendship. In order to perpetuate the memory of the king's visit, the rabbi placed a stone monument next to his home, a lion with a cluster of grapes.

In regard to the rabbi's life, there is also a wondrous legend that he created a golem out of clay. The rabbi himself kneaded the clay figure of a man, and he inserted the holy name of God into the golem's mouth. The golem promptly came to life.

The golem was very strong, and he performed the hardest tasks: sweeping, straightening, chopping wood, hauling water, and so forth. Yet he required no food and no rest. So he labored all week without a break. On Friday evenings, with the arrival of the Holy Sabbath, the rabbi would remove the holy name from the golem's mouth. The golem would then be turned back into a lump of clay.

With the closing of the Sabbath, the rabbi would reinsert the holy name in the golem's mouth, and the golem would come to life again.

One Friday evening the rabbi was in such a hurry to get to the synagogue that he forgot to remove the holy name from the golem's mouth. The worshipers were already ushering in the Sabbath. All at once the rabbi's guests and neighbors came dashing over, yelling and hollering. They shouted that the golem had rebelled. He allowed nobody to approach him, and he threatened to kill everyone! The rabbi stood there, at a loss as to what to do. It was already the Sabbath! But he had to figure out his next move. After all, the golem could wreak terrible havoc.

The crowd waited, shuddering.

At last the rabbi made up his mind. Without saying a word, he left the synagogue and hurried home. In the distance he could already hear the hubbub and the turmoil. The rabbi was followed by a huge throng. When he entered his home, he found total chaos. The dishes and the furnishings were smashed; the covers were strewn about; the sacred books were torn up!

The bedlam in the courtyard was even worse. The golem had killed all the poultry, slaughtered the dog, the cat, uprooted the century-old lilac tree by the porch. The golem's face was red from all the strain, and his black curls were ill kempt.

The rabbi strode directly toward him. He raised his arms aloft and glared straight into the golem's eyes.

The golem trembled. His eyes bulged at his creator, and all his limbs shut down.

The rabbi went over to him, and with a single wave of his hand he removed the Holy Name from the golem's mouth. The golem was virtually clipped. He collapsed and lay on the floor like a piece of cloth. The congregants couldn't help being amazed, and they shouted in delight. Upon seeing that the golem wasn't at all dangerous, they drew closer and started poking fun at him and ridiculing him. The rabbi took a deep breath, and without uttering a word, he returned to the synagogue to finish welcoming the Sabbath.

The Holy Sabbath was complete, but the rabbi never again inserted the holy name into the golem's mouth.

And so the golem remained a lump of clay. For a while he lay under the bench of the old synagogue. Eventually he crumbled into bits and pieces.

Dovid Frishman
(aka David Frischmann, 1859–1922)

The Golem

1922

Dovid Frishman was a multitalented, multilingual author, who wrote in Yiddish, German, and Hebrew. A major author in Hebrew, he focused on biblical rather than modern diction. Born in Poland, he resettled several times, including five years spent in Germany (1878–1883). He visited Palestine twice, in 1911 and 1912, but despite his excellent impression, he remained in Europe. In 1922, needing medical attention, he traveled to Berlin, where he died and was buried. A main theme of his fiction is the conflict between traditional Judaism and modernism, between religious faith and secular attitudes. This clash is described here in the sensuality of the girl and the golem.

For twenty-eight years the great Rabbi Leyb, known by the acronym of his name as the Maharal of Prague, locked himself up in his study, all by himself, absorbed in his isolation. He was tortured by the great mystery, which he wanted to fathom. Every day during the past few years, Eve, his daughter's daughter, had been slipping a bit of food through the tiny window of the tiny door of the tiny room. And when she came back to clean up, she found the food untouched except for a few missing crumbs. The great Rabbi Leyb had taken only enough to keep body and soul together.

One day a guest arrived, stubborn and obstinate, and he absolutely insisted on seeing the rabbi. Two or three scraggy, scrawny fingers reached through the tiny window, but no face emerged, and no voice was to be heard.

Sometimes, on a radiant day, a sunbeam slanted through the tiny room, hovered briefly in the air, then gradually faded, and finally vanished altogether, and no eye noticed the beam. Rabbi Leyb himself was too engrossed in seeking the great mystery,

Whenever it turned three o'clock on a summer morning, the trees would suddenly burst with the twittering of swallows. And again: "Twit, twit, twit!" And once again: "Trili, trili, trili!" And finally: "Girrr, girrr, girrrr!" But nobody heard their songs. Rabbi Leyb would be hunched over a thick holy tome, searching and searching. The great mystery would be weighing down on his head and on his heart and in the heavy air around and around him. In a corner of the ceiling a spider had been spinning a huge web for many years now, and the web dangled black and kept growing blacker all the time.

And when, after twenty-eight years, the great rabbi eventually emerged from his study, his salt-and-pepper beard and hair had grown wildly. The first thing to receive him was the bright sunlight, which happened to be shining through a window. The great rabbi had to shade his eyes with his right hand. The second thing he spotted was his granddaughter Eve. Again, he had to cup his eyes—for a whole minute. It was only a bit later that he moved closer.

"Who is that?" he asked. His voice sounded like that of a child learning how to talk.

"She's your granddaughter, Rivke's daughter," the rabbi's wife replied.

The rabbi had to cudgel his mind. Wait a moment, wait a

moment. Hadn't he once had a daughter? Yes, if he wasn't mistaken, and wasn't her name Rivke?

Eve stood in front of him, tall and haughty, gaping at the gray, wild miracle. She gave off the liveliest life, and everything about her boiled and seethed. Her blazing eyes flashed, and her face glowed, and her white teeth sparkled, and the room had something of sunlight, scattering now here, now there. And Eve just stood there, gazing at the clumsy, hairy old man. And then a smirk appeared in the corners of her mouth. The great rabbi drew one step closer. Something was attracting him. But then suddenly he turned away and hurried off. It struck him that he had forgotten God's name on the little table in his room. And so he rushed back. Eve burst out laughing!

Within several days, all Prague was simmering like a cauldron. The most wondrous tales were being told about the great Rabbi Leyb and God's name and about the rabbi's cabalistic studies and his cabalistic numerology. Some people claimed that he had gotten up one morning, washed his hands, recited prayers three times, had then taken God's name and resurrected a corpse. A young man had been standing between afternoon and evening prayers in Reb Mordkhe's synagogue, and he had told the other congregants that the rabbi had withdrawn into his seclusion. He had planted seeds in a bottle, and a human being had started growing there, and the human had grown and grown, until the bottle had burst. And the human being had developed and developed until he had become Rabbi Leyb's finest pupil. Furthermore, in the Old-New Synagogue, there was an elderly Jew who claimed that Rabbi Leyb had made a golem. If the rabbi inserted God's name into the golem's mouth, the golem would come alive, and he was able to destroy the entire world. And it was only when the rabbi removed God's name from the golem's mouth that the golem lay there as lifeless as a lump of clay.

Day after day the great rabbi, pensive and gloomy, left his room and reentered it, and a dark cloud weighed on his wrinkled face. He couldn't laugh, and he couldn't hear anyone else laugh. He could find no joy. What use was the great mystery? And what use was it when it was fathomed? Did that change the world at all? He sighed. It was useless when only one person fathomed it. Each person would have to fathom it himself. All people would have to fathom it together, at the same time, if they wanted to change the world and bring joy and happiness and could and would laugh.

Rabbi Leyb trudged on. Eve, laughing and delighting, came dancing toward him. She wasn't tormented by the great mystery, by how to live, by life itself. She simply lived. The rabbi halted, and he brooded for a minute. His eyes closed wearily. Then he energetically shook his head. Was *that* life? . . . Suddenly he trudged farther. He washed his hands and then stood and prayed.

All at once a carriage drawn by six white horses came barreling down Mount Hradcany and then stopped at the great rabbi's home. Emperor Rudolf II, who delved into mysticism and alchemy and similar things, also wanted to fathom the great mystery. Upon hearing about the rabbi's efforts, the ruler had grown curious to see the wondrous man, and so he had sent his adjutant to bring the rabbi to the imperial castle.

The following Friday was steeped in dazzling sunshine. The great rabbi was preparing himself for the Sabbath. He trimmed his nails, tore up paper, and finally went to the bathhouse. His elderly wife, sweaty and gasping, was busy in the kitchen. The smell of freshly cooked fish pervaded the house. Singing and deeply impatient, Eve was cleaning the rooms in honor of the Sabbath. A strange rushing and dashing arose from the Moldova River. At last Eve reached her grandfather's study.

Sporting a white kerchief that was knotted in back like a peasant girl's kerchief, Eve clutched a feather duster. And the white kerchief emitted two sparkling black eyes that flamed and fired. Eve sprang from nook to cranny, talking to herself. That is, she didn't talk, she chirped; and she didn't spring, she hovered and floated. Somewhere outside, in a hiding place on the roof, a songbird was warbling the melody of "How Lovely Is Life." Eve listened and joined in. She then climbed upon the table, upon the benches, upon the chairs, and she sprang from chair to chair and wielded the feather duster. Now on the balcony, in memory of the destruction of the Temple, Eve wiped intensely, and then she focused on the spider and the cobweb, and then on the bookshelf with the holy tomes, and she sang as she worked. But the room got too warm for her, and she opened her top buttons. Hot, unbuttoned life burst out.

Eve was holding and wiping a huge sacred tome. She stood there absorbed for a minute. Good Lord! Why so many books? Why does a person need them? Eve stood there, pensive. Her granddad was simply crazy! He had taken a long, blossoming life of seventy years and inundated it in such nonsense. Why, for one long minute, the dear, radiant world with the golden sun was a thousand times dearer and smarter than all these tomes put together.

But now Eve had already forgotten about the tomes and the long life and even the thought of the dear and radiant world with its golden sun. She was standing by the oven, wiping it all around. A figure with a rubbed-out nose was hacked out of the middle of the oven. Eve caught herself absorbed once again in her thoughts. What was wrong with her today, mulling and musing so often? She took her grandfather's fur hat down from the wall—his Sabbath hat—and she tried it on, bursting into raucous laughter. However, she was annoyed because the figure's nose was rubbed off, intentionally destroyed. Suddenly Eve recalled that there was some kind of Jewish law about a clear face. For it is written: "Thou shalt make no graven images!" The girl grew sad. But then she resumed her working and warbling. All she had left was to wipe the brass chandelier.

As she leaned over toward the nook in back of the oven, she virtually turned to stone, dropping the duster and staring hard. Her eyes flamed; her bosom heaved intensely; her breath blazed.

In the nook behind the stove, a figure lay stretched out, a human figure, not alive, but created, made of white clay: a plaster golem.

Eve gazed at the creature; she had never seen anything so beautiful. His face was alive, his lips were alive, all his limbs were alive. Eve couldn't tear her eyes from that creature. And it was a male! She couldn't help it. She had to lean down and touch him. For a minute a warm thrill flashed through her body. Eve stripped away the silk morning gown the figure was wrapped in; her burning eyes devoured him. Indeed, she especially liked his lips! They seemed ready to open and speak at any moment. Actually, she loved his forehead. Actually, she loved the tiny corners of his temples. Oh, God! How beautiful his temples were! She also appeared to see the fine blue artery in the fine temple. Suddenly she spotted the muscular upper arm. And his chest! Good Lord! How strong and tough it was. Suddenly her eyes wandered over to his ears and his fine earlobes. Only decent people have such earlobes. A hot blaze shivered through the girl. She couldn't help it, she had to place her warm bosom on his cold, artificial body and cool it for a minute. Gradually she closed her eyes, and everything was so sweet, so sweet. She would have liked to spend the rest of her life just lying there. Evidently a human created by human hands is a thousand times more perfect and more beautiful than a figure created by God. The figure couldn't help it; she snuggled closer to his body, and her lips pressed on his lips. Ah! If only he could also come alive! Suddenly she grew impatient, and she came to. She stamped her foot with all her might. "Life! Life! Life!"

Suddenly her mind grew clearer. She recalled what people had been muttering these past few days: Supposedly her grandfather had created a human being, a clay golem. She vaguely knew that her grandfather could also bring the golem to life and then strike him dead—whatever the rabbi wished. She now remembered sharply: She had to apply God's name. But who had the patience for all her grandfather's nonsense? Eve stamped her foot eagerly and excitedly. "Life! Life! Life!" But the golem didn't stir.

She hugged him and kissed him, and burning with passion, she said: "I love you! I love you! I do love you so much!"

And the miracle occurred. "Love brings life! When a golem hears the words 'I love you,' he stops being a golem."

God's name showed his strong devotion to the young girl in wondrous ways, the young girl showed her strong devotion to the word, and the figure showed his devotion to the word. Suddenly the figure stirred. And in the end he awoke.

The golem rubbed his eyes for a long time, and eventually he opened them. The first thing they encountered was a sunbeam. He had to shade his eyes with his right hand, like an awning, to keep them from going blind. Next he encountered Eve, and again he had to cup his eyes. He looked away, embarrassed, and he quickly donned her grandfather's silk morning gown. His face turned crimson. But soon he was lost in thought. Good Lord! Where was he? An ancient and forgotten world gradually arose in him. He recalled, each in turn: God, soul, heaven, sacred tomes, cabala, mortifications, divine service, Rabbi Leyb, paradise, afterlife. He was virtually surrounded by a fog. His heart grew so heavy, and his head dangled like lead. And he remembered that together with his rabbi, he had studied the Zohar, that basic text of the cabala. He also remembered that he had been awake now for several minutes without occupying himself with anything. A loud groaning came from him, as if he were lugging a heavy burden. He slowly got up and trudged over to the bookcase.

"What do you want to do now?"

He turned pale, and his eyes flickered. It was as if he were hearing a silver chime. But then it sounded as if a bird—the same bird that lived out in the tree—were tittering. The golem buried himself in the bookcase and whispered, almost inaudibly: "Study . . . I have to go and study . . ."

He was afraid to see where the voice was coming from. And again the silvery chimes jingled. But this time with no words whatsoever. Eve burst out laughing.

"Study." The word sounded so bizarre and so foolish that she was forced to laugh. So young and already doomed to study. So fresh and new and strong and already doomed to study. Still so lovely and charming and lively and already doomed to die. And she burst out laughing again. But suddenly she really lost her temper—at her grandfather.

She went over to the young man as if they were old friends, bright, and easy, and carefree. She placed her hand on his hand, which was clutching *The Splendor of Israel.*

"Oh, you silly golem, you! Look at me. . . . Look at the outdoors! . . . The sky is so blue, so blue! . . . And how vast is the garden, and how big and broad is the heart. And God's angels are in the garden, golden songbirds, and their songs are so sweet—do you know how sweetly the birds sing?"

She stamped her foot, and everything was fresh and delightful. And the thousand scents and the rustling of the trees and the minute of buzzing and humming, and nobody knew from where and for what. "And you, Golem, you want to bury yourself in books? In dust and mold?"

A blurry shiver flashed through his body. Feeble and barely perceptible, he whispered: "The sky is so blue, so blue, the garden so green." *The Splendor of Israel* slipped through his fingers, and he was lost in thought and shrouded in magic.

Then he wiped his eyes with his hand, wiped his entire forehead, as if he had awoken from a marvelous dream. He turned vigorously and pounced on his tome.

She gazed at him imperiously. Her eyes sucked him in, and the place where her eyes lingered was scorched as if by a burning glass. He raised his eyes reluctantly.

She began speaking to him slowly. The softness of her voice

reminded him of the roughness of his voice. Evidently only a female voice could speak to him as she was now speaking. And she spoke as if she were speaking about a wild, hairy oldster, who was burying himself in a dead alphabet. There, it was still understandable. Anything else did not remain in the world for him. But when such a young life, which knew how to live, which could live without a reckoning, when such a young life is upset and always tears itself and its deeds to shreds, and always examines its own works and its own groups, then it sins against its own purpose and against the true purpose of life overall, and you (she finished) are so young and beautiful. . . .

"Talk, keep talking."

And she poured the words out from her lips.

And she kept talking. He no longer heard her words; he heard only the sound of her voice. But suddenly she was lost in thought: What is life and why do we live? And wasn't the old man, with all his thousand sacred tomes and all his wisdom, wasn't he now seeking the purpose of life and the great mystery? Last night, at 3:00 A.M., when both of them were hunched over the sacred tomes, the old man suddenly awoke and then kept dashing to and fro, yelling: "No, no, no! No sooner did I find the great mystery, and imagined I was already at peace, than a new great mystery emerged. I would have to go and seek it and fathom it, and no sooner would I fathom it than a new great mystery would emerge, and there would never be an end!"

And that was all the rabbi had achieved with all his sacred tomes and all his wisdom! And while the old man was seeking, couldn't he, the golem, do something better and live life in the meantime? He, who had all the gifts for living? And could a thousand kinds of wisdom together give away what one feels in a single minute? Should one and must one then give away the entire mind for one minute of the heart? And she kept talking to him, and she felt as if his sick and lonely soul were wrapped in something soft to calm it and soothe it.

And when Eve and the golem came out in the open air, they walked hand in hand through the garden and across the bridge. The Moldova kept rustling, and they kept walking along the highway as far as the forest. The old dark trees loomed in front of them, drawing them on and on.

The forest stood hushed when they entered it. And when they reemerged, it rustled and resounded. It swallowed its great mystery, and it tried to worm it out of the trees. And the sun laughed as they returned. And the sand twinkled, and all the greenery sparkled and flickered and glowed and shone.

Half an hour later Rabbi Leyb came back from the bathhouse. The Holy Sabbath was already reposing on him. The rabbi looked bright and clean, and the edges of a fresh white shirt surrounded his neck. His wife served him a bit of fish and scrambled eggs. Then the great rabbi stepped into his study. At first he was terrified. The golem sat engrossed in a corner—though alive. He looked as if he had been left without God's name, without any life. But he couldn't remember. Hushed and wordless, the rabbi took hold of *The Book of the Angel Raziel* (a mystical work of the sixteenth century). He had to explain the mystery of creation to his favorite pupil, explain Adam and infinity. Indeed, infinity was the most important issue. The golem, however, didn't stir. Rabbi Leyb raised his eyes and gazed at him.

The golem, wrapped in dreams, whispered: "Outdoors . . ."

And the sky is so blue, so blue. . . . Green is the garden, and the field, and the forest. . . . And the heart is so big and broad, and the scents and the singing of birds . . . and sacred tomes are dust and mold. . . .

Sacred tomes lie on the table, more and more . . . And the golem utters strange words. The rabbi stood there as if his tongue were torn out. He didn't grasp a single word.

"How can that be? My golem and such language?"

Three days wore by.

During those three days the rabbi didn't exchange a single word with his pupil, as if the golem were excommunicated. And he trailed the rabbi like a shadow. Just a single word! Just a single word! He was drawn to the rabbi like a magnet. From minute to minute Eve's image grew paler and paler in the golem's fantasy. Just one single word! Just one single word! It was only on the third evening, between afternoon and evening prayers, that the rabbi opened his lips and spoke.

"Woe unto those," he said, "who abandon life everlasting and succumb to material life. Those who talk about the blue sky and the singing of birds and the green garden, and yet they desert perpetual life, leave it in a dark corner. What do the fools get out of it? Tomorrow a day is coming, and a heavy cloud will cover the sky. And the sky is already gray and not blue. And a cold wind will come and waft over the greenery, and nothing will be green, it will have faded. And a frost will come, and the bird will no longer sing, it will creep into some hole somewhere. And such foolish things, such empty fantasies, last no longer than a night, or a week, or a month. Then why do people wish to cling to the unchanging folly and draw their livelihood forever?"

The golem felt shattered in all his limbs. He wanted to raise his eyes to see the rabbi, but he couldn't. A kind of shame pressed him back. He tried to recall the forest, the darkness, and the way he was with her, and how her heart was different, and he absolutely couldn't remember why it was so sweet that time and how it kept remaining so sweet.

On the contrary, everything now appeared so foolish that he was surprised at himself, at how everything had taken place. After all, Rabbi Leyb was a fair man! What use were foolish things like a scent, a hue, a tone? They were no more than a momentary prickling of the senses, whereas what was eternal was simply eternal, and the Torah was the same as it had been for the past thousands of years, and it would remain the same for the next thousand years. "What I've learned," he thought, "I've learned, and it will be mine forever. And even after I'm gone, it will remain forever."

His wan face was so sad and disturbed and unhappy.

With a broken heart, he reentered his room. His hand stretched out, and it took hold of a mystical tome. The golem tried to absorb himself in the text and also in another tome, which bothered his brains. . . .

The men were praying in the study house. The golem was sitting with his thongs around his head. With his blond curls, he was propping his head on his hand.

"What did he make me into?

"The mistake is that the man who made me, the golem, made me with one body but two souls. Or is every man made like that? The world would look completely different if each person had one soul and two bodies, which could serve him now this way and now that way. But unfortunately, it's the other way around. Not only does he have just one body, but he also has two souls, one pulling him in one direction and the other pulling him in a different direction."

It seemed that when Eve was speaking, she was totally right, and there was no reply. But when Rabbi Leyb spoke, what he said appeared to be the core of truth. Would the war between him and himself go on for a long time? Was it the war inside every creature? Did the war end only when life ended?

The golem yanked the phylacteries off his head and hurled them on the table.

And who was in the lead? Heaven or earth? Heart or mind? Soul or body? Beauty or science? Poetry or philosophy? Faith or knowledge? Eve or the rabbi?

In the end the golem sat down again and propped his blond head on his lovely hands. The sunshine played on the tiny blue arteries of his fine fingers.

No one was in the lead. One man was created in one way, another in another way.

The trouble was only that it kept going. One minute was like this, and then one was like that. And that was the misfortune of the two souls! Good Lord! Wouldn't you have done a thousand times better, and wouldn't man have been a thousand times calmer, more peaceful internally, if you had given him two bodies and one soul? And if not, then at least only one soul?

Sabbath afternoon arrived. Everyone was tired and drowsy from too much pleasure. The golem was finishing the delights of the Sabbath. An acacia stood in the blazing heat, yearning for a drop of water. Exhausted and languishing, its eyes half open, half closed, a cat was lying on the windowsill. The sun was burning the back of the cat. The bench in front of the house was boiling hot. The yellow sand on the ground was baking like an oven. Several girls were playing in the street, sweating profusely. In the hush you could hear every rustle.

Intoxicating scents wafted over from the garden. A light beam broke through the glass prisms of the Sabbath chandelier, and a thousand changing colors poured out across the opposite wall.

The golem emerged from his room, wrapped in his silk caftan with his red handkerchief draped around his neck. He went toward the study house. However, while crossing the garden, he stopped for a minute. Then, approaching the garden booth, he could walk no farther. He sat down for a minute. The golem dreamed and dreamed, until he finally shut his eyes. When he reopened his eyes, he found Eve standing before him.

"Take care before you shut your eyes for even a minute. As soon as you shut your eyes, I'll kiss them."

His pale face blushed slightly.

He got up hastily and was about to leave. God's name shone—

along with a thought that a woman disturbed holiness. But his feet were so heavy, so heavy. He was unable to stir.

"Foolish man! From now on, I will be God's name for you. I will bring you pleasure, and I will bring you death." She seemed to be reading his mind.

He felt as if his strength had drained and he could no longer struggle.

And she spoke so softly to him, and she spoke so kindly to him. And the stirring in his soul paused for a minute and he felt so light, so light. Suddenly he couldn't understand how he could have felt and thought otherwise. Suddenly he felt that this was the sole and true life.

"The silly old man," cried Eve, and again her voice sounded like a silvery chime. What had the old man achieved in his whole lifetime? He was seventy, and he had wasted his life on empty dreams. And he had twenty-eight years robbed from his life. Had he gotten anything out of it?

After his death (may he live to 120 years!), his portrait will hang on the cellar walls of every cobbler and every tailor and on the garret walls back of their beds. But the world will remain the same. Just as the blade of grass sprouted a thousand years ago, so it will grow another thousand years, and nothing will have changed. Like the puppy that barks today, the same puppy will still bark in a hundred years. And just as the sun shines today, it darkens, but it will shine again for another thousand generations, and it will darken again and it will shine again, and everything will remain the same until the final generation. Whom has the old man helped with his seclusion and his reflection? How have we advanced with any kind of profound thought? And evil has remained the same as when "God had formed man's heart."

The golem felt his brains flipping over—but feebly, as if his lips weren't whispering about things that last forever and things that last only briefly.

"And he," Eve went on, "this old fool—he dares to talk to you about things that last forever and things that last only briefly? He? He should peer right into my eyes when he talks, and he should tell me that he knows about things that last forever and what they are! Doesn't he shudder often enough and doesn't he awaken often enough from the midst of his thoughts to ask himself on what he has spent his life?

"And honestly, are there such things that last forever? Aren't they simply flowery stuff? Look, my dear little fool, my dear blond little golem! Why, you're a man with five healthy senses, and you can examine and investigate on your own! On the contrary! You tell me! What does *eternal* mean? Is there anything else in life but the present moment—whatever lasts only briefly?

"Have you never let an hour slip by without using it for yourself, for your own life—that is, for your feeling, your sense? Then the hour is truly gone, and it will never come again. The hour that lasts only briefly is all that we really have. And the hour they call eternal is a kind of flowery stuff that can't be proved and that was invented by fools or liars or seducers. Pity the minute that you let pass without living, and without living a full life. Life is short enough as it is. You have to live and to enjoy life. . . ."

He felt as if he had felt it all before. All these words seemed mere echoes of what was shining in his own heart.

And he closed his eyes, and she kissed his eyelids and she kissed his lips and she kissed his forehead—and he was so light, so light.

The day was wet and rotten and gloomy. A slow and steady rain had fallen all night. The rocks were cleansed, the trees were dripping, and they poured and poured from minute to minute. Everything looked bleak and hopeless and deserted. A soaked chicken stood by a wet dung heap, pecking out seeds. The funeral of the town magnate—Reb Mordkhe Myzels—was scheduled for that afternoon. He had died quite suddenly, and the whole town was prepared for the interment of that great philanthropist. The black bier outside the door of the deceased spread an even greater deathly grief than usual through the dismal rain. The members of the Meetinghouse of the Sages, which the deceased had built, came to offer their final condolences. The children of his own yeshiva likewise came, and it all looked as if the whole world and his whole life were in his wet grave.

Standing by the grave, one of the great men of our age, Yom-Tov Lipman Heller, pronounced the eulogy. As is the custom, he spoke about what was still left to do after the dead man's passing. The deceased owned the treasures of King Solomon, thousands of ducats and thousands of precious stones. But now see what was happening. They didn't lower even a single ducat or even a precious stone into the grave with him. The crucial points were his good deeds, and the eulogist talked about them as well.

Next came Yitsik Leybish, Rabbi Leyb's son-in-law, and he talked about the "antechamber" and about what a man had to do in the antechamber. And he recalled a midrash [Talmudic and post-Talmudic interpretation of the Jewish Bible] about a builder who built a parlor using the bricks of the antechamber. Everyone loved the parlor. Suddenly they all fell silent. Rabbi Leyb, who earlier hadn't cared to speak at all, finally wished to deliver an oration. Each man tried to get closer to the rabbi.

And Rabbi Leyb spoke.

It was wondrous. The rabbi never even so much as mentioned the dead man. The golem stood in the crowd, and he felt as if the rabbi's every word were aimed at him alone and were prepared for him alone.

The rabbi spoke about the past and the future and explained that we had no choice: We were in the present, and we had no sense of the future. And when passion comes and seduces us, we convince ourselves that only the minute, the past, is the full truth. And we won't understand how foolish it is to balance the seventy brief years of the past with the millions of years of the future. We must be crazy or blinded by passion if we compare one with the other.

The golem stood up, and every part of him shuddered. For a minute he felt as if the dead man had died for him alone, so the golem should stand there, and so the great Rabbi Leyb should say all these things to him. Upon coming home from the interment, the rabbi took the golem aside and pleaded with him: "Child, do you see?" The rabbi spoke to him softly and kindly. "No matter where you turn, you cannot escape the fact that the earth you are standing on is all there is and that there is nothing more. Otherwise, you will keep asking about the purpose of life, about the whole machinery of life, and what use is it once you have drunk and eaten, and slept, and donned the finest garments? And for what does a rock live? It doesn't drink and doesn't eat and doesn't don the finest garments, yet it has a meaning. But I don't know its true purpose; I only know that its true purpose is yet to come. We can only conclude that all this is simply a preface and that true life begins only in the heavens above. . . ."

The rain was still drizzling slowly, the day was rotten and gloomy. Every word caught by the golem shattered worlds inside him and tortured him. At first glance it seemed as if not a single man capable of thought were able to achieve any other thought. Rabbi Leyb demonstrated that a divine man could speak words that only God could place on his lips.

And yet a kind of fog lay on the golem's heart and mind.

Early in the morning the golem and Eve climbed up the castle hill. She had kissed away the cloud from his forehead and the bitterness from his lips. She had also kissed away the heavy fog from his eyes, and she kicked away the stones from his path. She led him across green meadows, and she spoke every word as if it were a soothing balm for his sick mind, and soft as velvet she calmed his sick body.

When they reached the top of the hill, she stretched out on the grass and held his head in her lap. The eternal tempest swarming in his heart faded for a minute. He sat up and peered into her eyes. And when he put his arm around her waist, it was as if he were embracing life. Good for the man who hugs life and feels it!

And she talked about earth and heaven. "Ah, it's so foolish, my sweet golem, what they tell you about heaven! They've dreamed it up, and you have to believe that it really exists. But I next to you— don't you see?—I truly exist. I'm not air that can be called heaven. You can hold me and feel me and sense me. There, there, take hold of my breast. Hold it, feel it. This isn't air; it's yours. Anything you can't take hold of is a lie. You can't hold heaven in your hands. Anything you can't hold doesn't exist."

He would have liked her to continue speaking. Everything she said was true—like God's Torah—and it was impossible to deny it. Suddenly he failed to grasp what he had been through earlier. And how can a man with five healthy senses think any differently?

Around noon they arrived at the ancient ruins of St. Vitus Church on Mount Hradcany.

Upon entering the church, they were embraced in shadows. The old watchman, awoken from sleep, picked out his keys from their rusty bunch and led the visitors into the mortuary chapel. Empty skulls with empty eye sockets were arranged all around the walls. A worm was crawling through one of the sockets. The golem took hold of a skull. . . .

Out in the mortuary courtyard, lonesome and alone, they sat on rocks. There was no one left in the world aside from him and her. And what did they care about the rest of the world? Why should they bother about yesterday, today, or tomorrow? What did "time" mean? What did "place" mean? What did "life" mean? He embraced her profoundly, and he kissed her and kissed her. . . .

In the evening they sat under a cherry tree in the garden.

White cherry blossoms drifted down and covered them. The

blossoms drifted over their heads and over their shoulders and over their laps, and they were wrapped totally in white. They had to laugh aloud.

Suddenly he became serious. He sat stiffly, eyeing the ground. He was lost in thought.

The sky was so blue and the air so soft and the earth so green. What good did it do them to search every nook and cranny in order to spoil their joy in living? And yet the present is all that counts: the sheer moment. I let the minute pass, and I didn't use it to enjoy the bit of life. I lost it forever, forever, and it will never come again. What good do those people do, deliberately seeking goodness knows what, lamenting their lives with their dark thoughts? Who asks them to ponder and to embitter the little bit of pleasure for other people? And yet only the past is present, and no future exists now. Eat and drink and enjoy yourself. You can't get hold of heaven, and if you can't get hold of something, then it doesn't exist.

He hugged her and kissed her and kissed her.

He was happy!

In the evening they rowed a boat down the Moldova.

A gentle breeze wafted across their faces. She wielded the oar easily, while he sat calmly, with folded hands, lost in dreams. With every clap of the oar, the white foam gathered, and the foam and the water splashed into their faces and on their clothes, and they laughed aloud. They laughed like children. Then little by little the air grew stiller and stiller.

They dreamed, and they didn't know what they were dreaming.

They strolled through the night hand in hand.

Their footsteps echoed from minute to minute. Not a living soul could be heard aside from them, and they walked and walked. Then thousands of voices, vague and hazy, could be heard from the nocturnal ocean surrounding them. There was swarming, there was humming, there was murmuring, and nobody knew what, and nobody knew where. Tiny flames appeared in the field, on the way to the forest. Fireflies and summer chafers flickered from minute to minute.

They lay down on a grass bank, arm in arm, and hugged tightly. They were shrouded by the night. And the night was hushed and silent, burying its secret inside him.

And Rabbi Leyb snuggled against him like a sick child and smoothed his hair and smoothed his forehead.

Autumn lay, heavy, leaden, a deserted melancholy over hill and dale. From minute to minute yellow leaves drifted down from the trees. At times a raw wind blasted, and heavy, gloomy drops came down. At times it seemed as if everything were coming to an end, as if summer were coming to an end, as if humankind were coming to an end, as if life were coming to an end. The air was so heavy and mournful. A crow soared from a naked tree, across a rooftop, with a heartrending voice, cawing and cawing.

He snuggled like a sick person, but from minute to minute he leaned over him and peered into his eyes. And he talked to him the way you talk to a patient, mildly and softly, and he wove his thoughts and feelings into velvety words.

"And you see, my child," he said, "there are people who are not as strong as life and who cannot overcome it. There are passions that we grasp, but we cannot help ourselves. For instance, there is the lust a young man feels for a young girl. I know it; they call it love. They revel, they fulfill their passion, they enjoy it, and that is life. You don't think about eternity, about the future; you simply live.

"Now there's one thing that surprises me in this matter. How can it happen to a man with a good head on his shoulders? Why doesn't the thought occur in the right minute? 'Yes, now this young flesh is so beautiful, so enchanting that we would give away anything that smacks of eternity.' But what will ensue twenty or thirty years from now? The radiant face will be sallow and sunken; the bright eyes will be half snuffed and fading; the glittering white teeth will be yellow or gone.

"And will it be worth giving away the pleasures of days, of hours, of minutes, and sacrificing the everlasting and unchanging? Now I fulfill my lust, and I satisfy an entire minute. But after the minute, when I have sobered up, my soul will be filthy, and I will block my own path, and I will want to spit into my own face.

"I merely ask: 'How can someone with a good head on his shoulders do such a thing?'" He held him in his arms like a sick person, and he spoke so softly.

The golem sat there, with a pale face and a shivering body. A hopeless, desolate melancholy surrounded them. It was as if the autumn were ending the world. Everything was so bleak and weary. What good was life? What use was even a good life? And what good was a good life? And what good was a minute after a good life itself? Just go and kill yourself!

The golem sensed that every word was true, like the divine Torah. Suddenly he again failed to grasp how he could forget himself for even one minute.

That evening, when everyone was already asleep, the golem paced to and fro in his room, still haunted by the same thought. But when the scheduled hour came, the golem went out into the garden shed, where Eve was waiting for him.

For an entire year the golem wrote his memoirs. They became a marvelous book. One chapter seemed penned by the rabbi himself, and the second chapter seemed penned by Eve herself. But neither the rabbi nor Eve contributed even the slightest iota. The book was written purely by the golem.

And the golem had a torn life, a torn mind, two souls in one body, and not for a day and not for a year, but for an entire lifetime.

Why did the rabbi make the golem? And if he did make him, then why with two souls, one pulling him this way and one pulling him that way?

And to whom should man give the birthright: Earth or sky? Mind or heart? Wisdom or beauty? Philosophy or poetry? Knowledge or emotion? Body or soul? The rabbi or Eve?

The golem searched and searched, and he wrote and wrote. Once the rabbi exhausted his literary talent, and once Eve exhausted her literary talent.

Good Lord! What will become of all this? How will it end?

A winter passed and a summer arrived, and another winter drew up.

On the first day of Rosh Hashanah (New Year), a huge crowd came pouring out of the Jewish district in Prague and went down to the Moldova River, where they celebrated the annual Jewish custom of emptying their pockets—their sins, that is—into the water. The participants were young and old, big and little.

The sun was still shining and warming, but minds were already heavy and shuddering. The rabbi's elderly wife also went down to the river. She stood on the bank, emptying her pockets and reciting the prayers for women. The old rabbi likewise went down to the riverbank, where he prayed while emptying his pockets and throwing his sins into the water. Eve went strolling along the flow, where she shook out her pockets, not knowing what to do. A white cloudlet on the edge of the red sky drew her attention.

And the golem arrived. He stood there, gaping at the water, and the water drew and drew him. Sins were so grave, and they drew so intensely. They fell, they sank into the deep—oh, how heavy they were. Wouldn't it have been better to throw them all together instead of one by one? And join them? What good, what use was a torn life? But if his torn life ended here, what would become of other torn lives? He decided to leave the water. But a minute later someone suddenly shrieked! When the fishermen pulled out the golem, they carried him to the great rabbi.

He was revived a bit by the rabbi and God's name and a bit by Eve's words. Today it is said that the golem still lives in Prague, and not only in Prague but also in other Jewish communities. It is said that the golem lives everywhere and in all times.

H. Leivick (1888–1962)

The Golem

1920

H. Leivick's original name was Leivick Halper, but he changed it to avoid being confused with the poet M. L. Halpern. Born to a poor family near the Byelorussian town of Minsk, Leivick attended various yeshivas. He was expelled from one school for reading a modern Hebrew novel, Abraham Mapu's Love of Zion. *His radical political views and actions caused him to be arrested, convicted, and sentenced to four years of hard labor in Siberia. He described this period in his memoir,* In the Czar's Prison *(1959). Meanwhile, he had started writing first poems, then plays in Yiddish. After his release from prison, he eventually reached New York in 1913. Working as a paperhanger by day, he kept writing poems and plays, many of which were staged in America, in Europe, and even in Palestine and then Israel. Leivick became one of the most important Yiddish poets and playwrights, but little of his work is now available aside from* The Golem.

Cast of Characters

Rabbi Leyb of Prague
His wife
Deborah
The golem
Yitsik
Yankev
Avrom the Beadle
Bassevi
Tankhem
Tadeush
Monk

Wanderers
The old beggar
The young beggar

Paupers
The tall man
The redhead
The blind man
The peg leg
The spirit of Rabbi Leyb

The hunchback
The sick man

The invisible force
The spirit of the unborn person
The spirit of Tadeush
The man with the big cross
Healing spirits
The subterraneans
Jews
Cave spirits

Set in Prague during the seventeenth century

CLAY

(A deserted space along the river outside Prague. Daybreak. The surrounding area is dark and silent. Rabbi Leyb bar Bezalel, known as the Maharal and in his seventies, stands over an outlined heap of clay, kneading a human figure. The figure is completed. Next to the rabbi stands Avrom, the beadle, helping him in his labor. The rabbi stands up and addresses Avrom.)

RABBI. It's done. All done. Dash to the synagogue and go
Tell Yitsik and tell Yankev to get here!

AVROM. And you want me to stay there, Rabbi?

RABBI. Wait at the synagogue, but look, Avrom,
The secret you are privileged to know—
Just keep it locked forever in your heart,
And never say a word to anyone.

AVROM. Forever, Rabbi.

RABBI. For now don't tell them everything is done.
They have to see it for themselves, unbiased.
The day's already dawning, hurry up.

(AVROM exits.)

RABBI *(leaning over body)*. Yes, everything is done and wrapped
in darkness.
The splendid hour of wonder comes with daylight,
And I peer down at this enormous body,
Which has been kneaded, molded by my fingers.
And I can see the shadow striding toward me,
The shadow of a living human being . . . *(Raises his head skyward.)*
But who am I to say, "I mold and knead"?
My eyes were blind, and you—you made them see,
From heaven's height you hurt and harmed my brows,
You showed me, you revealed the sleeping body.
And who can say how many generations

The body has been sleeping there—who knows?—
While somewhere else his yearning soul is wandering?
Or has the endless wandering made the soul
Forget the road back to the sleeping body?
Or does the soul, so deep in special sleep,
Now keep you waiting, as the body does,
To open up my lids, expose my eyes. . . .
I hear the wings that whir around my head,
The night around is full of fluttering.
The waiting body lies there, all stretched out,
His face, uncovered, gapes up at the heavens,
And now a prayer rips from the lifeless lips. . . .
(*RABBI covers his face with his hands, stands there for a long time, steps back in fear.*)
Who fluttered past my eyes just now, who touched
My forehead, grazing it with something sharp,
And then who shrieked and screamed into my ears?
I hear dull echoes. Where do they come from? (*Peers around and listens.*)
I see nobody. Hush. The river flows.
The stars are fading, fading, one by one.
The eastern sky should be lit up by now.
Instead it keeps on growing darker, darker. . . .
Oh, strength, Creator of the Universe.
Amid proud joy, I saw a second shadow
Of this enormous, this tremendous body. . . . (*Suddenly he hears a distant rustle, and some pitch-black entity strides across the river surface, swaying and rotating.*)
Who's walking on the surface of the river?
Who's drawing near to me yet draws no nearer?
Drawing away yet doesn't draw away? (*The PHANTOM appears in front of the RABBI.*) Dark phantom, who are you?
PHANTOM. Why, don't you know me?

RABBI. I can't see your face
PHANTOM. Why, don't you know my voice?
RABBI. Your voice is like a stark and icy wind
Blasting and blasting through a deep dark pit
With no way in and yet with no way out.
PHANTOM. I have a voice that's not a voice as yet.
I have a heart that's not a heart as yet.
RABBI. Who are you? Tell me who. Tell me your name.
PHANTOM. My name will be called out much later, Rabbi,
But meanwhile I do not exist on earth.
I'm still the shadow of a shadow here.
RABBI. Where are you from?
PHANTOM. I've come to warn you, Rabbi: Don't create me,
And don't remove me from my crude condition.
RABBI. I order you to vanish, disappear.
PHANTOM. I warn you once again: Do not create me.
You can see all the stars are waning now!
And that's how every glow will fade away
The very moment it grazes the eyes.
And where my foot treads it will leave a blight,
And what my hand may touch disintegrates.
It yields and scatters into dust and ashes. . . .
Don't trade my darkness and my stillness for
The bustling of streets and human beings.
RABBI. Oh, help me in my harshest hour, God!
PHANTOM. I realize that you won't hear my prayer.
That's why I've come. I've come to warn you, Rabbi.
And now my warning must sound like a prayer.
You've spent the whole night kneading, shaping me,
And molding me with coldness, cruelty.
How wonderful it was to be mere clay,
To lie there, cold and lifeless, mingling
With all the grains of sand and tiny bits

Of pebbles from the earth and from the soil,
From all eternity to eternity. . . .
RABBI. Go, phantom, vanish to your hiding place.
Your sorrow and your fear of life, your terror
Should also vanish to your hiding place!
And when the hour of great wonders comes,
Just as the night melts in the eastern sky,
Your deep despair will also fade away.
God sent me here, to knead you and to shape you.
To raise you from the stony, pebbly soil,
And to lift breathing life into your life
At the first glint of dawn, first spark of day.
PHANTOM. I don't want it.
RABBI. Your own desire is nothing.
For all your roads, your days and nights have been
Decreed for you, decreed for all your deeds.
You are created for more than mere life,
To work great wonders here in hush and hiding,
To do your deeds in secrecy and silence.
No one shall know about your furtive strength,
You'll be a water carrier, a woodchopper.
PHANTOM. A golem.
RABBI. A nation's messenger, a man of might.
PHANTOM. A servant to be ordered, to be ruled.
RABBI. A living man.
PHANTOM. A living man? Why are you standing, waiting?
Where is the soul to be breathed into me?
Why don't you open up my eyes and see?
Where is the tongue, where are the teeth, where is
The blood that is to be poured into me?
What am I to become now? A blind man?
A crippled man, who's deaf and holds his tongue?
And maybe everything together? Tell me!

The night is turning pale and fading now.
The day is dawning, dim and dark and dismal.
Keep me in your abyss one moment more,
One moment more of what I've been till now,
A pile of lifeless, desiccated clay.

(PHANTOM *melts into the darkness.*)

RABBI. A darkness has assaulted the devotion
That I have tried to purge and purify.
My words of terror and my words of horror
Have left a flaw within the future heart.
Oh, I have failed to overcome resistance.
Nor have I kept my heart free of all sorrow,
Free of all pity, free of any anguish. . . .
Now heavier and heavier grows the load
Of every fearful, every frightful word.
My very own hands have turned aside his fate
Into a road of shock, dismay, confusion. . . .
And for long weeks, long weeks of days and nights,
I've purged my heart and purified my mind,
Sloughed off my self, sloughed off the world itself,
Transformed into a single thought, *your* thought.
I saw a single one, a single one,
And now he's coming, opening his eyes,
A secret smile that lingers on his lips,
His arms of iron strength and arms of might.
He sees, and no one knows that he can see.
He goes, and no one knows where he is going.
His life and death—are just a silent breath,
A calm, a quiet, and a hidden faith. . . .
He comes to no one, and he speaks to no one,
He lies, sprawled out in just some nook or other,
And waits until the moment he is summoned. . . .
What should he do now, now that doubt and dread

And bitter, unforgiving loneliness

Have spoiled and ruined and wrecked the living word? . . .

I see that I'm not worthy in your eyes.

Perhaps I bragged and boasted far too much,

Eager to see what no one had ever seen,

To see what no one has seen until now. . . .

I see! I see! And tell me, what am I

Before you? Just a very tiny worm,

A clod of soil, perhaps, a grain of sand.

(A long hush. THE PHANTOM OF TADEUSH, THE PRIEST, emerges. He instantly approaches the RABBI.)

RABBI. Tadeush, yes, it's he, he's coming toward me.

I just remembered him; he's on my mind.

Is this a further sign that God has sent? (*The PHANTOM OF TADEUSH bumps into the RABBI.*)

PHANTOM OF TADEUSH. What are you doing here in the thick of night?

RABBI. It's not the thick of night; the day is dawning.

PHANTOM OF TADEUSH. What are you doing in the dawning day?

RABBI. I'm doing what the Good Lord orders me

To do here in the dawning of the day.

PHANTOM OF TADEUSH. And what has God now ordered you to do

To have me join you in the dawning day?

RABBI. No need to stay; you can be on your way.

PHANTOM OF TADEUSH. I know that I can leave and go my way,

Tadeush—he can manage very well.

But what can cause your eyes to look so strange?

Your eyes shoot slaughter and spurt blackest strength!

How can a rabbi ever think of slaughter?

Throughout my life I've seen all kinds of dungeons,

Auto-da-fés ruled by the holy court.
And I have seen all sorts of Jewish faces,
And I have seen all kinds of Jewish eyes.
But I have never, ever chanced to see
A pair of Jewish eyes imbued with slaughter,
With truest hate as your eyes are now filled.
They look like the eyes of a savage golem. . . .
(RABBI *covers his face with his hands; his shoulders heave.*)

PHANTOM OF TADEUSH. Why have you suddenly covered your face?
And held your tongue? And who is this? Who lies here?
Who lies upon the ground? A corpse? I have
Been standing here but haven't noticed him. (*Leans over and peers at the clay figure.*) What do my eyes see? What is happening here?
A man of clay lies stretched out on the ground! (*Steps away and crosses himself.*)
Oh, holy Jesus!

RABBI. Till he's fit for life,
To lift his arm, to stand upon his feet,
Till then I bear the gazing of his eyes. . . .

PHANTOM OF TADEUSH. Protect me from the devil and from all
Unbaptized and accursed men—oh, Jesus . . . (*Vanishes.*)

RABBI (*silent for a time, wakes up as if from a spell, peers around*).
Is this a second sign that you have sent?
I see it has to be. The hand of God
He circled me inside a single circle
And coupled me with this small mound of clay. . . .
And all the images I now imagine
I see, and everything I see will come. . . .
It has to come, it must. . . .
And now my heart is clear and bright, for I—
Just what am I? . . . Your signs—they tell the truth.

It has to come, it must. . . .

(*The RABBI's two disciples, YITSIK THE COHEN and YANKEV THE LEVITE, come along the road to town. YANKEV is carrying a bundle of clothes. The two men walk softly, their feet barely grazing the ground.*)

RABBI (*going toward them*). You've come in time, my sons.

YITSIK. The day is dawning.

RABBI. And no one noticed you along the way?

YANKEV. We kept along the edges of the road.

RABBI. You spent the whole night in the synagogue?

YITSIK. The whole night, separated from each other,
We stood and prayed; we prayed there loud and clear.
And didn't light a candle until midnight.
The darkness barricaded us: a thick wall
That severed each of us from one another,
So far apart that each and every voice
Was powerless to reach a single ear.
At first the distance terrified my soul,
As if I were inside a pitch-black forest,
Seeking some path, some road I couldn't find.
I hurried faster to the forest's depth.
But suddenly I grew so calm, and then
I dashed far deeper, dashed far deeper still! . . .

YANKEV. And, Rabbi, listen to what happened then.
We thought that we were standing far apart
In darkness, and we didn't stir at all
As if we both were fettered to the floor
And felt as if each one of us were all
Alone, alone inside the synagogue. . . .
Now midnight was advancing, and as you
Had ordered us to do, we lit the candles
That each of us had earlier prepared.
And we saw miracles: The two of us
Were standing side by side, and each man's candle

Was lighting up the other person's face.

YITSIK. A wonder, an enormous miracle.

RABBI. A favorable sign, my sons. Your hearts
Were purged and purified by all your prayers
And you are worthy of the precious blessing
That now your lips and tongue must soon recite.

YITSIK. Rabbi, may we now have a look at him?

RABBI. You may. Go over now and have a look.

(*The two lean over the clay body and peer down at it.*)

YANKEV. For now there's nothing yet to see here. Clay.

YITSIK. But now the clay is opening its eyes. . . .

YANKEV. And now the clay is lifting one leg too. . . .

YITSIK. And now it's making faces and guffawing. . . . (*Jumping
back in terror.*)

RABBI. Yitsik, what's wrong?

YITSIK. I had a look, and it was horrifying!
It conjured up a nightmare I once had.

RABBI. A nightmare? When?

YITSIK. Rabbi, I've sinned. Forgive me!
At midnight, when we always light the candles,
We took a Torah from the Ark of the Covenant,
As you had ordered us. And we unrolled it
Until we reached the start of Genesis.
And each of us then called the other up
And read the opening section seven times.
And nobody impeded either reading.
We then returned the Torah to the ark
And started quietly reciting psalms.
And then, as I stood there, facing the wall,
Reciting, my eyelids grew very heavy.
I fought and fought to keep from dozing off,
And I recited psalms louder and louder. . . .
Suddenly I heard shouting, desperate weeping.

The clamor then came closer and came closer.
All doors and windows burst and opened up.
The synagogue was mobbed by panicky Jews,
Who threw themselves in every single corner,
Breathlessly tumbling under every table. . . .
And as they lay there, a strange man came in,
A tall man with a giant head, long hands,
With green eyes, piercing eyes, clutching a sword,
Jabbing and stabbing and slicing every which way,
Up and down and right and left.
And soon the Jews were gashed and bashed and bleeding,
Concealed in darkness, dying in their blood.
Then all at once the stranger raised his arm
And was about to strike me with his sword.
Then, Rabbi, suddenly you arrived.
RABBI. Who? I?
YITSIK. The very moment he set eyes on you,
He lowered his sword and headed toward the door.
But you stood in his way and grabbed his sword
And tried to strike his face but missed.
RABBI (*beside himself*). I missed?
YITSIK. You struck the air.
RABBI. And he then ran away?
YITISIK. He melted like a shadow, disappeared
The clay figure reminded me of him.
RABBI (*to himself*). So many signs! So many awful omens!
And won't a single ray shine through them all?
Lead me along all roads, along all roads,
But everything that is concealed from me—
Let now the one and only light shine through. . . .
YANKEV. In the synagogue they talked about bad times,
About the past and all the present rumors
Now circulating in the city of Prague.

About a slaughterer who has murdered Jews,
Masses of Jews, major and minor Jews!
And that was why I dreamed that dream, Rabbi.
RABBI, Yes, evil times are coming, my disciples,
And each of us will suffer harsh ordeals. . . .
Together with bad times great times will come. . . .
We must prepare for them; we must be ready. . . .
And now, you see, God's brought us to the start
Of the great times, the very callous times. . . .
I see that you are frightened, terrified,
With heavy hearts and deeply horrified.
YITSIK. Rabbi, my hands are shivering with fear.
Should I put down the bundle, Rabbi, now?
RABBI. Does it, my student, contain everything?
YITSIK. Everything, Rabbi.
YANKEV. Now the day is dawning.
YITSIK. Where will he stay? Inside the synagogue?
RABBI. Just ask no more, and stifle all your fears,
Repress them in your hearts, and with repression
Hide anything that you will see and hear.
Let's go find water now and wash our hands.
(*They go to the river.*)

WALLS

(The RABBI's private study. Dawn. The RABBI comes in. The created man halts at the threshold. He is tall, and the doorway is too low. He doesn't know that he should bend.)

RABBI. Just bend your head. The doorway's low, and you

Are tall. Remember, when a tall man wishes

To step through a low doorway, he must bend

His head. Just look—like this. *(RABBI bends his head. GOLEM enters with a bent head, pauses.)*

RABBI. Now lift your head and straighten out your body.

(GOLEM straightens out. Stands mute. A powerful gigantic build. Huge eyes. They seem dull, heavy, yet childlike. Thick lips, deeply indented corners. A frozen empty smile on the lips, empty yet twisted, virtually on the brink of weeping. Black, curly hair on his head, beard, and mustache. His eyes open wider and wider as he gapes at everything.)

RABBI. Your eyes are open, and you've seen the sky,

You've seen the sun, which rises in the east,

You've met Jews in the streets and in the courtyards.

I've talked to you; I'm talking to you now. *(GOLEM remains silent.)*

You've got a mouth and teeth, a tongue to talk with.

Why hold your tongue? *(GOLEM is mute.)*

I order you to speak. Your name is Yosl.

GOLEM *(terrified).* Yosl?

RABBI. You are a human being now.

GOLEM. A human being.

RABBI. You've got a heart to live by.

GOLEM. Live by.

RABBI. Don't be discouraged or despondent.

You do recall your name, you do remember—

(*GOLEM remains silent.*)

RABBI. Forgotten? Yosl is your name. Remember.

GOLEM. Yosl.

RABBI. And do you know what I'm called?

GOLEM. Rabbi. (*GOLEM walks around the room, clambers over benches and tables, knocking them over. Hugs the wall, pushes it. The windowpanes rattle.*)

RABBI. What are you doing? Stop! You'll wake the entire Household!

GOLEM. I want to get away from here! (*Pounds the wall.*)

RABBI. I tell you, stop! A man walks past a chair
Or table. He will never knock them over.
Nor can he ever walk through solid walls.
I tell you, stop! Stop pounding on the wall!

GOLEM. I want to get away from here!

RABBI. Haven't I told you
That you must follow every order I give?

GOLEM (*Sits down on floor, helpless*). I follow every order you give, Rabbi.

RABBI. You must always listen to all my words
And not forget them. Do you recall your name?

GOLEM. My name is Yosl. I have not forgotten.

RABBI. Stand up and then sit down upon a bench. (*RABBI takes GOLEM's hand, helps him up, and seats him on a bench.*)
I see you're tired; you come from far away.
Don't be afraid, here you're a welcome guest.

GOLEM. A welcome guest. (*GOLEM peers around and smiles.*)

RABBI. Why are you smiling, Yosl?

GOLEM. I don't know. Something's burning on the windows.
I don't know. Distant fire's reaching the panes.

RABBI. The sun is rising, rising in a blaze.

GOLEM. Your beard is long and white, and mine is black.

RABBI. I saw you lying on the edge of town,

And you were fast asleep.
GOLEM. I don't know, Rabbi.
Some distant fire's reaching the windowpanes.
It keeps getting bigger and redder now,
The walls are blazing, and so is your face. (GOLEM leaps up and
walks around again.)
RABBI. Where are you going?
GOLEM. To the fire, Rabbi.
Rabbi, I'm terrified of staying here.
RABBI. You may not go!
GOLEM. I want to, want to go.
You're very small and very old compared
With me, yes, and your head is very tiny.
You talk to me and tremble all the while,
And all the while your hands are shivering.
RABBI. Have you again forgotten who I am?
GOLEM. I don't know.
RABBI. You're to be my servant here.
And that is why you've come into my home,
To live completely under my control.
GOLEM. What do I have to do?
RABBI. Nothing for now.
You may live here or somewhere else perhaps.
Would you wish to live under my roof?
GOLEM. No.
RABBI. You cannot go away, you are a stranger,
And in my household you'll feel right at home.
GOLEM. Something inside me's rising, choking me—
A throbbing, pounding, ringing in my ears,
And red and green loom up before my eyes. . . .
My legs move up; they want to, wish to walk.
My hands—they want to, wish to grab your throat
And carry you away. Tell me, what's here?

I want to run, but I can't even walk. (*Shouts.*)
Tell me, what's here? I want my hand to hit
Your head, and yet I cannot move. . . . Watch me,
I'm staggering; the walls are spinning around.
The fire in the windows blazes bigger.
The walls are scheming with the door to hurl
Themselves upon me, catch a glimpse of me.
Do let me go. . . . I want to smash and shatter,
I want to twist my head off from my shoulders,
I want to twist my legs off, and my arms,
Snuff out the flames and take away the walls. (*He savagely pounds the walls, which wobble.*)
RABBI. I order you to be calm. The mighty forces
Are starting now to surge into your body,
Clearing a path, a road into your soul.
The pitch-black darkness and the transmigration
Have not released your head, released your heart
As yet, and from your depths of deepest darkness,
The filth and curses surge and spurt and shoot. (*RABBI places his hands on GOLEM's head, strokes him, calms him down.*)
Your shoulders now are heaving. Sit. And catch
Your breath. I prophesied this outburst of
Your hatred. Till the hour of lucid joy,
Of cleansed crying and of radiant calm—
Meanwhile make blind dread stop, blind panic stop,
Let my first blessing fall upon your heart,
My first assurance on your tangled mind.
You don't know who you are, and in your fear
You're dazed, astonished at yourself and at
Your arms and legs. Something has happened to you,
Erasing your entire lifetime from
Your memory until this very day.
You're starting now from scratch, starting anew. . . .

You're in my home, a guest, a welcome guest,
And that's enough for you to catch a glint,
The very first gleam of your very first hope.
Don't be so obstinate in your resistance.
Someone is coming here. You've woken up
The entire house. Just hold your tongue; don't talk.
You are a guest, you've come from far away:
That will be your response to any question.
GOLEM. I am a guest, I've come from far away,
Forgotten everything that's happened to me.
(*RABBI's WIFE and DEBORAH enter, awoken from sleep, terrified.*)
WIFE. What's wrong? Why did the house shudder and shake?
DEBORAH. Grandpa, such awful shrieks.
RABBI. You both had nightmares.
WIFE. Just nightmares? Why, I tumbled from my bed!
Such awful shrieks! Just look! Who's sitting there?
Who is that, Aryeh Leyb?
DEBORAH. A strange man.
RABBI. Why are the two of you so terrified?
Our visitor's a guest from very far
Away. As I was coming from the bathhouse,
I found him lying in the street, exhausted
From his long trek. Who is he? Where's he from?
I still have not determined that as yet.
He prattles and he babbles when he speaks.
It's better not to ask him any questions.
A poor man evidently.
DEBORAH. He looks wretched.
WIFE. He doesn't really seem to be a Jew.
Look at those shoulders, and look at those hands.
He scares me.
RABBI. There is no need to be scared.
He looks like that because of his long trek.

DEBORAH. Oh, Grandma, look! The way he gapes at me.

Grandpa, what does he want from me? Just ask him.

RABBI. Both of you go inside our home. He is

A silent man; he never answers questions.

DEBORAH. He lifts his head again and gawks at me.

What shiny eyes, what melancholy eyes.

WIFE. Don't stare at him. Come, Deborah, let's go.

A poor, pathetic man. He should be pitied.

And yet I do not care for him at all.

What is your name, what do they call you?

GOLEM. Yosl. (*Smiles. Rises and stares hard and amazed at DEBO-*
RAH.)

Rabbi, who is she? Why is she so frightened?

Why does she run away?

DEBORAH. Conceal me, Grandma.

Let's get out of here.

He's gazing at me. I feel petrified.

WIFE. The girl is scared. Is he insane or what—

To peer and gaze at somebody like that?

RABBI. Why are you staring, Yosl?

GOLEM. Who is she?

Rabbi, why does she want to run away?

RABBI. She is my grandchild, Yosl, do you hear?

And, Yosl, you must never talk about her.

GOLEM. Her long hair hangs over her shoulders, Rabbi.

DEBORAH. What is he saying? Grandma, I'm so sacred.

WIFE. Why, he should be ashamed to talk like that!

RABBI. He himself doesn't know what he is saying.

He's all confused. His mind is wandering. . . .

GOLEM (*suddenly*). Food!

RABBI. Food? Yes, go and get him some.

WIFE. Before

His morning prayers?

RABBI. Don't you see who he is?

WIFE. My girl, just go and sleep a little more.

Meanwhile I'll go and get him food myself. (*WIFE and DEBO-RAH leave.*)

GOLEM. Where is she going now?

RABBI. To get you food.

GOLEM. And then she won't leave me again.

RABBI. I've told you,

She is my child. You must not ever talk

About her, ever even think about her. (*Sharply.*)

I see a change has now come over you

As though you've shaken, shuddered, and jumped up!

GOLEM. I felt so fine whenever she looked at me.

RABBI. Silence!

GOLEM. And can't I even take hold of her hand?

RABBI. You mustn't even catch a glimpse of her. . . .

A very different life's marked out for you,

A different air to breathe, a different language.

In time you'll see it, and you'll sense it too.

Meanwhile be silent, locked up in your silence.

Do you hear? Hush!

GOLEM. Not talk to anyone?

RABBI. Just answer any question; say no more!

And keep away from people. When you come

Into the synagogue or somewhere else,

Settle in a secluded corner there.

If somebody should come and ask you something,

Answer without anger. Your isolation

Is neither punishment nor misfortune.

It is the pathway that eventually

Will lead you, take you to your joys and wonders.

GOLEM (*sits down, turns his head*).

Now all at once I'm in the depths of darkness.

I can't see anything, Rabbi. Hold me tight,

I'm falling.

RABBI. You're not falling; you're just hungry.

(*WIFE enters, followed by DEBORAH. WIFE brings milk, bread, and a pitcher of water. GOLEM is hunched over the table.*)

WIFE. Honored guest, wash your hands before you eat.

(*GOLEM sits immobile.*)

What's wrong with him, Aryeh Leyb? Just look,

He doesn't lift his head.

DEBORAH. Is he asleep?

WIFE. Honored guest, wash your hands now; here is water.

Why is he silent, Aryeh Leyb? You ask him.

(*GOLEM looks up silently.*)

WIFE. You want to eat, don't you? Then wash your hands.

RABBI. Just serve, he'll wash. Yosl, now wash your hands.

(*GOLEM pours water over his hands, wipes his hands silently and clumsily with the towel held out to him by the WIFE, and starts to eat.*)

WIFE. No blessing, no benediction on the bread.

Just look at how he's hungrily gulping down

The bread. What a heartrending sight to see.

RABBI. Should I invite him to remain with us?

WIFE. With us?

RABBI. I need a servant after all.

And for the synagogue we also need

A woodchopper and water carrier.

WIFE. He shocked the girl. God knows—may we be spared!

Who is this man?

RABBI. A human being, see?

A decent and a lonely human being.

WIFE. If you think so, then maybe you know better,

But I—

RABBI. You're scared.

WIFE. I am. May God forgive me!

RABBI. There's nothing to be scared of. God has sent him

Across my path at just the right time now.

WIFE. What are you saying, Aryeh Leyb?

RABBI. I've looked for

A servant like him for the longest time. . . .

A man of might, a man of strength like him. . . .

WIFE. Well, maybe you know better, but I'm leaving.

(*To GOLEM.*) Would you perhaps care for more food meanwhile?

(*GOLEM shakes his head no.*)

WIFE (*to DEBORAH*). Why do you keep on following me? Go to bed.

DEBORAH. Grandma, I'm scared.

WIFE. Are you a child or what?

RABBI (*putting his hand on DEBORAH'S head*).

There's nothing to be scared of, Deborah.

DEBORAH. Will he live here forever?

RABBI. I don't know.

DEBORAH. And still his eyes are gaping at me now.

(*She leaves with RABBI'S WIFE.*)

RABBI (*to GOLEM*). Have you already had enough to eat?

GOLEM. Rabbi, my eyelids feel so very heavy.

RABBI. They're heavy? Good! You'll get your fill of sleep.

And when you wake, you'll see a different world.

GOLEM (*nods, drowsing, suddenly wakes up with a start*).

I must leave; something urges me to go.

RABBI. You're starting yet again; you may not leave here.

GOLEM. And where is Deborah?

RABBI. Haven't I warned you?

GOLEM. She looked at me. Rabbi, why did she leave?

And why are you so angry with me, Rabbi?

RABBI. I'm not angry at all. I only seem to be.

I warn you, never mention Deborah. (*GOLEM is silent.*)

And do you hear my warning, Yosl?

GOLEM. Yes,

I hear it, Rabbi, and I will obey. . . .

My lids are growing heavy once again. (*GOLEM falls asleep while sitting.*)

RABBI. He's sleeping. (*Sits down opposite GOLEM and gazes at him in his sleep, then stands up, looms over him while his eyes are glued to the sleeper's face.*)

So much dumb sorrow in that face. . . . (*Trembles.*)

Is that the man I dreamed into existence?

My champion? My envoy? . . . He? Such arms!

Such legs, such shoulders! . . . So much body, flesh!

So much dumb sorrow, anguish in that face. (*Faces the wall, absorbed in his grief.*)

(*WIFE enters softly, gapes in amazement.*)

WIFE. Why is the building so hushed, so silent now?

(*RABBI turns away from the wall and motions for her to be silent and leave.*)

WIFE. You're terribly pale, Aryeh Leyb.

RABBI. Don't say a word. He's sleeping.

WIFE. Sitting up?

RABBI. No matter. . . . He should sleep his fill. He must!

WIFE. Should I bring him a pillow?

RABBI. No, you mustn't!

But I'll be with you soon enough. Just wait.

(*WIFE tiptoes away.*)

(*RABBI stands over GOLEM, listening to his deep and heavy breathing.*)

THROUGH DARKNESS

(*RABBI's private study. Evening. RABBI sits dozing over an open book. A frightened DEBORAH stands at his side, trying to wake him.*)

DEBORAH. Grandpa, Grandpa, wake up!

RABBI (*wakes up*). What is it, ha?

DEBORAH. You're yelling in your sleep—so loudly, Grandpa!

RABBI. Loudly, you say? I was just napping, napping. . . .

Deborah, that's all, a dream took hold of me.

DEBORAH. You shouted: "Fire, blood!" And something else

About the Fifth Tower.

RABBI. Deborah, a dream,

A nasty nightmare. Go, my dear, it's nothing!

Deborah, it's nothing, just a dream, a nightmare.

(*She exits.*) *RABBI sits there, leaning over the table, burying his face in his hands. GOLEM enters softly and halts at the door, clutching an ax. The longer he peers, the more GOLEM-like are his features. A sudden broad smile exposes two rows of white teeth. Then his face freezes into a stiff expression. He goes over to the table where the RABBI sits, lost in thought. GOLEM settles on the bench right across from RABBI, assuming his position and expression. Several moments later the RABBI suddenly wakes up, sees the GOLEM, and is frightened,*

RABBI. Oh, God, oh, God, it's you! How did you get here?

And who told you to sit down at my table?

GOLEM. I don't know, I just saw you sleeping, sitting. . . .

RABBI. You needn't mimic everything I do.

Why have you come here now into my study?

GOLEM. You've called me, Rabbi.

RABBI. When?

GOLEM. Why, all this time.

Rabbi, I heard you calling Yosl, Yosl!

RABBI (*glares at him*). I've never called you, never called at all.

Get back to work, have you split all the wood?
GOLEM. They won't allow me to split wood.
RABBI. Who won't?
GOLEM. They tease and taunt me.
RABBI. Again I ask you, who?
GOLEM. The children taunt me—and the grown men too.
They stand around me, and they stare and stare—
And ask me for my name and where I come from.
RABBI. Don't answer them.
GOLEM. I don't. I hold my tongue.
Why, after all, you told me to keep silent.
RABBI. They'll never harm you.
GOLEM. How I hate them all!
RABBI. You ought to live in peace with everyone.
GOLEM. I look at no one, and I talk to no one.
Just see them gazing, staring through the window.
RABBI (*goes to window, looks out*).
Stop worrying, and get your work.
I'll go myself and tell them all to stop.
GOLEM. Well, Rabbi, none of them fear you at all.
I say: "The rabbi will now come and scold you!"
And when I say that, they start laughing harder!
RABBI. Just go on out, and I'll come presently.
GOLEM. I would've let one have it with my ax.
RABBI. What are you saying? You?
GOLEM. Take them away, just drive them all away.
What are they saying? What are they looking at?
Such talk, such eyes. Get all of them away!
The ax glides lightly, calmly in my hands.
Up, down, up, down, and I'm so tall—the tallest.
And the ax glides and slides, higher and higher. . . .
Why do you say we shouldn't raise an ax?
The ax flies from my hands all on its own . . .

RABBI. All on its own? I see now. It will flee
No longer. For I lent your arms their lightness,
A labor to relieve your loneliness.
"The ax should fly into your hands—a feather!"
That was the benediction that I gave you.
But now I see it must be different.
Let each stroke of the ax strike you with sweat,
With strenuous effort and with great exertion.
And every time the blade attacks the wood,
Your breath will sink just like a heavy load. . . .
This is no castigation; it is more
A favor—to keep the lightness of your arm
From tempting you and from enticing you.
GOLEM. I hate them, hate them all. I hate you too.
RABBI. Me too?
GOLEM. I'm frightened of your glaring eyes.
I'm terrified of every word you utter.
I always think that I can hear your voice:
"Where are you now?" I smash the ax into
The wood, and then I answer you: "I'm here!"
And everyone laughs and mimics me: "I'm here!"
RABBI. Get back to work, and don't look at the others.
GOLEM. I never look at them; my eyes are lowered.
But then the onlookers keep forcing me
To lift my head and look into their eyes.
RABBI. Didn't I put a charm around your throat
To draw your eyes in friendship to all faces?
GOLEM. It worked for just a moment. When I was
Splitting the wood for the very first time
And when I raised the ax, I saw so many
Faces and eyes, and all encircling me,
And smiling at me kindly, smiling gently.
Not speaking, no, just staring tenderly. . . .

Then all at once they all began to talk,
To scamper back and forth and fling their arms.
They yelled strange words and started laughing loudly,
Dashing and darting in and backing out
And then I heard your laughter too.
RABBI. My laughter?
GOLEM. As if you were concealed behind the others,
Compelling them to howl and holler: "Golem!"
I dropped what I was doing and fled here.
RABBI. And are you calm?
GOLEM. I feel so good with you.
If you wished to be with me constantly,
You wouldn't leave me by myself, I wouldn't
Be scared of anyone, I wouldn't be
Alarmed at hearing my own name. . . . Do not
Send me away from you ever again.
RABBI. Who says I'm sending you away at all?
You see me here a dozen times a day!
And if you need me, you can seek me out.
GOLEM. I want to be with you forever, yes,
Forever. When the others stand around me
And watch me all the while, just splitting wood,
Why aren't you among them? After all,
You can be like them, standing, watching me.
RABBI (*smiling to himself*).
What? All the while? Does he grasp what he's saying?
He reasons like a child, and he is blind,
Yet fear emerges from his reasoning,
A fear that's anything at all but childlike. . . .
(*To the GOLEM.*) And do you know where you'll be sleeping here?
In the Fifth Tower. Lots of Jews sleep there.
My beadle will be taking you, and he'll

Prepare a place where you can spend the night.
You surely wouldn't want me to sleep near you?
GOLEM. Why not? Isn't there room enough for two?
(RABBI *smiles. Then his face saddens. He goes over to the wall and halts
thoughtfully. GOLEM stares and stares and likewise goes over to the wall.*)
RABBI (*turns away from the wall*).
I can't be with you all the time. And you
Must know that you've come here to be alone.
So then I tell you, go about the work
That you must do. And then, when you are done,
Just go and sleep where you are told to sleep. . . .
You must be all alone and not with me.
It's harsh for you and dark. The darkness is yours,
And it will then pursue you step by step
Until it shines for you, bursts into brightness.
I took you on to serve me, work for me.
It's not my job to follow you and guard you
And watch you while you eat and while you sleep.
I'll call you when I need you. Meanwhile leave.
(*GOLEM leaves, clutching the ax.*)
RABBI (*alone*). Now my impatience keeps on growing,
nourished
By vicious rumors and by my restless dreams.
Who will interpret, clarify my dreams?
You show me signs that follow one another:
Great dangers lie in ambush on our road.
They are arriving now; they lurk before us.
You open up my eyes, and I can see them:
Blood libels, blood and fire and . . . destruction.
I know that rescue comes with misery
And that the sword brings comfort and relief.
And the black flame contains the brightest brilliance.
But my heart's filled with turmoil and impatience—

Impatience with myself—my greatest sin
Before you. And you sent him to me, sent
This helpless servant, all helpless himself,
To help us. Darkness itself, he is to bring
Us brightness. All of us are hanging by
A single thread above the chasm's edge,
And he, he, the redeemer, is the first
To weep for help. . . . I sent him out in anger.
Yet he'd done nothing wrong. Was he at fault?
(*He looks out the window.*)
I still appear to fear his glaring eyes. . . .
You've spread the sorrow of a feeble mind
Across his face, cold and uncanny strangeness.
So that we all, including you, might not
See his true shape. . . . Perhaps that should be so.
I'll wait. I'll rip impatience from my heart,
So that the terror facing us will not
Confuse my mind or cloud my eyes in my
Old age, so that I may perceive the face
Of his true shape. . . . His truth must be revealed.
For his true shape is . . . yours. . . .
(*He stands there, leaning against the window. REB BASSEVI, an elderly,
richly clad Jew enters.*)
BASSEVI. Good evening, Rabbi.
RABBI. A guest, a guest. Good evening, Reb Bassevi.
Please have a seat.
BASSEVI. The rabbi must forgive me
For coming here without an invitation.
RABBI. Nonsense, Reb Bassevi. A welcome guest . . .
BASSEVI. I crossed the courtyard of the synagogue.
Clusters of men were standing all around,
All of them wondering and worrying,
With rumors rushing round from mouth to mouth,

And I—I hope that my words aren't sinful—
I myself, Rabbi, feel so queasy now.
RABBI. Why don't you have a seat now, Reb Bassevi?
BASSEVI (*sits down*). Rabbi, I hope I'm not disturbing you.
RABBI. Not at all, Reb Bassevi
BASSEVI. Yes, I figured
I might drop in on you for just a minute
Or two and chat awhile.
RABBI. A good idea.
How very thoughtful, of you, Reb Bassevi.
Yet you seem out of sorts; you look distracted.
Might something else have brought you here today?
BASSEVI. Something else? No! I just don't know myself.
You should have seen the turmoil, Rabbi, in
The courtyard of the synagogue. It wasn't
The normal hustle and bustle there.
Tankhem, that melancholy man, was clad
In tatters and in gloom. God only knows
Where he had gotten all the words he spewed.
Blasting and blighting all the groups around him,
He flung his hands and talked and talked and talked. . . .
On top of everything, who should come along
But him, the woodchopper? And, Rabbi,
He cast a shroud of fear upon the Jews. . . .
RABBI. You're just like all the others, Reb Bassevi?
A man is standing, drudging, chopping wood!
What can be scary about that? Why, we've
Been looking for a good woodchopper for ages.
You know that, Reb Bassevi, very well.
BASSEVI. Yes, but nobody seems to like this man.
Rabbi, you ought to go and watch them. Young
And old come pouring from each house into
The courtyard of the synagogue to gaze

At some amazing sight. And frankly, Rabbi,
When I myself saw him just now, I couldn't
Help it. I stopped, entranced; I had to stop
And gape at him heaving his ax. . . . I've never
Seen such a man before in all my life.

(*RABBI sits pensive, alarmed.*)

BASSEVI. Rabbi, do you know who he is? A local?
RABBI. Do I know who he is? Of course I do!
He's not a local; he's a stranger here.
It doesn't matter.
BASSEVI. Then we have no reason
To fear him, Rabbi, since you know the man.
RABBI. Tell everybody that we have no reason
To fear him.
BASSEVI. Rabbi, I will spread the word.
RABBI. Yet you still seem uneasy, Reb Bassevi.
I see it in your face.
BASSEVI. Forgive me, Rabbi.
I may be sinning. Too much anxiety
Has gathered in my heart these past few days.
And yet far more than anything, that same
Anxiety has brought me here to you,
RABBI. The Good Lord is our Father, Reb Bassevi.
BASSEVI. Rabbi, I've come to hear those very words
From you, those words of hope and faith and solace.
My hair is gray now, and my heart itself
Should carry words of solace constantly.
I shouldn't be afraid or yield to fear.
And yet what can we do? We're sinners, Rabbi,
And times are evil—God have mercy on us!
Rabbi, I couldn't sleep a wink all night,
My eyes were open till the crack of dawn.
RABBI. What are you saying, Reb Bassevi? Tell me.

BASSEVI. I must confess that talking now would tear
The terror from my heart.
RABBI. Well, could it be
That we're exaggerating all that danger,
That we're exaggerating it ourselves?
BASSEVI. Ourselves? Perhaps we're overstating it.
But then, perhaps the opposite is true;
The danger may be greater than we think.
Who knows, who knows what's going on behind
Our very backs? And who knows in which nets
Our feet may get entwined, entangled—if
Not now, today, then possibly tomorrow?
Who knows whose hands are sending out misfortune?
Rabbi, what do they want of us? Please tell me.
I simply wish to grasp, to understand,
To comprehend: What do they want of us?
RABBI. They want a great deal of us, Reb Bassevi.
But we can give them nothing, do you hear?
Yet if we can—oh, Reb Bassevi, if
We can, we do not want to, do not want to. . . .
With a mere fingertip we touched the world
And everything and everyone it holds.
Standing aside, we merely breathed a breath
On the entire world, and everything
And everyone it holds will bear the imprint
Of our touch until the end of time.
And storms will rage and whirlwinds will erupt
From our mild and our gentle breathing.
Then why must we uncover any causes?
Why must we ask, What do they want of us?
If any cause is needed, let them look!
Just let them look; they look and truly find.
But what good are they and their arduous

And ardent looking and their fervent finding?
And we—we stand aside from all the causes,
We are both light and hard, both near and far.
If we desire it, we face the world;
If we desire it, we turn our backs.
The world is nothing but a passageway;
It's nothing but an anteroom for us.
The passage may be far too long and twisted.
It may be bristling with spears and axes.
But who will try to clear away those axes
If, with the axes, we must also clear
Away our touch and our crimson steps? . . .
BASSEVI. Must the road stretch forever and forever? . . .
RABBI. And we forevermore—redeem the world. . . .
We can, but we refuse.
BASSEVI. What? We refuse?
RABBI. For this, precisely, is what *they* would want.
BASSEVI. I hear you, and each word intensifies
The anguish and the agony I feel.
RABBI. Anguish? Just what is anguish, Reb Bassevi?
Why, we have grown together into anguish,
Grown part of it, swathed it, set it on fire,
Made it blaze up and spread across all worlds. . . .
Look at yourself now, Reb Bassevi, look.
Anguish is flaring in your face, your features. . . .
But then an hour of impatience may
Arrive, greater than all your agony,
An hour that will be far greater still
Than all your stubbornness. And I, or you,
Or anyone on our street—why, even Tankhem—
Instead of grazing the entire world
With just a single fingertip, he should
Raise his entire hand with all its fingers.

What do you think would happen, Reb Bassevi?
BASSEVI. A tragedy for us, a tragedy.
RABBI. A tragedy? Imagine not just me,
Or you, or someone somewhere else, but him,
That woodman in the yard—imagine him
Raising his hand with all its fingers. Then
Would they still want us— (*breaks off, terrified.*)
BASSEVI. Rabbi, what's wrong with you? You've turned so pale!
RABBI. It sounds just like a riot. Don't you hear it?
BASSEVI. A riot, Rabbi? I don't hear a thing.
RABBI. It must be my imagination then. (*Looks out the window.*)
Imagination, yes. The courtyard's clearing.
BASSEVI. What should I say now, Rabbi, when I see
The fear that's flaming in your features too?
RABBI. What should you say now, Reb Bassevi? Nothing.
There is a time for silence—do you know? . . .
The Jews now in the synagogue will finish
Praying and will then scatter to their homes
And will, as usual, go quietly to bed.
Perhaps, like you, they will not get a wink
Of sleep. And yet not one of them will rise
From bed and will capitulate to fear.
BASSEVI. Rabbi, are your words meant as a rebuke?
RABBI. No, Reb Bassevi, my words aren't meant
As a rebuke. You haven't caught my drift.
BASSEVI. I hoped to hear your consolation, Rabbi.
RABBI. And words of consolation still are here,
For all the fears are pointless, Reb Bassevi.
BASSEVI. Pointless?
RABBI. Yes, fears with no foundations to them.
BASSEVI. I want to understand you fully, Rabbi,
Clearly. You say there is a time for silence.
And yet I sense that your fear is not silent,

That your—forgive me, Rabbi, for these words.
RABBI. Indeed, I do forgive you, Reb Bassevi.
But bear in mind my word of warning: Never
Spend the whole night without a wink of sleep.
A Jew should never drive his sleep away. . . .
The two of us are old now, Reb Bassevi,
But we must never, ever grow too old
To apprehend all wonders. Do you catch
My drift? I mean *all* wonders, Reb Bassevi.
BASSEVI. Rabbi, your words are wise. Perhaps like you
I'll be found worthy to live till that moment. . . .

(*A tumult is heard outside the door. RABBI opens the door and looks out.*)
RABBI. Who's there? Oh, Tankhem. Let him in, my girl.
BASSEVI. Tankhem? Too much!
RABBI. No matter, Reb Bassevi.

(*TANKHEM enters, tattered and disheveled. A ripped coat lapel is a sign of mourning.*)
TANKHEM. What rudeness! Tankhem wants to see the rabbi,
And they won't let him pass!
RABBI. Sit down, Reb Tankhem.
TANKHEM. Rabbi, no time to sit—
I have to hurry, hurry!
My fiery chariot is waiting for me.
BASSEVI. And what will be the limit of your grief?
TANKHEM. A limit? There's no limit!
For all lapels are waiting for my touch
To rip them. . . .
If not for our grand festival, Passover,
My son Yokanan would be alive today.
Should we then give up Passover forever?
You're silent? Should we then give up Passover?
I'll send my fiery chariot for you.
BASSEVI. I've heard all that before, Reb Tankhem.

TANKHEM. You've heard?
You may have heard it all a thousand times,
But you have never heard it.
Deaf, how can you hear?
Blind, how can you see?
You see my features in the blackest night?
You hear my voice?
I spread my arms out wide;
I turn my eyes inside;
I crane my neck so far away. . . .
Over the top of the tower,
Through all its shattered windows,
I dash in and out. . . .
Five is the number of Towers—
Five,
One for east and one for west,
One for north and one for south,
And the Fifth Tower—for me.
Who endures the sorrow of the towers?
I.
I am the lord of the ruins. . . .
RABBI. Relax, sit down, Reb Tankhem.
(*TANKHEM sits down, panting wearily.*)
RABBI? Reb Tankhem, no one's left now in the courtyard?
TANKHEM. No one, no one. They've scattered
Inside the synagogue for evening prayers,
Leaving Tankhem alone with him—that killer!
But Tankhem isn't scared of any killer.
I've come to tell you now
That Tankhem isn't scared of any ax.
BASSEVI. Rabbi, did you hear that?
RABBI. Why do you say such things, Reb Tankhem?
TANKHEM. Why say such things?

You, of all people, Rabbi!
Darkness is spreading over us, darkness,
From all sides.
And who can stop my fiery chariot?
Not even you.
For nobody will dare,
For nobody has sat in it as yet,
Or roasted in its flames,
Or rolled beneath its wheels.
No one has breathed its dizziness.
Let hands reach far, reach out for me;
Let axes heave;
Let throats now scream.
Hands become weary,
Axes rust,
And throats turn silent,
And if not silent, they are slit. . . . (*Jumps over to RABBI.*)
And who's the master here?
The rabbi or Tadeush—who?
RABBI. Tadeush?
TANKHEM. You don't know who Tadeush is?
The rabbi certainly should know.
And he must know: Tadeush was in the
Fifth Tower.
RABBI. I know, Reb Tankhem.
TANKHEM. The rabbi knows. (*Rests his head on the table.*)
BASSEVI. Rabbi, is that the truth?
RABBI. He wants to drive the paupers out from there.
TANKHEM. But who's the master here?
The woodchopper perhaps? (*Jumps up.*)
Drive us out? What's he waiting for?
I've got more ruins than needed in our village.
Ruins of the whole world

Have been waiting for me
For a long time.
They gape at the world through gawking holes;
They breath to me;
They call for me to come and rule.
And should I come,
What joy for them,
A singing
And a dancing. . . .
So should I turn my face and never hear
That prayer?
Who else should hear it except me?
Me—
Because my heart is filled with mercy for the world.
(*He stops flailing his arms and stands there as if congealed.*)
The huge eyes of the world
Are filled with yearning.
Who sees the huge eyes of the world?
I.
Who can appease the yearning of the world?
I.
Because my heart is filled with mercy for the world. . . .
In my fiery chariot I rush around.
I rush around the towers
In thick of night.
My son lies
In the fiery chariot—
My son, to celebrate Passover. . . .
His left eye, it is pierced through by a spear,
His right eye—closed.
His right arm is hacked off up to his shoulder,
His left arm, to his elbow.
Each first Passover night I tell my son:

"Stand up and live.
Regain your eyes and arms
Because the whole world's thirsty with its lust
And hungry with its yearning."
My son stands up,
And he waits.
Until we hear those footsteps,
Hear them.
They pierce his left eye once again,
They chop his right arm once again up to his shoulder,
His left arm, to his elbow
I lay him back inside the chariot,
And I say:
"Until next year. . . ."
Because my heart is filled with mercy for the world . . .

(*TANKHEM dashes out. RABBI and BASSEVI sit there, stunned. A long hush.*)

BASSEVI. Such chatter, chatter.

(*RABBI starts pacing to and fro, stops at the window, and peers out.*)

BASSEVI (*stands up*).

I hear the worshipers going to evening prayers,
Rabbi, good night.

RABBI. Good night, good night, I'll join them very soon.

(*Paces to and fro, stops at the window again, peers out, puts his head out, and peers anxiously. Uneasy voices of men and women are heard from the courtyard. They hurry past the RABBI's window, yelling, "Where's the rabbi? Make him come out!" Female voices: "God help us! What a terrible misfortune has come upon us!" The RABBI heads toward the door. His WIFE comes hurrying in, holding DEBORAH's hand. Both women are terrified. DEBORAH is crying.*)

RABBI. What's wrong?

WIFE. That stranger—the woodsman! Heaven help us!

RABBI. What has he done?

WIFE. A new misfortune on us, Aryeh Leyb, I tell you.
He terrified the girl. Now heaven help us!
She went outside to draw a pail of water,
But he dashed over to her, and he wouldn't
Allow her to get over to the well.
DEBORAH (*weeping*).
He said that carrying water was *his* job.
RABBI. And what did he do then?
WIFE. Oh, Aryeh Leyb,
I'm so ashamed even to talk about it.
In front of everyone he grabbed her, kissed her!
If there had been no throng of witnesses,
He would have choked her.
RABBI. What's he doing now?
WIFE. What should he do? A golem, not a man!
He's standing still as if he were made of stone.
DEBORAH. Drive him away. Just drive him far away!
(*RABBI, WIFE, AND DEBORAH leave. A turmoil is heard from the courtyard. Then it fades. RABBI enters, followed by GOLEM, clutching his ax, GOLEM stands in the center of the room, strangely rigid, his hands dangling at his sides. RABBI scrutinizes him for a while, then removes the ax from his hands. GOLEM is immobile. He looks as if he were standing asleep with open eyes.*)
RABBI. You stand in stone and do not see
That I am nearing you.
(*GOLEM stands inflexible.*)
RABBI. Lift up your head and your eyes too.
I want to peer inside them.
The uproar you aroused is resonating,
Terror is lurking still behind your back,
Peering across your shoulder, ready now
To pounce. With many thousands upon thousands
Of eyes and mouths and tongues, it still keeps whirling

Around your head.
(GOLEM *stands motionless.*)

RABBI. For you I prayed to God for wonders.
I prayed through pain and tears,
So you'd see where nobody else can see,
So you'd hear everything
Nobody else can hear,
So that your steps would sense
Nine cubits in the depth,
So that your body wouldn't burn in fire,
So that you wouldn't drown in deepest water,
So that your nostrils would detect
The scents blown by the farthest winds.
And if need be, your body might become
Transparent like a ray or like the air,
Or be transformed into another person,
So that you'd see but not be seen.
I grant you glory for your life
And blessed power for your hands,
And you—you stand stock-still like wood,
Your eyes are dull; your mouth is warped.
Your shoulders are like broad walls, and
They bear the lifeless grief of clay.
And long-lain, dust-encrusted worms
Are twisting still upon your arms,
And still for miles around, your breath
Emits the reek of rotten rock.
You're now alive, you're only one day old,
And yet how fast the human being in you
Has hurried to reveal himself
In hatred, and in passion, and in anguish.
But have I brought you to me so you'd be
Like any other human being here?

Well, let's just say that you've been overwhelmed
By all the dread and all the darkness felt
By all the human desperation now.
But where upon your face is there the song,
The vast glow of our universal faith?
Why are you silent? Answer me!
Don't you now see—before
I lift my staff against you!
(*GOLEM comes to, joyfully stretches out his hands to RABBI.*)
GOLEM. Where am I, Rabbi, ha, where am I now?
And where did everybody disappear?
They all were shouting, weeping,
Crowding around me,
And I couldn't tell why.
Then everything went silent all at one,
My eyelids stuck together, and
I slept, Rabbi.
RABBI. You slept?
GOLEM. I'm not sure, Rabbi.
The earth began to sway beneath my feet.
A hand then yanked me out
And hurtled me so high,
Then hurled me deep, deep down.
I plunged. And suddenly the earth
Crumbled and cracked apart
Into two halves.
I flew into the chasm,
But there was no place to alight. . . .
And as I flew, I noticed you
Riding on me and urging me
Deeper and deeper into the abyss.
RABBI. Just tell me everything.
GOLEM. I saw your features in a double image.

One half was as big as mine,
The other half, smaller than mine.
You had four eyes, all of them dead.
There was a speck of red in one,
With hot blood oozing out. . . .
And suddenly I saw your head
Begin to toss and bob about
And bang and beat against my head,
And with the oozing, bleeding eye
It burned into my brow,
And it sank bit by bit into
My brain, until it reached my throat.
And as you sank inside me, I saw that
Your neck was long and white and supple.
And now I grabbed you by the throat
And started fiercely strangling, strangling. . . .
RABBI. Let words rebuke you for your rage.
GOLEM. That's all I know, that's all I saw;
I didn't see your face, your eyes.
Someone was strangling *my* throat,
And I thought that it was *your* throat. . . .
Oh, stay with me, don't go away.
(*GOLEM lies down on the ground, at RABBI's feet.*)
Oh, stay with me—or else drive me away.
RABBI. Stand up. I see your grief.
I do forgive you.
GOLEM. Don't go away.
RABBI. Stand up.
GOLEM. Oh, let me lie a little longer
At your feet.
RABBI. Stand up.
GOLEM. Oh, just a single moment, Rabbi.
I feel so good, I feel so easy,

It's all so bright.
RABBI (*joyfully*). Bright?
What do you see?
GOLEM. You.
RABBI. And now?
GOLEM. Your hands are touching me.
RABBI. I'm blessing you. And now what do you see?
GOLEM. Fire! Fire!
A huge flame billowing and flurrying,
It's trying to ignite me, but it can't.
RABBI. And now?
GOLEM. A torrent whirls and frenzies.
I sink, yet I don't drown.
And rocks hail down upon my head
And bounce away. . . .
RABBI. What else?
GOLEM. And vicious dogs keep tearing me.
But my flesh isn't torn. . . .
RABBI. What do you hear?
GOLEM. I hear gagged voices
Deep down in the earth.
The conversation between rocks and roots,
And steps of scurrying feet. . . .
I hear a wind, it wafts and whirls,
It calls me by my name,
And I'm not worried by that wind. . . .
And, Rabbi, look, a face is gazing at me,
A face made up entirely of light,
A body huge like mine.
It floats, it flutters over me
And sways as if on wings.
It grows out from my shoulders
And spreads out from my arms. . . .

RABBI. Stand up.

(*GOLEM stands up.*)

RABBI. And now what do you see?

GOLEM. I see a man dressed all in black,

He's coming here with silent steps,

With steps that lurk for prey. . . .

RABBI. Now, open up your eyes again

And see the light again,

The wings of an invisible person

That spread out from you.

Go to the Fifth Tower,

And stay there now, and sleep there now.

(*GOLEM rushes from room in a single leap. RABBI, himself amazed, leans his face against the wall, his shoulders heaving.*)

BEGGARS

(In the Fifth Tower. A large room with a high ceiling. The room is a shambles. Each side has an entrance to another room. One wall is broken through; the others are blackened, covered with cobwebs, rain-soaked. No doors, wobbly thresholds, shattered windows. Here and there, unbroken panes in various colors. In a few places there are signs of leftover murals. They all are smeared, stained, carelessly scratched. In one corner we see the chains of sacred Christian lamps. Paupers and beggars live in this room. The floor where they sleep is covered with old rags, bundles, a few pillows. Beggars' bags hang on the walls. Night is setting in. A cold spring wind is blasting through the shattered windows. The room is dark. A sick, feverish PAUPER lies in a tangle of rags on the floor. The other inhabitants haven't arrived as yet.)

SICK MAN. My bones are breaking, all my bones.

If I died, nobody would know.

I'm cold. *(Sits up.)*

Nobody's here.

Someone should bring a little warm water.

I haven't had a bite to eat all day. . . .

Oh, my bones! Oh, my bones! *(Lies down again.)*

What's taking them so long? Isn't the day

Enough for them? They'd gulp down the whole world!

And what would they have then? My bag is hanging

There, stuffed with bread, with challah. . . . Oh, my bones! . . .

(Sits up again.)

A deep darkness. I haven't got the strength

To stand and light the lamp or fill the holes

In windowpanes with something, anything. . . .

(Stands up, shuffles in the dark, falls back down.)

Oh, God of Abraham, of Isaac, and of Jacob!

(Covers himself with the rags lying near him, huddles under them, trem-

bling. Silence. GOLEM enters, pauses in the middle of the room, doesn't know which way to turn. Remains silent.)

SICK MAN (*raises his head*).

Has someone come? Oh, God! Has someone come?

(*GOLEM remains silent.*)

SICK MAN. Have you no tongue to answer an invalid?

Why are you silent? Ha! Who are you? Who?

(*GOLEM remains silent.*)

SICK MAN (*more and more scared*).

Why, don't you see I'm shaking in the cold?

(*Jumps up and stares at GOLEM. Shouts.*)

Fire! Fire!

Who are you? Answer me! Just wait a moment!

I'll light the lamp.

(*Lights smoky lamp. His fears grow.*)

What do you want? Why won't you talk?

Are you a pauper?

(*GOLEM silently sits down on the floor.*)

SICK MAN. You want to sleep here?

GOLEM. Don't talk to me.

SICK MAN. Where are you from? And with no bag at that!

Is this your first visit to Prague?

GOLEM. Don't talk to me.

(*SICK MAN collapses on his pad and fearfully gazes at GOLEM. GOLEM stands up, goes into the adjacent room, sits down by a wall, facing the doorway. He is barely visible in the darkness. REDHEAD and BLIND MAN enter.*)

REDHEAD. You understand?

BLIND MAN. Did you see right?

REDHEAD. A heretic is spotted right away.

BLIND MAN. Why, then, it must be true!

If everybody says so, then it's true.

BLIND MAN. You say he walked behind us?

REDHEAD. No more than twenty paces,
Bent over, wordlessly gripping his staff,
And all at once he turned off to a side. . . .
BLIND MAN. Ah, God has punished me, so I can't see
The footsteps of the man pursuing us.
REDHEAD. Punished? Perhaps he's blessed you.
I'm not a coward, as you know,
But something took my breath away.
BLIND MAN. Somebody who was not a beggar
Has never walked the path to the Fifth Tower.
REDHEAD. Well, just try to get someone to come here.
The sole reply: a pair of bulging eyes,
For everyone is terrified of ruins.
BLIND MAN. And we? Aren't we terrified as well?
We're only here to stay the night—that's all.
Sleep covers and conceals us and protects us.
REDHEAD. And suddenly, when you hear a stranger's steps
Behind you, do you grasp the meaning of
The stranger's steps?
BLIND MAN. The meaning of those steps?
Only the living God knows. He's our father.
(*Both at once.*) Are we alone here?
REDHEAD. The sick man is here.
He's lying on the floor; he's fast asleep.
BLIND MAN. Aside from the sick man?
REDHEAD. I told you, he's
The only other person here.
BLIND MAN. Am I
Imagining it? Scrutinize the room.
REDHEAD. What do you mean?
(*BLIND MAN gropes around and bumps into SICK MAN, who awakens.*)
SICK MAN. A little water, get me
A little water.

REDHEAD. There's no water here.

SICK MAN. There's water in the adjacent room—oh, no!
Don't go there now. A stranger's sitting there.

REDHEAD. A stranger?

BLIND MAN. Don't you listen? I did tell you!
(*He gropes his way to the threshold of the next room.*)
A stranger? Ha, why, who's the stranger now?

REDHEAD (*looks in and then jumps back*).
It's him, it's him, the woodchopper. It's him.

BLIND MAN. The person who grabbed hold of Deborah?
He's here now? What's he doing in this place?

REDHEAD. Some sort of clown.

BLIND MAN. Don't holler, speak more softly.
The rabbi warned us not to tease the stranger.

REDHEAD. I wasn't teasing him. I was just talking.
Now, just who is it who has brought him here?

SICK MAN. He came alone and cast a pall on me.

REDHEAD. Someone like him can truly cast a pall.

BLIND MAN. Keep quiet now, don't play the sage.

GOLEM (*appears in doorway*).
I heard somebody mentioning my name.

REDHEAD. Your name? . . . No, no! I said—that is, I meant—

GOLEM. Don't mention me again. (*Returns to adjacent room.*)

REDHEAD. You understand? Why, you could thank the Lord
That you are blind and that you don't see *him*.

BLIND MAN. The rabbi has befriended him himself.

REDHEAD. There's something fishy here. Just mark my word.

SICK MAN. Stuff up the panes.

REDHEAD. I think you mean the holes.

SICK MAN. Well, stuff them up before I freeze to death.

REDHEAD. Our rags are few; the holes are many.
What should I stuff them with?

SICK MAN. Oh, God of Abraham, of Isaac, and of Jacob . . .

(*BLIND MAN sits down on the floor, removes coins from his breast pocket, and ties them up in a knotted rag.*)

REDHEAD (*takes down a bag from the wall, shakes out some crumbs. To BLIND MAN*). You've earned a lot? I haven't made a kopeck.

BLIND MAN (*wraps up the rag and returns it to his breast pocket*).
A lot. How do I know if it's a lot?
Just ask these blinded eyes of mine.
They are what earns the alms, not I.
If day and night are all the same for me,
Then let me at least have a knot of coins. . . .
Well, yes! Just ask these blinded eyes of mine.

REDHEAD. The bread's all gone. But there will be
Fresh challahs in the morning, Friday morning.
(*Packs rags into his bag and ties it up.*)
The bag should be all ready now, packed full.

BLIND MAN. What's that you're saying? I can't hear you.

REDHEAD. Talking—what do I have to talk about?
The bag should be all ready now, packed full. . . .

BLIND MAN. What do you think of that?
Why, I forgot to say my evening prayers.
(*He stands there, facing the wall.*)
"And he who is merciful and therefore forgives sin." . . .
(*He prays softly. OTHERS enter: HUNCHBACK, PEG LEG, TALL MAN, SHORT MAN—all with full bags. REDHEAD goes toward them.*

REDHEAD. We've got a guest tonight, a guest.
The man that's in the courtyard—

ALL. What kind of guest?

REDHEAD. Where've you been that you haven't heard?
The woodchopper in the synagogue courtyard.

TALL MAN. Is that for real? He's here?
Why, all of Prague is buzzing about him.

REDHEAD. And there he sits, concealed in darkness, gaping.
(*They all peer inside.*)

SHORT MAN. He's huge.

REDHEAD. Stop yelling, he could hear you. It's not safe.

PEG LEG. Why? Does he fight?

REDHEAD. He doesn't have to fight.

He glares at you; that's frightening enough!

TALL MAN. What is his name?

REDHEAD (*very softly*). They say his name is Yosl.

(*GOLEM comes striding in; others back off to the side.*)

GOLEM. I heard somebody mentioning my name.

Don't mention it again. (*Goes back.*)

REDHEAD. The second time

Today. And twice to me. When have you heard

Such nonsense? I thought I was whispering.

SHORT MAN. What's wrong? Why can't his name be mentioned ever?

(*They all look at one another, astonished.*)

Why, every good-for-nothing winds up in

This ruin.

REDHEAD. The rabbi sent him here himself.

ALL. The rabbi?

(*They sit down and untie their bags.*)

REDHEAD. Coming here, did you meet someone?

The priest . . .

ALL. What priest? Tadeush?

BLIND MAN (*while praying, he motions to the others to keep silent*).

Shhh! Shhh!!

(*They all stop talking and they display what they have gotten when begging.*)

REDHEAD. My bag is full. And you're unpacking yours? . . .

A waste of time, a waste of toil and trouble.

TALL MAN. Well, what's he saying there?

REDHEAD. I told you what.

Or are you hard of hearing now? They want

To drive us out of here, expel us soon.

BLIND MAN. Shh, oh, shh!

TALL MAN. What? Drive us out? From here? From this ruin
here?

The whole of Prague is envious of us.

No matter where you go these days, they ask:

Isn't there any room in the Fifth Tower?

Now do you catch my drift? The whole Fifth Tower

Will soon be mobbed by Jews, Jews who have been

Expelled from all their houses, driven out.

You catch my drift? You can be driven from

A house but not be driven from a ruin.

Now, do you finally see why the Fifth Tower

Will soon be mobbed by Jews?

BLIND MAN. Ah, well, now, shh.

HUNCHBACK. And what if they come here

And drive us out? God help us!

TALL MAN. We'll open all the bags we've filled.

"Take us; take everything!"

And when they take it all away,

Well then, they'll take it all away:

The challahs and the hunks of bread,

The clothing and—what else? What else?

Well, they'll take everything away!

BLIND MAN (*finishes praying, stands by the wall*).

There is a God in heaven, Jews.

SICK MAN (*sits up*).

There *is* a God in heaven, certainly!

He watches as the beggars settle down, and

After a day of begging they complain

About the challahs and about the bread.

And when they wearily drop down and shut

Their eyes and fall asleep, leaving the challahs

Unguarded. . . . Anyone could take them then. . . .
Not necessarily an enemy
But anybody happening to pass by.
For any passerby—he never sleeps.
He sits there, gloomy, and he never sleeps,
While beggars are exhausted and they slumber. . . .
There is a God in heaven, and he watches.
TALL MAN. What's wrong with him? What is he babbling?
SICK MAN. I haven't begged for two entire days.
So what? My bag is tied up and untouched.
And anybody who has wanted to
Could have untied it long ago and taken
The contents and then carried them away. . . .
But no one's come as yet. So what! Who cares?
Someone may come tomorrow or the next day.
Because it's never too late. . . .
Someone might even come today—
There is a God in heaven and he watches. . . .
BLIND MAN. What's he babbling about? Huh?
SICK MAN. I've now been lying here all day, all day,
And I've seen everything, heard everything.
The man who can see and hear everything
Must lie in one location. . . . And the man
I loudly called: He never came. . . . The man
I never called: He was the man who came. . . .
There was no one to sip the final drop
Of water on my palate. I lit a fire
Only because of fear. I fell facedown
Upon the ground; my thirst was still unquenched. . . .
For he—the man I didn't call—he came. . . .
ALL. What's wrong with him? What is he blabbering?
SICK MAN. I'll speak no more! I'll speak no more.
Let the man speak, the man I haven't called.

There is a God in heaven, and he watches. . . .

(Lies down again, burrowing into his pallet.)

(GOLEM appears, standing by the doorway. All the others are too fright-ened to stir. Now Tankhem arrives, and he scrutinizes everyone. Upon spotting GOLEM, he is petrified.)

REDHEAD. Things will be cheerful soon.

(TANKHEM glares at him silently. Walks over to GOLEM and bursts out laughing.)

TALL MAN. Lunatic! What's so funny?

TANKHEM. You know them? *(Points at the others.)*

You know who they are? You know what they do?

You've got big hands—beat them up!

You've got large feet—trample them!

I saw you had an ax—where is it now?

You see the hump? You see the red beard now?

You see the foot—split it.

You do know how to split wood.

(GOLEM silently goes back into the darkness. TANKHEM settles on the floor and takes his head in his hands.)

REDHEAD. He laughs out loud—the lunatic.

TALL MAN. Just draw his tongue out—why, that's all you need.

(All remain silent.)

TANKHEM. But meanwhile I'm the master here—

The sills are mine,

The chopped-out panes are mine,

And I allowed you all to enter here—

I!

In seven days and seven nights

He will arise,

He'll come down from the fiery chariot,

And all of you will have to leave,

The Fifth Tower belongs to him,

To him, my heir.

Now can't you hear the ruins all hollering?
And all the windows calling,
"When will he come?"
Pick up your rags,
Tie up your bags,
Clean up my home, my heir.

(*Two strangers enter: YOUNG BEGGAR and OLD BEGGAR, dusty from the long road, weary, clutching staffs, bags on their backs.*)

TWO BEGGARS. Good evening, Jews.

ALL. Good evening.

OLD BEGGAR. Why, we're in luck. You see? Jews everywhere.
And can we spend the night? What do you say, Jews?

TALL MAN. Grandpa, of course.

(*He welcomes the strangers, shaking hands and greeting them. Others do likewise except for TANKHEM and SICK MAN.*)

OLD BEGGAR. Good evening to you, Jews, good evening to you. . . .
You sleep upon the bare floor, don't you now?
Then we will do the same as all of you.
We'll spend one night here, just one single night. . . .

REDHEAD. You can spend many, many nights here, Grandpa.
The ruins are large enough for everyone.

OLD BEGGAR. We only need to spend a *single* night.
That's all. Then we'll go on again at noon.
We're both exhausted, and especially he—
He's young, he isn't used to traveling.
His feet, moreover—

(*They take off their bags and sit down.*)

TALL MAN. Yes, I see. He's limping.

OLD BEGGAR. From the long road. His feet are filled with sores,
He needs to rest, but there's no time as yet.

TALL MAN. Are you in any hurry?

OLD BEGGAR. No, we're not.

We've hurried up till now. These past few days
We've hurried day and night without a rest.
But we won't hurry after we leave here. . . .
TALL MAN. You need something in Prague?
OLD BEGGAR. Yes, yes . . . we need . . .
We need . . . What's new among you now in Prague?
TALL MAN. It isn't cheerful, Grandpa; it isn't cheerful.
OLD BEGGAR. Not cheerful? Really now? Not cheerful?
(*Hush. YOUNG BEGGAR sits down on the floor and starts unbinding his
sores. He unwinds the rags on his feet and winds them on again.*)
HUNCHBACK. You know, he doesn't look like any beggar.
Jews, what a noble face.
TALL MAN. Grandpa, you seem
To come from far, from very far away.
OLD BEGGAR. From very far away. The night had come.
We trudged, and then the castle loomed before us.
We saw deserted doors, deserted windows.
And so we thought that we might go inside. . . .
Tonight we'd rest up and we'd sleep our fill.
YOUNG BEGGAR. I'm so worn out, I'm really so worn out.
OLD BEGGAR (*points at TANKHEM*).
Why does he sit there like a man in mourning?
TALL MAN. Grandpa, he's sort of not all there.
(*All watch YOUNG BEGGAR bind his sores.*)
YOUNG BEGGAR. They keep on spreading, and they keep on
bursting,
They come up to my knees. . . . I'm so worn out.
My eyelids are so heavy. . . . (*Collapses on the ground and falls
asleep.*)
OLD BEGGAR (*inserts a bag under YOUNG BEGGAR'S head*).
Well, then, sleep, then sleep. . . .
TANKHEM (*jumps up*). Now guests are coming here to spend
the night,

And no one asks for my authorization?
Yet I'm the master here of this domain. . . .
REDHEAD. Be quiet! Can't you see this man's asleep?
TANKHEM. Asleep? How does he get to be asleep?
He must wake up and pry his eyelids open.
This is a place for being wide awake,
For trembling,
For fevering,
For lurking. . . .
The dead must soon arise,
And he—he sleeps?
REDHEAD. Just shut your trap, you lunatic!
(*He pushes TANKHEM, who falls down.*)
OLD BEGGAR. Don't hit him, Jews!
REDHEAD. Nobody can endure him here, I tell you.
We've got predicaments enough without him.
TANKHEM (*lies there, yelling*).
The dead must soon arise,
And he should sleep?
(*RABBI hurries in, scowling severely.*)
ALL (*surprised*). The rabbi! The rabbi!
RABBI (*exchanges looks with OLD BEGGAR. A long hush. To
STRANGERS*).
What are you doing here? The two of you?
Who sent for you? Who told you to come here?
OLD BEGGAR. We need to spend *one* single night, that's all.
To sleep one night after our long, long journey.
RABBI. You've come here on your own? At no one's bidding?
Grab up your bags at once,
And wake him up and leave!
I order you!
OLD BEGGAR. We're both exhausted from our long, long
journey.

We hurried here.

RABBI. You hurried? Then turn back.

I order you.

OLD BEGGAR. He's sound asleep. Don't wake him.

RABBI. Are there no other ruins in the world?

Are these the only ones you like? Wake him up!

(*Bangs his staff on the ground.*)

You've come here on your own, come on your own.

(*GOLEM enters. Upon seeing him, OLD BEGGAR changes totally. He turns pale, shudders, quickly wakes up YOUNG BEGGAR.*)

OLD BEGGAR. Wake up! Wake up! Hurry! Wake up!

We have to leave! We have to leave! (*Starts gathering his things.*)

YOUNG BEGGAR (*drowsy*). Oh, let me sleep some more, just sleep some more.

(*Spots the GOLEM, starts shuddering and hastening.*)

Let's get right out of here, right out of here.

(*They grab their belongings and rush out. GOLEM tries to dash after them.*)

RABBI (*holding him back*). Where to? (*To the Jews.*)

GOLEM. With them. I want to be with them.

RABBI. Stay here! I order you to stay. Their time

Has not yet come. This time right now is yours.

(*To the Jews.*) Tadeush is coming. (*A frightened uproar.*)

ALL THE BEGGARS. What does he plan to do?

RABBI. He plans to drive you out from here.

The Fifth Tower does not belong to us.

(*They all start filling their bags. Only SICK MAN and TANKHEM remain as before.*)

RABBI (*whispers to GOLEM*). Will you know what you have to do?

GOLEM. I'll know, Rabbi.

RABBI. But not to death.

GOLEM. I'll know, Rabbi.

RABBI. Your power of invisibility—

Let it emerge! Now go inside and wait.

(*GOLEM returns to his earlier place. RABBI goes out. BEGGARS, occupied with packing and with fear, have noticed nothing. TADEUSH enters, accompanied by a MONK.*)

TADEUSH. You see these beggars—fakers every one.

They're richer than the two of us—take my word.

You see the hump. The hump is false. It's nothing

But an enormous mound of rags—no more.

MONK. If so, the hunchback must be quite an artist.

TADEUSH. And he, the *blind man*, isn't blind at all.

We know them well—those eyes that he keeps closed. . . .

MONK (*points to PEG LEG*).

You can't suspect him, Father; there's no basis.

His wooden leg sticks out.

TADEUSH. Don't you believe him.

Not even if you touch the wood itself.

His kind can actually cut off a leg

And hide it in a beggar's bag. And when

They need it, they can pull it out again.

They live like lords as if they owned this tower.

The walls are caked with filth and filled with nails;

The air is so polluted that you choke.

To think that our heroes, our nobles,

And our princes lived here in their glory.

To think that royal and imperial feet

Once trod these twisted, termite-ridden floors.

Can't you now hear them shouting from the walls—

Those rubbed-off, spat-on mural images?

And there still hanging in the corners, see

Those slender chains of holy lamps. whose eyes

Once lit his look of love, the tears that dripped

In sorrow from his crown of thorns, which they,

Hushed nonbelievers, stuck into his brow.
Now everything is ruined. He's been expelled.
The oil is gone. Only the chains remain,
Mocking and dangling, and those bags . . . those bags.
(*To BEGGARS.*)
Why do you gaze and stare? Why don't you speak?
You live among us, furious and embittered.
And wear your fury as he wears his hump.
Haven't we tortured and tormented you
Enough? Plagued you and persecuted you?
Broke you, burned you, and slaughtered you enough?
We've grown so tired of our hate for you
And rage for you and cruelty for you.
And yet the more you make a spectacle
Of your resilience, your tenacity,
Your stubbornness, your firm determination,
The more you shatter our dream of peace,
The more you set our hate for you in blazes.
We'll never ever make our peace with you
Because you're our nightmare, our terror.
We cannot ever share the earth with you,
Shone on by the same sun, breathing the same air.
The air your lungs inhale is venom for
Our hearts. For our hearts yearn for peace and quiet,
For respite from you, for release from you.
You lie upon our minds, our consciences
Like murky spiders twisted up in knots,
And weaving, weaving webs and nets of nightmares. . . .
We've hounded you. That's not enough; we'll hound
You more. Our thirst for love, for peace and quiet,
For good can be quenched only by your blood,
By our dance around the flaming stake.
We'll set more stakes on fire, more stakes on fire,

Till you release us from yourselves at last.
You say that we accuse you of blood libels,
And you—you rush about to prove we're liars. . . .
Why do you lack the courage to proclaim
Proudly and publicly and with dignity,
"It's true! We do drink blood at Passover.
We've always drunk it, and we always will!"
Although you're innocent, we burn you at
The stake. Why do you go there to the fire
As if you were now going to a dance?
Why don't you then strike us as we strike you,
Attack with axes and with blazing torches?
And now, this very moment that I speak,
Why do you hear me out, why don't you answer?
Isn't there one among you with the courage
To step forth and to grab my staff from me
And smash it on my skull? You hold your tongues.
You wait for me to holler now, "Get out!"
You're always, always ready to go away—
Then go!

(*BEGGARS leave silently, with their bags on their backs. SICK MAN and TANKHEM remain to the end, then jump up and dash out as if from a fire.*)

TADEUSH. Such dogs! You order them to leave,
and so they leave without another word. (*Terrified.*)
Don't you hear? Footsteps. Has someone remained?

MONK. Not one of them is left, oh, Holy Father.

TADEUSH (*peers into next room*).
No one is there, but can't you hear the footsteps?
Somebody seems to be trudging around.

MONK. Father, it's only your imagination.

TADEUSH. I do hear footsteps. What is going on?
The air is roused.

MONK. My legs are buckling.

TADEUSH. Oh, Holy Jesus, please protect us now.

(*They cross themselves. The surrounding air whirls and whistles as if somebody were beating it with long, wet rods. Steps of gigantic unseen feet can be heard trudging about. Dreadful blows are inflicted in turn on the heads of TADEUSH and MONK. The two men spin about in wild terror, drop to the floor, dash toward the doors. But no matter where they rush, they are hounded by the blows of unseen hands.*)

TADEUSH. This place is haunted—by the demons! Run!

(*But they are stopped at every doorway, hurled back, while the blows keep pelting down on their heads. Their noses start bleeding. The two men collapse on the floor, moaning with pain and fear. All at once they are lifted and thrown out a window. We hear the crash of their bodies on the ground. Then silence reigns again. The quivering lamp resumes its quiet burning. GOLEM enters from the next room. He is feverish with excitement. He is pale; his eyes are blazing. His breathing is heavy; his nostrils are flaring. He leans against a wall, turning his head aside.*)

GOLEM. Where are you, Rabbi? Tell me where you are.

RABBI (*hurries in*). I'm here, I'm here. I'm here.

GOLEM. Oh, Rabbi, Rabbi.

RABBI. Go ahead, talk to me. I'm listening.

GOLEM. Don't leave me here, don't leave me. Take my hand.

RABBI. What's wrong with you?

GOLEM. Rabbi, it's dark, it's dark.

Don't leave me here, don't go away from here.

RABBI. I have to go away. Lie down and sleep.

GOLEM. Don't go away from here, don't leave me here.

RABBI. There's lots you'll have to do. Now go to sleep. (*Leaves.*)

GOLEM. Oh, Rabbi. Stay with me here, stay with me. (*Peers around.*)

He's left. What is this sudden silence?

A darkness, darkness, Rabbi. Now, where are you? (*Lies down on the floor.*)

Where are you, Rabbi, where? It's dark, it's dark. . . .

UNBIDDEN

(A field outside Prague. Night. Heavy clouds drifting around. OLD BEGGAR and YOUNG BEGGAR sit at the side of a road leading into the distance.)
YOUNG BEGGAR.
No one wants to hear me out.
I'm a stranger, unknown here.
And my outstretched hands are sick,
Like the sickness on my feet.

Dark and cold like lifeless tears,
Now tomorrow dashes in.
No one will obstruct the road
Freely leading into Prague.

No one comes to greet me there,
Welcome me in joy or grief.
Night has fallen on all roads
To the city gates of Prague.
(OLD BEGGAR remains silent.)
YOUNG BEGGAR.
Six long days and nights have waned,
This is now the seventh day.
All are feverishly waiting
For the golem's miracle.

From the man who bears the cross
To the beggar with his pack,
Comes the golem, the redeemer,
With his fist and with his ax.

OLD BEGGAR.
Don't speak bitterly, my son.
Maybe that's how things must be,
God-protected, God-defended.
Lie down, rest, and get some sleep.
YOUNG BEGGAR.
Let's get out of here; let's flee.
Look, the smoke's already rising
From the burning stakes in Prague
Upward toward the evening sky.
I can't help the suffering victim,
I can't go and die with him.
Now he's dead, and now the flames
Of the stakes are fading out. . . .
OLD BEGGAR.
Why this talk of death and victims?
You can picture them. Imagine!
Springtime breezes waft all over,
And the moon comes drifting out.
YOUNG BEGGAR.
Don't you hear a smothered cry
Puffing toward us from somewhere?
Countless feet are cautiously
Marching in an army: *they.*
OLD BEGGAR.
Whose feet?
YOUNG BEGGAR.
Those of enemies,
In a cave, preparing something.
And a masked and twisted face
Shouts from far away, "Don't talk! . . ."

Shut my eyes, and hold my tongue,
Ah, and mute my mouth as well.
Fears of pogroms spread a pall
On my eve of Passover. . . .
OLD BEGGAR.
Just lie down and go to sleep.
This will be our final night.
See? A gleam has flickered past,
Bringing us release, relief.

And that gleam is yours forever,
It goes with you, step by step.
For it knows your heart is faithful,
Chosen by Almighty God.

Your despondence comes from grieving,
And your love from hurt and harm.
Your impatience is duration,
And your darkness is a luster.

No one, no one is at fault
That we sit here on the side,
That we fail in our patience,
That we've come before our time.
(Both men sit silent.)
OLD BEGGAR.
Go to sleep, and let my knees
Be your pillow for your head
Till the earliest drops of dew
Tell us that the day is dawning.

I will guard you in the hush,
Guard your miserable sleep.

And however much you've suffered,
None of this is punishment.

Not a punishment, a hidden,
A mysterious vocation.
Not tomorrow, then the day
After, and the call will come. . . .
YOUNG BEGGAR.
Silence, silence, hurry up.
Take me back, back to the desert;
As the night grows stiller, clearer,
My eyes bulge in greater dread.

I see hands wrung, hands on hands,
Eyes are bursting, falling out,
Lopped-off heads and chopped-off bones,
Flames and smoke in every house.

By the doorways of the houses
Two men stand and check their watches,
See the watch hands creeping, creeping.
Two men standing: I and you.

Every throat has long been slit.
In the blend of blood and ashes,
We two men stand, guarding, guarding,
Never miss a single minute. . . .

For we are the mute observers,
Watching mayhem, murder, havoc,
Mute observers, mysteries,
Spread throughout the deep, dense darkness. . . . (*Grabs the knees
of the OLD BEGGAR.*)

Please forgive me now for ripping
My wounds open, rip by rip.
Please forgive me now for biting
My lips bloody, bite by bite.

Please forgive me now for waiting
For the words of joy and pleasure.
I have trapped and tricked myself
With a glee that turns to gloom.
(*Long hush.*)
    YOUNG BEGGAR (*lying with his head drooping*).
Sway and sway
On my chain
Old and blind
Eternity.

Circle, circle,
Take my steps,
Twist them tight
And twirl them taut.

From the wild
And rowdy rush
Gather hours,
Gather moments.

Winds that drowse you
Till you die
On the links of
My own chain.

I myself
In my disguise

Rock and sway
Upon my chain.
(*YOUNG BEGGAR falls asleep. OLD BEGGAR sits there, guarding him,
dozes off himself. RABBI hurries in, impatient, trembling with rage.*)
RABBI. You two still here? Must you be ordered more
Than once?
OLD BEGGAR (*awakes with a start*).
Please don't be angry. We are staying
One final night, and then we'll leave tomorrow.
RABBI. I tell you, not a single moment more,
No moment more.
OLD BEGGAR. The road is long and dark.
RABBI. Don't tell me about darkness, and don't try
To stir a deep compassion in my heart.
Whom do you beg for mercy and for whom?
For him? It's all enough for me to stifle
And suffocate my weeping and my wailing,
And keep my knees from buckling and bending,
From falling down before him, crying, "Mercy!"
It would be sad, it would be sorrowful
If I drove out the harshness from my heart
And opened up my heart to pity, mercy.
Don't tell me about darkness. . . . Why did you
Have to bring him here, here, of all places,
And let him see the face of death and danger?
What can he do for us, what should he do?
Now that the world has poured out all its hatred
On us, all of its loathing and disgust?
Has each of us from land to land to land
Now felt the butcher's blade upon his throat?
Has he already sensed the final edge
And seen the final lifting of the sword?
How could he ever say he's sensed or seen—

If I'm not slaughtered yet, if my own body,
If my own flesh has not been burned alive?
OLD BEGGAR. Oh, Leyb, Leyb . . .
RABBI. Take him away! Escape!
Do not pollute his heart with our panic.
How can we go and greet him, welcome him,
If every road is bristling with corpses . . . ?
And everybody walks on pointed spears?
And who should laud him, who should sing his praises?
The victim with no gullet slit or slashed?
And who should open all the doors for him?
The slaughterer with his blood-smeared hands? And what
Should shine and what should glow above his head?
The burning flames of blazing goods and riches?
He has to leave; he can't stay in our realm.
And can his fingers coil in iron fists
And crush and bash and smash and shatter skulls?
And can he even stand the stench of blood
And spill it? And can he exact a tooth
For every tooth, an eye for every eye,
A head for every head? And can his hands,
His delicate hands, scratch in the filth of pits,
Looking for limbs, looking for bones and ashes?
His hands cannot! And even if they could,
I'd be against it. He must be the last!
God help the man who tries to intervene,
Who tries to block our path with violence.
OLD BEGGAR. We've only come here now to have a look.
His heart is filled with yearning for you, longing.
RABBI. Then let him stifle, muffle deep his craving. . . .
I have a second man to do my bidding,
The only one permitted to be dark,
Permitted to shed blood, spill blood for blood. . . .

The world's not worth another nemesis,
Nor we as yet another to defend it. . . .
OLD BEGGAR (*wakes YOUNG BEGGAR*).
Get up, get up. We've got to go again.
YOUNG BEGGAR (*stands up*).
You come again to drive us on again?
(*RABBI is silent.*)
YOUNG BEGGAR. Why do you persecute us? Why?
RABBI. I must.
YOUNG BEGGAR. Why won't you let me sleep here this one
night?
RABBI. This night will be a night of blood for us.
YOUNG BEGGAR. My eyes are yearning for the deep red night.
RABBI. They would be better off if they were blinded.
YOUNG BEGGAR. My ears crave vulnerable lamentations.
RABBI. They would be better off if they were deafened.
YOUNG BEGGAR. My lips are thirsting to confess my sins,
Confess it with the man who's dying here.
RABBI. They would be better off if they were muted.
YOUNG BEGGAR. Don't you have any warmer words for me?
(*RABBI is silent.*)
YOUNG BEGGAR. You talk to me in harsh and callous words.
But I'll put up with it. I've come alone,
Waiting at no one's call, at no one's summons.
I wanted to walk all across the world,
To hear the echoes of my steps alone.
And then, perhaps, perhaps, I also hoped
That everyone else would also hear their echoes.
I've peered and stared into so many eyes,
I've seen so many steps on all these roads.
But all the eyes were peering somewhere else,
My glances all were left in great suspense,
And so were all my footsteps on these roads. . . .

And all I want now is one thing: to rest,
To keep my eyes from peering at the world,
And hide them back inside myself as always,
And rock upon my restlessness. . . . Who knows?
Perhaps I've come one moment here too soon,
Perhaps I dozed off for a single minute.
Who knows? Since it was I who chose to come
Alone, to walk and wander through the world,
How can we blame, how can we fault the world?
Is it obliged to put an end to hatred,
To stop all killing, stop all murdering,
To halt all civil wars, all national wars?
For after all, I've come here all alone,
Simply to walk and wander through the world. . . .
I'm going on, I'll find inside the desert
The slumber that I've lost in hounded nights.
And peace be unto you, each one of you.

(*BEGGARS exit.*)

RABBI (*impulsively holds out his arms to them and remains standing, hunched over his stick*).

Not with honor,
As befits him,
Did we welcome
Our guest.

Nor with any roof
Did we shelter him.
Not with bread
And not with water.

Not with rags
To bind his wound,

Nor a blessing:
Nor a farewell.

On he hurries,
On his footsteps,
He won't dare
To turn around. . . .

Far and farther,
Stride by stride,
Costumed as
A beggarman.

Tightly shut,
His lips are split.
One lip grieves,
And one lip laughs.

And his eyes—
His brows are arching,
One is rigid,
One is glaring.

And his ears—
Sound by sound,
Hear lamenting,
Hear a singing.

His shape is
No longer visible,
Not for young
And not for old. . . .

(*RABBI leans on his stick in deep sadness. The entire sky is overcast with dense clouds. A strong wind starts to blast; a storm is brewing. RABBI collapses.*)

RABBI. Oh, oh! They're gone already. . . . (*With a drooping head, he starts out for Prague. The wind rips at his clothes.*)

Gone, gone, gone. . . .

(*His figure melts into the darkness. The storm erupts.*)

REVELATIONS

(In the Fifth Tower. GOLEM lies facedown, asleep. The rain blasts in through the windows. We hear the echo of a distant, quivering voice: "Gone, gone, gone. . . ." As if summoned by that voice in his sleep, GOLEM starts tossing and turning, muttering, suffocating, then lies motionless again. TANKHEM, soaked with rain, appears in the doorway. He pokes in his head, tiptoes in, shakes off the rain. He fails to notice GOLEM.)

TANKHEM. Cowards! They won't let me in anywhere!
All thresholds are now barred, all doors and windows
Are shut, and all the shutters are now hooked.
Tankhem keeps knocking, but no one responds.
Cowards! They think I need to spend the night here.
(Chortles, covering his mouth with his hands.)
Everyone's dead. They think that I don't know.
Didn't I knock on each door of each house?
Didn't I stride and saunter through each street?
Didn't I whack on every single shutter?
Didn't I shout, "Prepare a welcome! Come!"
But Prague is dead; the city has died out.
No rhyme or reason, without any warning—
And Prague is dead, the city has died out.
(A thunderclap.)
Should I change into holiday clothes? And wait?
Yes, I can sit and I can rest a time,
While all the ruins are made ready here,
While they are cleared and cleaned and cleansed and tidied.
My orders are: Uncover the covered tables
And chairs; remove them from their hiding places.
Unlock the coffers with their carvings, and
Take out the gold, take out the silver too,
The polished cups,

The candelabra
With their seven branches,
The painted trays.
Open the chests,
Take out the cushions
And the shrouds,
The embroidered mantles,
And then bring each and everything to me. . . .
Cover the tables with the tablecloths,
And then set up the cups and candelabra,
Spread out the special Passover couch
In purest white.
I've brought the candles too—
Now here they are. . . .
And he will bring the wine, yes, he,
The last of all my heirs,
The reddest and most radiant,
The shiniest—far shinier than blood.
I've brought the candles too.
Now here they are. . . .
(*Produces candles from his bosom.*)
Have I forgotten anything at all?
I don't think so. . . .
By now attendants stand at every door,
Stand there in darkness and stand there in storm,
Faithful and vigilant
And patient too.
They do not wish to waste a single second.
Isn't there some command I should repeat?
My servants, listen, let me say again:
Cover the festive couch in purest white,
In purest white. . . . (*Lights a candle, spots GOLEM, edges toward the
door.*)

The same one,
The only one,
The surviving one. . . .
Since all the Jews have died,
Since no one else comes to rejoice here,
He has come. . . .
He's fast asleep now, but he'll soon wake up
And be a witness here,
A one and only one,
For all Prague has died,
And he alone is left asleep,
A survivor,
An eternal one,
A one and only one. . . .

(*He is about to step into the other rooms when GOLEM starts tossing and turning again, muttering eerily in his slumber, "Gone, gone, gone. . . ."*)

TANKHEM. What's gone? Who's gone?

GOLEM (*awakens, sits up*).

Gone, gone, gone. . . .
He drove them both away, and now
He stands alone and mourns.
Gone, gone, gone. . . .

(*TANKHEM tries to dash out. GOLEM jumps up and blocks his path.*)

GOLEM. Don't run away. Stay here. I want to talk.
You see me rising, see me growing bigger.
And now I spread my wings and stand before you,
Sharp and profound, distinctive in my darkness. . . .
Now let me stretch my hands and arms to you,
Now let me pull them back, let me withdraw them. . . .
Now let my fingers untwist and unbraid. . . .
I must not speak, and yet I speak. . . .

TANKHEM. Who are you?

GOLEM. You don't know? I am deepest in my sleep.

The deepest man, who heard the cry,
Gone, gone, gone!
And if you wish, I'll throw myself much deeper,
Much deeper into sleep,
Much deeper. . . .
TANKHEM. Now be alert. It's my wish. I'm not scared.
And as for who you are, I do not know.
If all are dead, one must remain behind.
Let that be you.
GOLEM. I am the one, I am.
TANKHEM. And then you'll be permitted to bear witness,
And one to share my celebration—do
You know about my coming celebration?
And if you don't know now, then you'll know soon.
I'll force you then to join my celebration.
There won't be any klezmers making music,
So you yourself will have to be the klezmer.
I haven't yet invited any dancer,
So you yourself will have to do the dancing.
Well, can you dance at any celebration,
Or clash the cymbals here, or dance a round?
Do you know how a bridegroom's welcomed here,
Or how he's circled with a ring of candles—
Lit candles at his head and at his feet? (*Spins around.*)
Do you see how to dance and how to whirl? (*Dizzily drops on the*
floor.)
GOLEM. You don't see who I am? I'll be another.
Beware of looking at my face, my features.
I am condemned to lie here on the ground.
I do not want to lie here any longer.
I am repelled, disgusted by my flesh,
Revolted by my glassy, bulging eyes,
By my own muteness, by my dark sign language.

I roam and ramble through the days and nights,
I tear myself away by my own strength—
Into the distances so far away. . . .
The moment now has come. See, I repel
Myself as I would repel any worm. . . .
TANKHEM (*lying on the ground, afraid to lift his head*).
Who are you? Tell me. Tell me who you are!
Through all the nights that I've spent in the tower,
The darkness has revealed its deepest secrets.
Tell me, are you one of its secrets too?
GOLEM. I am the mystery of light, not darkness.
Not always but now. Do not gaze at me.
For you will not see anything at all,
Even if you pop both your eyes in gawking,
For every darkness is now open for me,
And every darkness is now shut for you.
And I hear distant voices, distant singing.
And shaky breathing now and soaring steps. . . .
I go—go where? To stride across the rivers,
To rest upon the brinks of gulfs, to follow
Hard on the heels of all the banished beggars. . . .
TANKHEM (*raises himself to peer at GOLEM, then falls back in mortal dread*).
Another one, another, not the same.
A luminous, a radiant one, a glowing,
A gleaming, glimmering, a glittering face.
GOLEM (*surrounded by a brightness of invisibility*).
I told you not to look at me at all.
If you glance up at me a second time,
You'll die. Terror grabs hold of you, grabs tight.
If you glance at me a second time,
It's not a dream. . . . Don't you know I'm eternal
And not from here? And not the klezmer here

Upon your celebration, not your dancer
Or your witness? . . . I turn away from you,
For I am everlasting, I am eternal.
TANKHEM. A sole and single survivor was left,
And now he too is leaving me, leaving
Myself. . . .
Myself—the father,
Myself—the klezmer,
Myself—the dancer,
Myself—the witness,
Myself—the mourner.
GOLEM. I'm going there, where meadows stretch and sweep,
Untouched by cries of sorrow: "Gone, gone, gone. . . ."
I'm going east. I hear a voice from the west,
A voice from the north, then one from the south.
I'm going to all corners of the world,
For all are calling, calling me at once,
Hard on the heels of both the banished beggars,
Calling to me, "Come back, come back, come back!"

(*He flies through a door and vanishes. TANKHEM stands there, clutching a candle. Rain is lashing through the windows, and the wind is blowing the candle flame, TANKHEM hugs a wall. Suddenly he bursts into wild laughter.*)

TANKHEM. Tankhem hoodwinked, Tankhem hoodwinked.
And Tankhem let himself be hoodwinked here.
And who is the hoodwinker? Who is he?
Tankhem has been hoodwinked here by a golem. . . .

(*A female voice is heard from a distant area of the tower, weeping and calling for help. Her cries reverberate through the ruins and then are abruptly cut off.*)

TANKHEM. Help? Who should help?
VOICE (*a second time*). Help!
TANKHEM. Who can help? Who?

Who wants to help? Huh?

Who must help? Who?

(*TANKHEM dashes out and vanishes. DEBORAH and RABBI's WIFE hurry in from a distant room. Terrified and barely able to catch their breath, they cling to each other to keep from falling.*)

WIFE. Demons and devils have brought us here! Demons!

We cannot leave, we do not know the way!

Oh, we are doomed, my child, oh, we are doomed.

DEBORAH. So many doors and caverns—who can help?

WIFE. Now I can barely feel my head, for all

Its bumping, banging, battering against

The wall! And whose fault is it? Tell me! Yours!

Insane to come here in the dead of night. . . .

DEBORAH. Who would have thought?

WIFE. Insane! I've never heard

Of such a thing! To seek Grandfather here!

Just what could he be doing in these ruins?

DEBORAH. Well, who would have thought it? And now you scold,

Yet you yourself suggested that we come here.

WIFE. I did? Of course I did. Since everybody

Is sitting behind barred and bolted doors.

It's midnight now, but your grandfather still

Hasn't as yet returned from evening prayers.

DEBORAH. My dress is torn to tatters in the darkness. . . .

WIFE. And both my hands are raw and rough; the walls

Are filled with nails. It's thundering again.

DEBORAH. If only *he*'d respond. Here's where he sleeps!

WIFE. Hush, hush, don't say a word, that's all we need! . . .

Oh, God of Abraham, of Isaac, and

Of Jacob, pity us, be merciful.

DEBORAH. Come on, come on, let's have another look.

There has to be a door to lead us out. . . .

WIFE. How could we get so lost and so confused?

(*She tries the various doors, gropes through the darkness. They search and then return.*)

RABBI'S WIFE. Tell me, my child, tell me, what should we do? How awful!

DEBORAH. Please don't cry, don't cry, my darling! (*She herself weeps.*)

WIFE. We must do something. Try and shout again!

DEBORAH (*shouts tearfully*). Help!

WIFE. Aryeh Leyb, Aryeh Leyb!

DEBORAH. Don't shout, don't shout!

WIFE. Hush, I think I can hear an answer.

TANKHEM (*in the distance*).

Who should help?

Who can help?

Who must help?

Who? Ha-ha-ha!

(*The two women, barely breathing, huddle in a corner.*)

WIFE. Let us be quiet. Let us pray to God.

DEBORAH. My head is spinning. I'm about to fall.

WIFE. Hold on to me, my child, my darling child. . . .

(*GOLEM rushes in with the glow of invisibility above him. The two women bury their faces in their hands and shriek in terror.*)

GOLEM. Why do you shriek in fright? I have come here

To help you, to redeem you, guide you out,

The wind has brought me all your cries for help,

And I did spot you here from far away.

One step, and all roads leap toward me. Darkness

Dissolves, and brightness spreads before my eyes,

And everything I touch becomes transparent

And pure. And when my arms stretch out, they reach

Across the earth from corner to far corner.

TWO WOMEN. Leave us.

GOLEM. Why leave you? I've come to redeem you,
And yet you're scared of me. Where should I go?
And who else, do you think, can save you now?
Do you believe the beggar will be coming?
Your hopes are useless. Let me say that I
Myself sprang up from my sleep when I heard
The sad and mournful outcry: "Gone, gone, gone!"
I started after it to turn it back.
My springing up, my dashing out were useless,
The shattering of my tower sleep was useless.
If I've returned here empty-handed, then
How can you still be hoping that he'll come?
Yes, I alone can save you—I alone. . . .
TWO WOMEN. Leave! Aren't you the one called Yosl? Tell us!
GOLEM. My name is different now, for Yosl is
Somebody else, someone who isn't flung
Upon the floor, who doesn't lie full length,
And who no longer sleeps his strange, dark slumber.
I got up silently and stole away.
I knew the rabbi wouldn't let me go,
And so I didn't ask him for permission.
I've dreamed so long about myself. . . . Why do
You both glare at me now in deathly terror?
You didn't here expect me? Isn't it true?
No one can see me, and no one can hear me,
And I myself must not reveal myself.
I must remain unseen, obscure forever,
Until the man who manages my fate
Will tell me, "Go and grasp, and look and listen."
Do you two know who manages my fate?
TWO WOMEN. Oh, leave, you frighten us, oh, go away.
GOLEM. You do not know who manages my fate?
I'll tell you if you like—don't be afraid. . . .

This is the very first time and the last
That I display my outer shell or speak
To any person, peer into his eyes,
Or cross his threshold as an unforeseen,
An unexpected visitor at midnight,
Or speak such words here or hear such a hush.
This is the very first time and the last. . . .
Do you know who keeps following me and calling,
Forcing me to come back here? Do you know
What "first time" or what "last time" signifies?
You don't know? If you want me to, I'll tell you.
I lay asleep and didn't even see
The glowing in a dream. And if I opened
My eyes, I didn't even see myself.
And if I yelled or if I shouted something,
I couldn't even hear my very own voice.
But then I heard and saw a thousand leagues.
I saw with eyes shut tight and heard with ears
Gone deaf. I cried and yelled with a mute tongue.
And can't you hear that moaning in the ruins?
It's calling me. . . . I thought I wouldn't care.
I thought I'd leave the ruins to themselves
And let the moaning wane and fade away
Into the hush and hollowness of the tower.
Those were my thoughts. But see, inside my heart
A love awoke, a longing shook my frame.
I'm looking forward to the moment when
I can fling myself out again and stretch
And lie, and I can hug and squeeze the floors,
And I can lie in darkness, hollowness. . . .
I really love it, the Fifth Tower. . . . You know? (*Sits on the ground.*)
I'll sit here for awhile—awhile. I'm weary.
I need to rest. The darkness, hollowness—

Well, they can wait. Meanwhile may I sit down?
DEBORAH. Why does he ask us, why—why does he ask us?
GOLEM. Don't be afraid. I won't hurt you. Look at me!
Why do you shudder—Why? Your hands, your lips—
Since you will never see me again, never?
I am so radiant, the most radiant now,
More radiant than he, the young wanderer.
More radiant than the rabbi. If you like,
Should I tell where the young man's feet are treading?
And where the rabbi's?
WIFE. Have you seen the rabbi?
GOLEM. Have I seen him? I see him all the time.
The footsteps of the wanderer disappear,
They're swallowed up by thunder that booms down
From heaven. Do you think the thunder's pointless?
The rabbi's coming, coming home, he'll soon
Be here. . . .
WIFE. Where is the rabbi coming from?
GOLEM. He's coming from the fields beyond the city.
I'm coming from those fields as well, where all
The roads are shut for both the wanderers.
I saw the rabbi standing there in sorrow,
Bowing his head, while he, the wanderer,
Went trudging step by step on wounded feet,
Where all the roads were urging, driving him
Along. . . . Oh, how I yearned to follow him,
To slog ahead now and to be with him,
To stretch out at his feet and be his shadow,
And yet how could I if my heart blazed out
In deepest longing? . . . Yes, the rabbi's coming,
The rabbi's coming home now. And if I
Have to come home, then surely so must he.
The rabbi's late because his steps are heavy,

Because his head sinks mournfully in pain.
For me the road back was a single step,
For me the darkness was a single blink.
The rabbi plods in lightning and in thunder.
The brewing tempest was the first to grab him.
It hurls him back and forth, it yanks his clothes.
The rain is lashing in through every hole. . . .
WIFE. Oh, God! Be merciful, be merciful.
DEBORAH. Escape! We must escape!
GOLEM. Don't leave! Don't leave!
No one must see me at this very moment.
No one must hear my words except the people
To whom I have revealed my outer shell
On purpose. . . . Can you tell who is sitting
Among you? You're familiar with my face
And with my name, and yet you've never seen me.
You would be blinded in a single moment,
If you looked at me without my permission. . . .
For death and dazzling and fiery brilliance
And boundless perishing—those are my eyes. . . .
I live and I myself don't know how long—
Upon the earth or underneath the earth,
With worms and animals and human beings,
In fire and in water and in rock.
And I can never see the start or end of
My boundless perishing. . . . Relieve me, please,
Relieve me of my state of wonderment.
But who can hear me here, can hear my prayer?
Now that I've come here, flying from the fields,
I suddenly hear a strange ringing in
My ears, and weird flames burst inside my eyes. . . .
But maybe— No! What am I saying? I'd
Step into every house no matter which,

For every house would welcome me with fear,
And every house would drive me off in dread. . . .
(*His head droops as he sits down. Thunder and lightning outside.*)
DEBORAH. Be merciful to us, be merciful.
GOLEM. You're still afraid? The rabbi's coming soon.
I see him, he's close by. The rain is pouring,
And yet rain has no power over him,
While lightning lights his path. He's coming, coming. . . .
He mustn't know what I've been saying here.
I see outlandish terror on your face.
You peer into my eyes, and I remember
That moment when I hugged you, when I squeezed
You, clutched you, when I pressed you close to me.
I still can feel your warmth upon my fingers,
I still can hear your shivering on my bosom. . . .
But then I couldn't talk, I couldn't catch
My breath. . . . Well, things are different now. I don't
Want to touch you. It's quite enough for me
To sit here face-to-face with you like this
And speak such nimbly dancing, dazzling words.
If I wished, then—astounded and astonished
As both of you are sitting there—I'd grab you
And heave and hurl you high into the air,
Then pitch you to my feet and pick you up,
And whirl you round my head with dizzying rush,
And whirl and swirl and twirl you until both
Your hands grabbed me and grasped me by my neck,
And then your flaming lips would burn and blaze
With hurt and harm and melt into *my* lips.
(*Both women desperately hide their faces and wring their hands.*)
GOLEM. What's more, I'd sling you then across my shoulders
And carry you into another tower
Through all the flashes of tempestuous darkness,

And we would twirl into a single twine,
And clutch under the cover of the void. . . .
And I would open up my eyes and see
The winds tearing and tattering my clothes,
The bolts of lightning baring your white skin,
The void intoxicated with your warmth. . . .
I'd bite into your limbs, suck in your whiteness.
Then silence rules again; the rain keeps lashing
Through every hole. The lightning bolts keep twisting
And untwisting, and bricks keep dropping down
And falling one by one, each one in turn. (*Gets up.*)
Come, let me lead you out. I'm sickened by
Your fear, still more by your self-revelation.
I've humbled myself quite enough so that
I couldn't pass you now without recalling
Your warmth upon my fingers and without
Recalling that I've revealed so many secrets
To you, two frightened women, lost, forlorn. (*Goes over to door
and halts.*)
  The moaning in the ruins has abruptly
Stopped. Just one step of mine, and peace has spread
Over each wall and cavern, for each step
Of mine is joy, and every gesture is peace. . . .
You shudder, and your faces are all white,
Your features are all dreamy and all drowsy. . . .
Like you, I myself now forget my words
And feel my eyelids drooping. And I could
Lie down and fall asleep right here. However,
I don't. And I could move my sleep elsewhere,
But you can go nowhere, nowhere at all. . . .
From every side the long-expected things
Come upon you with all their flames and fires
So well prepared and with the sharpest axes.

And now the very first red drops, still warm,
Still freshly dripping from the sword, pour, one
By one, into the very heart of night.
And suddenly the drops now rage and roar,
Surging and streaming into storms, a storm
For every door . . . a storm for your door too.
And the red torrents carry you away,
Sweeping you far and farther. Buildings burn,
Falling into the dying flames and fires.
And with the buildings, heads are burned and drowned.
They ring around you, floating on the streams. . . .
The monastery bells keep clanging, tolling;
The crosses glow. And mouths still red from fire
Catch up the clanging and the clashing of
The bells and swallow them and hurl them back
In long and twisting tongues. They ring you round.
They drown you, and they toss you out again
And drown you once again. . . . And you—you sit
There as you sit there now, sleeping and dreaming,
And lulled in peace, my peace. You only paint
Sadness and terror for me now. I tell you,
Lift up your head and see how high and wide
And deep I spread my arms, how lightly I breathe.
I raise my feet and float above the floor.
My paces carry me like outstretched wings. . . .
Get up and leave, and I will lead the way.
(*Both women, faint with fear, have sunk to the floor and now sit there with covered faces, refusing to budge.*)
    GOLEM. Wake up, come on, I'll show you how to leave.
    Confused, bewildered women, follow me.
(*He takes them by the hand and helps them up. Women follow him as if in a trance.*)
    GOLEM. Don't be afraid, I'll touch only your hands. . . .

I'll only lead the way, I'll guide you. . . .

(*He leads the way. A moment later he returns, settles in a corner, and rocks with his hands crossed over his heart.*)

GOLEM.

Gone, gone, gone. . . .

Why are you mute, walls,

My walls?

Why do you sleep,

Caves,

My caves?

Why don't you ask me

Where I'm from?

Risen up and radiant,

I released all my words,

Spoke them into emptiness. . . .

Now, as then,

The rain is beating

On the rocks of my castle. . . .

Did anybody

Order me:

"Go and chase after the shadows

Of the two?"

No one, no one, no one.

When they cried

And called for help,

Was it then I

They called upon?

Did they hope

That I would hear? . . .

Why are you mute,

Walls, my walls?

Why are you mute,

Caves, my caves?

TANKHEM (*sliding in*). Who should rescue? Who?
Who can rescue? Who?

GOLEM. I!

TANKHEM (*laughing wildly*). Who are you? (*Astounded*).
Now you've come back! How fast! The very same.
Not long ago he was a different person,
And now, and now, he is the very same. (*Angrily.*)
You fooled old Tankhem, yes, you fooled old Tankhem.

(*GOLEM grows darker and darker.*)

TANKHEM. He's back from all the corners of the world.
(*Laughs.*)
What's happening in all corners of the world?

GOLEM. Shush, do you hear?

TANKHEM. I hear, of course I hear.

GOLEM. Come closer to me, closer to me now.

(*TANKHEM moves up against GOLEM. They sit down*).

GOLEM. Well, now I'm back again, you see, I'm back.
What does a moment earlier or later
Much matter in a night of endless thunder,
Of storms, of distant places unattained?

TANKHEM. What does it truly matter, truly matter?

GOLEM. I feel so much at home here. What about you?

TANKHEM. I do, of course.

GOLEM. I even felt the warmth there,
While dashing through the forests and across
The fields, seeing and hearing everything.
I knew that somewhere there were walls, four walls.
You know it too.

TANKHEM. I do, of course I do.

GOLEM. And what if *these* four walls were bright, transparent?
Where could I flee from everything I've seen?
And where could I find hardness for my skin,
And icy trembling and prickly darkness,

And bound and bordered anguish, desolation? . . .
As I left, I said angry things to you,
But even in my anger, didn't you hear
A hint of my return, a trace, a touch,
A sign of all my love and all my longing?
TANKHEM. I heard each hint, I heard, I really did.
GOLEM. My light has eaten away at my own eyes,
And all the people whom I've met all through
The night have been dispersed and scattered in
My glow. But every single person will
Be found. Each has a private corner of
His own, a place to rest his head, a place
To press his brow and dig into the ground
With both his eyes and lie in utter silence. . . .
The rabbi has a study all his own,
And the young wanderer has his nest of rocks
Out in the desert there. . . . One night and then
Another night. He dashes over there,
And he will come to it as I've come here.
And just like me, he'll fall so joyously
To kiss the pointed stones. And they will hug
Him with their sharpness and caress him with
Their hardness and their total desolation. . . .
By now the rabbi is at home, and now
He sees wonders and horrors both revealed. . . .
And now he slumps across his table and
Falls silent and turns happy just like me
In stoniness. And now he stands and walks
And comes this way like me to find some warmth
Inside *these* walls, four walls like me, where he
Is always sure to find somebody—me—
Waiting for him and then forever his. . . .
TANKHEM. His?

GOLEM. Just don't ask. Come closer to me now.

TANKHEM. Are you asleep or what?

GOLEM. Don't talk, don't question!. . . .

Darken the light, and hide the brightness of

My eyes. You rain-washed floors, come closer to me,

Send all your iciness through all my limbs. . . .

And let me hear the breathing of my thunder,

And let the wind and rain come whipping in. . . .

And let me move away and stay away. . . .

(*He collapses, lies prone, in the same position as at the start. TANKHEM, terrified, tiptoes away slowly. Reaching a door, he vanishes swiftly. His hasty, horrified steps resonate to the distant rooms of the tower, growing fainter and fainter and then fading altogether. Sheer darkness. RABBI enters, clutching a lantern.*)

RABBI (*illuminates GOLEM with his lantern*).

No change. He's still the same as I left him. (*Silence.*)

The rain is pouring in on him.

Get up! It's time! Get up!

(*GOLEM sits up.*)

RABBI. You've slept your fill.

GOLEM. Rabbi.

RABBI. You've slept two days and nights—enough.

GOLEM. I wanted to awaken long ago.

I wanted to sit up so often, but

I couldn't open up my eyes at all.

I'm drenched now and I'm freezing—freezing cold.

RABBI. The rain's been pouring on you all this time.

GOLEM. I was asleep. I didn't feel the rain.

Where am I?

RABBI. Don't you know? In the Fifth Tower.

GOLEM. And I kept dreaming that I was somewhere

Beyond the town, striding across the vast

And shadowy meadows, striding and striding.

People were coming toward me, and I—
I started walking toward them. They came closer.
I sprang across so I could see their faces.
And yet no matter where I turned or stood,
I saw no faces, only napes of necks. . . .
No eyes, no brows, no noses, only napes.
No mouths at all, and yet I heard them talk. . . .
I asked, "Who are you?" And they answered, "You."
"Where do you come from?" They replied, "From you."
I asked, "Where are you going?" And they said,
"To you. . . ." And while they spoke, they wheeled around
And started dashing one after another
To the Fifth Tower. I followed them. And as
I ran, I noticed there were five of them:
Two women and three men. I finally
Caught up with them, and then I grabbed one with
Both hands. I looked, Rabbi, and it was—you.
RABBI. Was I?
GOLEM. You were totally drenched and frozen.
Your clothes were sticking to your skin, your beard
Was thoroughly disheveled, and your arms
Were dead and dangling every which way.
And there where your face ought to be were two
Big gashes. One ran down from your forehead;
The other ran across. And both of them
Were glowing like red flames. They glowed; they faded,
They turned black . . . and you dropped upon your knees
And wept, "Oh, save me, Yosl, save me from
The gashes, save me from the cross. My face
Has carried them a thousand years already.
No skin, no flesh has ever healed upon them."
RABBI. What then?
GOLEM. Well, when the others saw me lying

And weeping there, they pounced upon me then
And flung me to the floor and spit into
My face. One man, with bruised and wounded feet,
Trampled on me and shouted, "Golem! Golem!"
I jumped from under them and captured him
With both my hands and hurled him in the air.
I tried to smash him on the floor—that's all.
But furiously and unexpectedly
You struck your staff across your head and stammered,
"Do you know whom you want to batter? Golem!"
A darkness shrouded me and I collapsed.
All five of them lifted you high and held
You by your arms and legs and carried you
And dragged you over to a pit and threw
Me in and scooped handfuls of soil in turn
Upon me one by one and buried me.
Just half my head stuck out, and suddenly
I heard one of the women, Deborah—
RABBI. Who?
GOLEM. I recognized her voice, she burst out sobbing.
She fell upon my half head and embraced it
With both her hands, pressed me against her heart,
And wept. And she was also weeping now,
And everyone kept shoveling and kept on.
And then I heard you shout in your own voice,
"Do you know whom you're grieving for today?
A golem isn't grieved and isn't mourned."
RABBI. Enough. You hear? I'm all alone. Alone.
As you can see, I come to you at midnight.
I bring you calm and peace. You've slept for two
Whole days and nights. I've come here several times
To see you and to summon you for food
And drink. But you have never heard me here.

GOLEM. I'm still not hungry. I was very cold.

But now I'm not, Rabbi, because you're here.

RABBI (*places his hands on GOLEM's shoulders*).

You have to come with me. I need you now.

GOLEM. I'm ready, Rabbi, you can summon me.

RABBI. We mustn't meet at midnight in this place.

We have to plumb the depths of the Fifth Tower—

Far deeper than upon all graves you've gazed at

Here in your dreams. Now listen to the word

That I reveal to you; now grasp it well.

Now see its redness, and make out its warmth,

Its trembling and sharpness: the word is *blood*.

GOLEM. Blood.

RABBI. Do you understand? Will you recall?

Say it again, but louder, louder: blood.

And now say it again, but softer.

GOLEM. Blood.

RABBI. And now prepare to come along with me.

GOLEM. I'm all prepared, Rabbi, now come along.

RABBI. I call you. Come.

(*They both go over to the door leading deeper into the tower. TANKHEM glides across the stage, clutching lighted candles.*)

TANKHEM (*breathless, in a fit of coughing*).

Res-cue us!

Who will res-cue? Who?

Who can res-cue? Ha?

Who can res-cue? Who?

IN THE CAVE

(In the underground caverns of the Fifth Tower. The darkness is almost palpable. TADEUSH, accompanied by MONK, emerges from the depths of the cave. MONK clutches a small torch. They both are gasping from their long underground climb.)

TADEUSH. Your hand now. Steady. If it weren't for
The stifling air and the thick darkness, we
Would have fulfilled our mission long ago,
As was ordained for us by God and Jesus,
our king. As you can see, the cave is vast,
Deserted, and so alien. Yet our hearts
Refused to fear, and our hands refused
To shiver. God himself evenly guided
Our footsteps till they reached their synagogue.
MONK. I'm falling. Hold me, Father.
TADEUSH. Straighten up
And catch your breath. The air is better here.
MONK. I've done whatever you've told me to do.
I wasn't scared. My right hand clutched the knife,
My left hand clamped my throat. . . . No shout, no shudder!
I corked the bottles tight, put them away.
I still can feel their warmth upon my hand. . . .
Catch me, my head is spinning once again.
TADEUSH. Scared? Coward! Can't you see who's leading you?
Can't you see my gray beard, my old-age staff,
And in my eyes the nights I haven't slept?
For whose sake did I lie awake? For mine?
Who shines in the reflected glory of
The cross? Just I? Do you shine more than I?
And who's done more to whet and wield the knife?
I or else you? And who inhaled more of

The warmth, although I stood beside her: I or
Else you? I did everything that was done,
Not you. So I should be the one who totters,
For you've done nothing whatsoever, a
Mere swiping with the knife blade, and that's all.
MONK. Forgive me. (*Kisses TADEUSH's hands.*)
TADEUSH. I forgive you. I am kind.
You can go calmly to your cell and sleep.
And I am more than calm, I am so blissful
For watching you fill every flask with blood.
And right before my eyes I saw those visions
That no one else has ever seen but him. . . .
And he, nailed to the cross and hanging there,
And seeing the same visions that I saw,
He raised a single corner of his brow
And sent a very soft and loving glance.
For even then this cave was ready, and
So was this knife. Gleaming and glistening
And sharp, the knife shone on him from inside
The cave. It shone, caressed his open eyelid,
And gleaming, glistening, his eyelid closed.
You think, Revenge? No! Only love. For blood
Is love; the blood of children too, for he
Was once a child himself. . . . And every knife
Since that time has been blessed. And never will
Those crucifiers dispossess us of
The sanctity of knives. For never will
The blood stop pouring out: the blood of those
Who couldn't see the gentle glow cast by
His closing lid.
MONK. Someone seems to be coming.
TADEUSH. You fashion fears of every kind—you coward!
Who would be coming here? Who on earth knows

The secret entrance? Let me say again,
Don't be afraid. You hear footsteps? Indeed!
Those steps are his. He hovers over us,
Quiet and yearning, yes, inhaling deep
And strong the red aroma. And he comes
Alive not only in the heavens above
But also with us here on earth as well.
He's coming now. His pallid cheeks are flushing.
His joy of love, his childlike tenderness
And pity are now streaming from his eyes.
He bears the cross upon his back, he dances
With it, he sings with it, he lives with it,
he plays with it. He's with us—don't you see?
Just lift your eyes.
MONK (*crosses himself in terror and falls upon the floor*).
Oh, come, I'm scared. I'm scared!
TADEUSH. Now do you see?
MONK. Merciful Jesus! Take pity!
Oh, Holy Father! Carry me away!
Away, away from my eyes—I tell you,
now see, but you are deaf and you are blind.
(*MONK starts to run, followed by TADEUSH. Both vanish. RABBI and
GOLEM enter from opposite side. RABBI is carrying a lantern, GOLEM an
ax and a spade.*)
RABBI. Stop here and look. What do you see?
GOLEM: I see
The cavern's length from end to end. A narrow
Path on the right, a broad path on the left.
A hundred paces in I see a third path
Forking away and barely useful here.
RABBI. Where do the first two end?
GOLEM. The narrow path
Leads all the way up to the synagogue.

The broad path leads all the way to the priest.

RABBI. Now listen hard, and tell me what you hear.

GOLEM. I hear the last breath of a man who's dead.

RABBI. What do you smell?

GOLEM (*shuddering*).

The Word, the Word you gave me

In secret: red and sharp and warm and still.

I feel it, and I hear it, and I see it.

RABBI. Stop shuddering. And now, pronounce the Word.

GOLEM. Blood.

RABBI. Blood? From which side?

GOLEM. From the right, along

The narrow path.

RABBI. Come on, let's go there now.

We mustn't speak to one another, but

We have to keep repeating to ourselves,

"Through death and blood and final breath!" And step

By step, we walk ahead and don't look back.

Start walking now, and say in unison

With me: "Through death and blood and final breath."

GOLEM. With you: "Through death and blood and final
breath."

(*They begin to walk, but suddenly an invisible being shoves RABBI back
and blocks his path.*)

RABBI. You have to go alone. The evil spirits

That haunt the cave are hindering me now.

Go on alone! You're not within their power!

And take the spade and take the ax along.

You don't need any torch at all. Go to

The square that's underneath the synagogue,

And grasp whatever you may find. Then take

Each thing back to its rightful owner, for

Your strides are long, and radiant are your eyes. . . .

GOLEM. Are you now leaving me?

RABBI. Are you afraid?

GOLEM. Oh, no! But come with me, you'll see what happens
If someone tries to block your way again.

RABBI. I mustn't go. For with a thousand eyes
Peril seeks pretext. You must go alone.

GOLEM. Whenever you come to me, you then leave
At once. I lay above us in the tower,
I lay there day and night, waiting for you
To come to me and stay with me. I thought
Each rustle was a herald of your coming.
You'd ordered me to speak to no one and
To go nowhere. And so I spoke to no one
And went nowhere. But with each passing moment
I heard the cries inside me, I heard words
That I had never heard before. I had
To grit my teeth to keep from shrieking out.
I had to tie my legs, bend them in half,
So that they wouldn't rise and run away.
That was how urgent I felt and how driven!
And yet no sooner did you look at me
Or even speak a word or two than you
Turned round and left me all alone again. . . .
Don't leave! I see this darkness as if through
A glow. I see the caverns in their length
And breadth. I hear the rocks conversing, stirring.
From all the cracks the shadows start to slither
And twist like snakes. And closer come the noises
Of barking, howling, the grinding of teeth.
I'm not afraid. But stay with me. I need
To have you near me, simply need you near me.

RABBI. We follow trails along the roads that rule
Themselves. They seek every which way to sow

Confusion on us, to seduce, mislead us.
And they'll incite still greater dread upon you.
But though you are alone, you must pass through.
You must, for you've been sent. You have no choice.
Whatever you may see or you may hear,
Must not distract your eyes, divert your ears.
Pierce through whatever you have seen and heard.
Now see and hear that other, distant thing
That you must still uncover. Stay alone.
GOLEM. Oh, Rabbi, just one moment longer, please.
RABBI. The peril grows with every passing moment,
And you—what are you in the face of danger
That we should now delay for even half
An instant the redemption of a nation?
GOLEM. How often have you come only for you
To send me on some errands, rouse me from
My stillness and my drowsiness, and change
Me into an entirely different being?
Do you really believe that I don't know?
RABBI. Your whole life is an expectation of
Those moments when I need you. And now that
A moment has arrived, you still don't sense
The vital meaning of each single day,
Which has the honor to expect all this. . . .
The accidental and superfluous
Elements of your life lead you away,
Great deeds and heroism summon you.
Your life is granted you. See, it is spreading
Upon you, yes, and Providence protects you,
It spreads its wings, unfolds them over you.
(*RABBI exits. Darkness. A soft glow gradually starts to surround GOLEM. His eyes grow big and bright, his face becomes sharp; his whole body is lithe like a tiger all set to pounce.*)

GOLEM. The endless depth and distance—just one stride,
One leap, one glance, one flutter. Those are all
It takes: through death, through blood, through final breath.
(GOLEM is about to leap when all at once a great din erupts in the cave.
Savage roaring winds blast up. A hail of rocks pours from above and over
his head. He shakes them off and backs up. As he retreats, the storm quiets
down. He waits a few minutes, then strides forward again, yelling wildly.)
We pass through death, through blood, through final breath.
(A dreadful howling, a thumping of dog paws on the ground. The cave is
full of moaning and turmoil. GOLEM swings his ax every which way. The
howling stops. Flames and smoke appear, twisting and coiling around him.
His clothes catch fire. He flails about like a lunatic, emitting repressed
shouts. He collapses. The flames vanish. He lies panting on the ground. He
stands up, raging. His clothes are scorched, but he is unharmed.)
GOLEM. Where are you, Rabbi, please, where are you now?
(He kneels. All kinds of shadows, cave spirits begin to stir in the surround-
ing brightness. They dance and whirl and swirl above his head.)
GOLEM. Where are you? Come and see how everything
Rises against me, Rabbi, in sheer anger.
The fire is snuffed already, and the storm
Has faded, Rabbi. But the silent horrors
Are creeping from their hiding places now.
They weave and whirl and hug and ring around me.
They pierce my eyes and dazzle them with double
Fires. They pierce my ears with double sounds.
This very cavern has turned double, Rabbi.
And now the glow around my head is dimming.
(GOLEM wishes to start walking, but he doesn't know what direction to
take. He keeps turning in one spot, and a wild circle of CAVE SPIRITS
swivels around him.)
CAVE SPIRITS.
Round and round,
Round and round,

Who is he who's in our midst?
Who now designates his steps?
Who now shields and shelters him?
No one,
No one.
He is not in our might,
Who's been brought here tonight
On the eve of Passover,
In our midst,
In our midst?

Round and round,
Round and round.
He himself's awakened us,
Made us known despite the blackness.
Who is he who could be?
No one,
No one.

Sway and swirl into a chain,
Sing the song of dread and death.
Twist and twirl him, tangle him
In our midst,
In our midst.
GOLEM (*virtually tethered*).
The fire hasn't consumed me,
The rocks haven't felled me.
Now shatter, whirling wheel,
Now smash, double dance.
I've been sent to walk
And not to stand in your midst.
CAVE SPIRITS. Coil and curl in double,
Pleat and plait in triple,

Till you shield and shelter
Him who's in your midst
And who twists alone,
Separates in two. . . .

He is lost forever,
Grab him, strangle him.
Stifle, smother him.
Then break half from half.
Let this broken thing
Fall within our midst.
Who has sent him here?

You picked up an ax,
Split your head—that's that,
Before he who issues
These commands now comes,
And he brings them here.
Now he grabs the ax,
And he grips it hard. . . .

Make way, we already
Hear his steps draw close.
Pallid glows are lit,
Blazing bloody red,
In a rising column.
Let who's in the midst
Hear and listen too.

Twist and twirl in pairs,
Break and smash the chain,
Stand in sturdy rows,
Mute and shut in death;

Pour the bloody red.

Let the man who's dead

Spin around on his own.

(CAVE SPIRITS stop dancing. The cave is filled with blood-red brightness. A hush. GOLEM collapses, horrified by what he suddenly sees. From the path he was to follow a figure emerges: RABBI, an icy rage on his features, his eyes piercing, his lips clenched. He trudges with short, ridged steps, and he is soaked in red radiance. With each step he takes, he hits his staff on the ground, and each blow reverberates throughout the cave.)

FIGURE. Didn't you call for me before?

GOLEM *(lifts his head)*. Who are you?

FIGURE. Who am I? You don't know? Don't know at all?

GOLEM. Oh, no! Oh, no! Oh, no! You're not the rabbi.

You are somebody else; you're not the rabbi.

FIGURE. I'm not? *(Laughs nastily.)*

What insolence! And you don't know whose hands

Command your fate? Those are my hands. Why did

You summon me before? I ask again.

GOLEM. Oh, go away from me! Just go—I'm scared.

You are somebody else; you're not the rabbi.

FIGURE. Again you're insolent! Just try again,

And you will feel my stick!

GOLEM. Take pity on me.

FIGURE. I am the rabbi!

GOLEM. Please take pity on me!

What do you want to do to me? Please tell me!

Someone misled me here: the rabbi. You.

FIGURE. Now why should that involve me? I will never

Let you flee. You'll stay forever, forever.

(GOLEM is about to run, SPIRIT blocks his path.)

SPIRIT. Don't run. Stand still. We're doomed. There's no escape

From here.

GOLEM. Let go! You hear? Let go! Let go!

FIGURE. Hold back your insolence. You see this stick?
Now should we poke your eyes out, both of us?
Or should we pluck your hair out, hair by hair?
Or knock all of your teeth out from your mouth,
A tooth for every word?
GOLEM. Let go, let go! (*Swings his fists and then leaps back.*)
FIGURE. You raise your fists to me, to me, your rabbi?
Hey, just come here, come here now, all of you!
Tear out his tongue so that he'll never talk!
Chop up his legs so that he'll never run!
Throw him upon the ground, chew up his flesh,
And slit his throat!
GOLEM. Whom are you calling? Stop!
Don't call, don't call! Whom are you calling? Stop!
FIGURE. Silence! Do you see now that I'm your rabbi?
GOLEM. Yes, I see now.
FIGURE. And now you know that it
Was I who brought you here!
GOLEM. Yes, you! Yes, you!
FIGURE. Then hear and hold your tongue: I am your master.
I can do anything to you my heart
Desires. I won't harm you. I'm just toying
With you and with your dread and with your grief.
I don't have any need of you beyond that. . . .
What are you peering at, you golem, chunk
Of flesh, you dimwit? Close your bulging eyes.
Drop down upon the ground and lie there! Down!
(*GOLEM sinks to the ground.*)
That's right! Just lie there with your drooping head—
Lower and lower, facedown, deeper, deeper.
Bend over triple, and stay seated there,
Stay day and night, stay day and night again.
(*GOLEM thrusts his head between his knees. FIGURE disappears. CAVE*

SPIRITS come crawling out, shape into serried ranks. They move lightly, barely grazing the ground.)

CAVE SPIRITS.
Snuff the flame
With stormy winds.
Sic the dogs
To tame the storm.
Hurl the rocks
Upon the dogs.
Fling the rocks
Upon the child.
The child lies
Inside a sack.
Take the rope,
Tie up the sack.

Peer into
The deep, deep sack.
You'll find bottles
Of wine there.

Let's drink
Bottle after bottle
When the turmoil
Has died down.

He will sit there,
He will sway
In his stupor
Hour by hour.

(*They exit. GOLEM remains seated and alone. He lifts his head and peers around.*)

GOLEM. Where am I? What has happened? How did I

Plunge to these depths? With whom did I whirl in
A dance? I must go somewhere. Where? And why?
Why has it grown so silent suddenly?
And tell me, what are these? An ax? A spade?
Where am I? Where? And who has brought me here?
(*GOLEM shrieks until he is out of breath.*)
I shriek, no one responds. Should I stop shrieking?
Should I stretch out and call no more at all?
Something is shining there before my eyes.
(*He huddles close to the ground and remains there. THE INVISIBLE FORCE appears overhead. He grabs his shoulders and shakes them.*)
INVISIBLE FORCE. Just look at me once and for all. Just look.
(*GOLEM jumps up and looks.*)
INVISIBLE FORCE. Don't run. Wherever you may go, I follow.
Look at me joyfully. Your earlier fear
Confused you, and the dancing dizzied you.
I watched it, and now you can watch it too.
GOLEM. Who are you? Tell me now?
How can it be?
INVISIBLE FORCE. Don't ask. . . . Just look. And that will all
be all.
GOLEM. Your face is radiant as it was before,
Yet everything is darkness for me now.
INVISIBLE FORCE. It had to happen once. You should have
looked
Just once and never looked again.
GOLEM. What am
I doing here? I don't know. Might you know?
INVISIBLE FORCE. You've come to watch the dance of madness here,
And all you've seen is the beginning. So
Let me divulge the end. You clutch an ax,
A spade—you don't need them. The flasks are ready.

Just stretch your arm out—all you need to know.
GOLEM. Ah. Now I know, and now I do remember.
INVISIBLE FORCE. Why bother to remember anything?
So what if you forget? It's all the same.
You'll carry out your mission come what may.
For what else can an emissary do
But what he must do—must sooner or later,
Must here or there? And when it's done, it's done.
It may be far too late for someone else.
But how can it be too late for yourself?
Stretch out your hand, your arm. No more than that.
It scarcely pays to stir a step.
GOLEM. From here?
INVISIBLE FORCE. From here! And what is distance? Nothing,
nothing.
And hidden mysteries grow manifest
From always to forever, and each road
Is just a step. And barriers are simply
Playthings for anyone who wants to leave
Insanity for even a split second.
And what are blood and death and final breath?
GOLEM. Ah, now I can remember everything!
INVISIBLE FORCE. Everything?
And just how much are you alone?
And I, who am like you, like you yourself?
Not blood, not death, not final breath—all told.
You understand? Not even final breath.
Hold out your hand. If anything lies hidden
Anywhere, it will surface by itself
And grip your fingers. For whatever's buried
Deep in this cave has long since shown itself
To every single eye. . . . And there it lies.
You see? Bend over. Pick it up. You see?

GOLEM (*looks down and sees a tied-up sack at his feet*).
How come I didn't notice it before?

INVISIBLE FORCE. You didn't see it any earlier.

GOLEM. Well, should I pick it up?

INVISIBLE FORCE. Why? Let it be.

GOLEM. You're making fun of me. You look like me,
And yet you're making fun of me.

INVISIBLE FORCE. Should I leave?

GOLEM. Yes. I'm afraid. The cave is whirling once
Again. Oh, no! stay here.

INVISIBLE FORCE Untie the sack,
And then I'll go away.

(*GOLEM unties sack and produces two flasks of red liquid.*)

INVISIBLE FORCE. Now do you see?

GOLEM (*yells*). Blood! Blood!

INVISIBLE FORCE. Why yell? Just put them down and let them
stand.

(*Vanishes suddenly. A waxy yellow brightness fills the cave. The ground opens, and SUBTERRANEANS come pouring out. Their long, scrawny hands clutch big, lighted tapers. After a long, profound sleep in their graves, their clothes are ragged and rotten. They dance a very quiet circle around the flasks, barely stirring and holding out the tapers. GOLEM hugs a wall, watching anxiously.*)

FIRST SUBTERRANEAN.
Each one sings for the first time
In a voice that's purified.

We are risen from our rest
To bring the end of everything.

Radiant in our delight,
In the very face of death.

ALL THE REST.
And the tapers are prepared,
Waiting for the dead to wake,
Till the tapers are burned up,
Worn out in our outstretched hands.

We don't weep, and we don't wail.
We just carry, carry tapers
Till the tapers are burned up,
Worn out in our outstretched hands.

When we sing and we have sung,
We lie down upon the ground,
With the tapers not burned up,
Worn out in our outstretched hands.
FIRST SUBTERRANEAN.
Count the steps, and don't miscount,
For this place is hallowed ground.
And we circle seven times with
Death's eternal signet ring.
And no doubt you know who's coming,
Coming here so very soon.
ALL.
Yes, we know who has to come.
That's why we took all the tapers,
Till the tapers are burned up,
Worn out in our outstretched hands,

When we hear them, hear their steps,
Let the tapers be snuffed out,
Till the tapers are burned up,
Worn out in our outstretched hands.

For we do not wish to speak.
We just carry, carry tapers,
Till the tapers are burned up,
Worn out in our outstretched hands.
FIRST SUBTERRANEAN.
Bow your head one final time
To the circling boundary string.
Then go back to sleep again,
For the end is coming soon.
ALL.
Now we close the seventh turn,
Clutching all the burning tapers.
Tapers that are not burned up,
Worn out in our outstretched hands.
FIRST SUBTERRANEAN.
I hear others in the night,
And their names are mentioned all.

And their names pass by, pass by,
Since they number one in three.

One of them has long been listening,
Hearing our radiant singing.

There he stands and watches us,
Knowing neither what nor where.
See, his clothes are singed and scorched,
He's a stranger in this cave.
ALL.
Let the stranger stand and watch,
Tapers swaying, swaying, swaying,
Tapers that are soon burned up,
Worn out in our outstretched hands.

For we swear upon his head
He'll be dying, dying, dying—
Snuff the tapers, though still burning,
Soon worn out in outstretched hands.

(*All snuff the tapers and sink back into the nooks from which they appeared.*)

GOLEM.
Since I'm staying here forever,
I'll be sitting in the middle,
At the chosen center here,
Measuring the chosen ground.

I hear no more spirits now,
Only one, who lit the taper.
Death is lying on my hands,
And my hands are on my face.

(*GOLEM sits down inside the marked-off circle. An invisible hand pushes YOUNG BEGGAR into the cave; he is fettered to a long chain. Shoved so hard, he collapses on the ground. After lying there awhile, he gets up.*)

YOUNG BEGGAR.
Finally I'm here,
Finally I'm free.
In the final hour,
I am one of three.

Now my feet are tangled
In the circling chain.
Every open wound
Brings me to my death.

Here is where I've come,
Not to leave again.
In my final sorrow,
I console myself.

Torment of my flesh,
Dig into the rock,
I'll remain, remain,
I console myself. (*Groping in the dark.*)

Where are you? Reply.
We must be three, three,
Three,
Sit here head to head,
And be friends again.

The world goes its own way,
And we go our way,
No one in the middle.
The madness of the final, final, final
Wonders
Will itself defend us.
Hear my voice, where are you,
You nailed to the cross?
We make peace, peace, peace
Now and still forever,
And where are you, Golem? (*He bumps into GOLEM.*)
GOLEM.
Leave! I sit inside the circle
Since I'm staying here forever.
YOUNG BEGGAR.
Take me too inside the circle
Since I'm staying here forever.
GOLEM.
Sit, and tell me, Where is he,
He who has to be the third?
YOUNG BEGGAR.
He who has to be the third

Will be coming soon enough.

GOLEM.

You repeat the words I speak

As I speak them—word for word.

YOUNG BEGGAR.

Everything you speak and say

I repeat it word for word.

GOLEM.

Yet you bandage your old wounds?

YOUNG BEGGAR.

Yes, I still dress my old wounds.

GOLEM.

You exude the stench of rot.

YOUNG BEGGAR.

Yes, it is the stench of rot.

GOLEM (*shouts*).

Silence!

(*Both sit in silence.*)

YOUNG BEGGAR.

Two whole days my parching palate

Hasn't touched a drop of water.

GOLEM.

Drink! Two bottles now are waiting,

Two full bottles, filled for you.

YOUNG BEGGAR (*takes bottle, opens it, is about to drink but yells*).

Blood!

GOLEM.

Why the hollering and shouting?

Put it back and let it stay.

(*An invisible hand shoves in MAN WITH BIG CROSS on his shoulders. He buckles under the load of the cross.*)

MAN WITH BIG CROSS.

Finally I'm here,

Finally I'm free.
In my final hour
I am one of three.

Press me to the ground,
As I've been forever.
I've already heard
What I have to do.

Now I hug the walls,
Seeking my redemption,
Waiting on the floor,
In the final pain.

Nails that pierce my hands,
Thorns around my head—
Scrape and scratch the walls
Till I grate you down.

(*Gropes in the dark, shouting.*)
    Where are you? Reply.
    I'm alone, alone, alone—
    Abandoned.
    My Lord told me to bear the cross
    And never throw it down.

    Blessed be his lips that gave—
    I can only be blessed, blessed, blessed
    And forgive.
    My Lord has now become my slave,
    My kingdom is at hand. (*Bumps into the seated two.*)
    GOLEM.
    Stop! We're sitting in the center,

I too will be here forever.
MAN WITH BIG CROSS.
Take me too inside the center,
I'll stay here forever too.
GOLEM.
Sit down. Well, we number three,
Now that we're all here forever.
YOUNG BEGGAR.
Now that we're all here forever.
MAN WITH BIG CROSS.
Since the three of us are here,
We're all here forever too.
GOLEM.
You too speak the way he speaks,
Speak and speak—and word for word.
MAN WITH BIG CROSS.
What you say is what I say.
Speak and speak—and word for word.
GOLEM.
Do you still carry the cross?
MAN WITH BIG CROSS.
Yes, I still carry the cross.
GOLEM.
You give off the stench of death.
MAN WITH BIG CROSS.
I give off the stench of death.
GOLEM.
Silence! Sit and do not speak.
MAN WITH BIG CROSS.
I am thirsty.
GOLEM.
Drink. We have here
Two full bottles.

MAN WITH BIG CROSS (*puts bottle to mouth*).
Blood!
GOLEM.
Why your yelling? Can't you drink?
Put the bottle back and be.
(*CAVE SPIRITS return and ring around them again.*)
CAVE SPIRITS.
Again
And once again.
Now all three are here already,
Here to meet the final hour,
And aside from them, nobody—
No one's here, no one's here.

And the cross lies on the ax,
And the fetters on the sack.
Closer, closer, nearer, nearer,
In the center,
In the center.

All around,
All around,
Once again and yet again,
And we dance away your woe.
And you know just who we are.
No one's here,
No one's here.

And your deathly footsteps are
All well guarded, well protected,
All three sitting and embracing
In the center,
In the center.

(Their dancing grows dizzier and dizzier.)

> Oh, redeemers, you redeemers,
> Be redeemed!
> Listen, hear our own decree,
> Do not wring your hands at all,
> And do not gouge out your eyes
> In great distress.
>
> Finally you've found your way here,
> Finally rest.
> You have borne your burden well,
> And what else can you have brought?
> Sit and see how we can hang,
> How we shed and carry off
> Dead blood.
>
> And your kingdom, yes, your rule
> Is now crowned,
> We, as loyal subjects here,
> Circle round you at the center,
> Entertain you and protect you
> Without profit.
>
> And anoint your heads, yes, you who
> Are redeemed.
> Bow down to the ground—exalted—
> Press your temples till they faint,
> Till a fire blazes round your crown.

(CAVE SPIRITS exit. SUBTERRANEANS return, clutching unconsumed candles. They dance around the three as quietly as before.)

With our voices purified
We now sing one final time.

We, awoken from our sleep,
Now move closer to the end.

Look, all three are sitting there,
Never stirring, never speaking.

You must know just who they are,
Sing the story of their anguish.
ALL.
There is nothing more to sing.
There the cross lies, not to carry.
There the chain lies, not to clatter.
There the ax lies, not to strike with.

So we sing the song of nothing.

No one's lids are shut by us.
They are shut without our help.
No one's tears are caused by us.
They are shed without our help.

So we sing the song of nothing.

We leave steps on no one's road.
We don't waken; we don't kill.
No one comes to welcome us,
No one to accompany us.

So we sing the song of nothing.

If we have no need to hurry,
Then we softly whirl and swirl.
And we carry, carry, carry
Candles that will never burn.

So we sing the song of nothing.
FIRST SUBTERRANEAN.
No one weeping, no one wailing,
Sitting as if carved in stone.

Dead worms creep and crawl and skulk
In the heart of all their glory.

He who waited for them was
Not delighted, just deceived.

He who trusted in them was
Not rewarded, only punished.

Just a pretext, just a trick
For the last fool in the street.
ALL.
Since they sit there, mute and sunken,
Our tongues can only tangle.
We should only beckon, signal,
But our fingers all have stiffened.

So we sing the song of nonsense.

Everything that's been begun
Ended long and long ago.
Where a foot has left its print
It was swept away long since.

So we sing the song of madness.
Hands that wring and twist in anger—
They stay wrung in all their wrath.
For whatever has been promised
Has already been fulfilled.

So we sing the song of nonsense.
FIRST SUBTERRANEAN.
Slowly, slowly footsteps fade,
Hide your faces, all of you.

We won't come here anymore,
Never stay here anymore.

Keep your voices soft and silent,
This is now the final time.

Spit on all the candles here,
And then leave the silent three. . . .
ALL.
We don't need to spit at all,
For the flames die on their own.
Now let's take and scatter wicks—
Dead wicks on this trio here.

So we go back to the grave,

Shake and shake and shake your fingers;
Take a pace, and turn around.
Draw your tongues back in your throats;
Hush forever—evermore.

So we go back to the grave.

(*The candles fade in their hands. Darkness. Everything vanishes. A few moments wear by. Steps sound, and a light appears. RABBI hurries in, clutching a lantern. GOLEM sits alone, guarding the two flasks. His eyes gape; his features are insane. He doesn't move a muscle.*)

RABBI.

You're sitting? Why? What's going on?

Why won't you speak? (*RABBI spots the flasks.*)

You've found it! Quick! Get it away!

You're sitting?

(*GOLEM doesn't move his head. Says nothing.*)

RABBI.

Answer me! Speak!

What's happened here?

(*GOLEM remains mute.*)

RABBI.

Well, can't you see who's talking to you? (*Shakes GOLEM's shoulders.*)

I order you to speak!

You don't remember me? Have you gone mute?

GOLEM (*looks up, then lowers his head again*).

Who are you? Go away.

RABBI.

You don't know who I am?

GOLEM.

I don't know. Nothing. Leave. (*Jumps up, screaming.*)

You've come to torture me again? Just go away!

RABBI. What's wrong with you? You're blackened and you're scorched!

What are you doing?

GOLEM (*sinking to ground*). Leave me, leave me.

Don't talk to me! I don't know, something burned

And barked and stormed and danced

And sang and died. Just take away the blood!

Take it away, away from here!

RABBI (*takes him by the hand*). Calm down and see me. Be yourself again.

(*GOLEM sinks back into his rigidity.*)

RABBI. You still don't recognize me?

GOLEM. Who are you?

RABBI. I am the rabbi.

GOLEM. The rabbi? Who? What rabbi? Do you want
To sit? It is forbidden. Don't come near me.
Don't touch me. For this spot is marked and bounded
And surrounded for me and for nobody else.

RABBI. If madness has twisted your face,
Let madness leave you. Hear and understand.
You're gambling with your life. Your mission is
Still unfulfilled, and yet how deeply swamped
You are in terror and insanity—
Poor man! What have you done with joy and brightness?
Where have you scattered and where have you lost them?
You are obsessed with darkness and with fear!
Wake up! And if your eyes are blinded now,
Then search with blinded eyes. Restore the light,
The brightness that I've given you! Wake up!

GOLEM. Don't wake me up. I feel so good like this.
Let me lie down, I'll like it. There! You see? (*Lies down and
curls up.*)

RABBI. I order you to stand and be what you
Have been. Remove this blindness from your eyes,
And then smooth out your twisted face and features.

GOLEM. Whoever you may be, don't torture me.

RABBI. Go quickly, end your mission here.

GOLEM. What mission?
You are a stranger, what can I do for you?
Now everything is spinning once again.

And now I'm well, and now I'm radiant—look!
And I'm no longer frightened anymore,
For I know everything there is to know,
And now my heart is fully out of breath.

RABBI. You must fulfill your mission here, you must!

GOLEM. Don't call me anymore. Leave me forever.

RABBI. You must fulfill your mission here, you must!

GOLEM. Be silent. Here they come, they come to me.

RABBI. Who's coming?

GOLEM. Can't you see them, can't you hear them?
Be silent, silent, silent. . . . (*GOLEM rises all at once, gapes, embraces*
RABBI.)

Oh, Rabbi, Rabbi—you are here, my rabbi?

THE FINAL MISSION

(*Anteroom of old synagogue. It is Friday evening, and the Jews are welcoming the Sabbath. Part of the synagogue is visible through the open door: the holy ark, chandeliers, and the gathering worshipers. At left, a door to the courtyard. GOLEM is lying on a bench. He looks shabby, ill kempt, scraggly, and sleepy. He wears only one shoe. His other foot is bare, and the ripped shoe lies where it was dropped. GOLEM jumps up with all his might, shuts the synagogue door, and falls back on his bench.*)

AVROM (*He enters*). You heard that slam? Where do you think you are?

Why are you bothered by an open door?

GOLEM. If I close, let it stay closed! And they—

Well, all they do is open it and keep opening it.

If it is closed, let it stay closed.

AVROM. Indeed! If he shuts it! And who are you?

Why, have you ever heard such insolence?

GOLEM (*mutters*). If it is closed, let it stay closed—stay closed.

AVROM. What are you muttering about? Speak up!

GOLEM. None of your business. (*Turns with his face to the wall.*)

AVROM. How long will you lie there?

It's nearly time to pray and greet the Sabbath.

The rabbi's coming now, he'll be here and—

You haven't even put your shoes on yet.

GOLEM. What shoes?

AVROM. What do you mean, "What shoes"? Your shoes! Not mine!

GOLEM. I'm wearing one shoe, can't you see?

AVROM. A waste of time talking to you, a waste!

GOLEM. Hand me the shoe. I'll put it on.

AVROM. Hand you?

GOLEM. If you don't want to, don't. Just go away!

AVROM. Bare feet are banned in any synagogue.

(*GOLEM is silent.*)

AVROM. You don't hear what you're told now? Are you deaf?
It's almost time to pray—

GOLEM. I don't know how.

AVROM. You are a savage; they should drive you off.

GOLEM. The rabbi isn't here as yet? As yet?

AVROM. Why do you ask?

GOLEM. No reason. Tell him that I want him.
Go tell him to hand me the single shoe.

AVROM. The shoe? The rabbi?

GOLEM. Why keep repeating? Can't you hear? (*Leaps up.*)
Go tell him that I want him. Yosl wants him.

AVROM. What rudeness! Did you hear that? Lunacy!

GOLEM. I told you, go! (*Jumps toward him.*)

AVROM (*runs toward the door, shouting*). Come hurry, Jews, come
hurry! Do you hear me?

(*GOLEM flops back on his bench.*)

AVROM (*at the door*). He's lost his mind, that's sure, in the Fifth
Tower.
He was to chop our wood, carry our water.
A fine state I'd be in if I must wait
For our wood, for our water too.
We put him in the foreroom, gave him a bench
And food and drink, and guarded him, and he
Is quite indifferent. Either he sleeps
Two days and nights without a single pause
Or lies three nights without a wink of sleep.
Fearful indeed!

GOLEM. Tonight I won't shout. I'll be still.

AVROM. You will be still? That's what you said last night,
And yet you howled and yelled all through the night.
No one could catch a wink. The courtyard was crowded.

GOLEM. Tonight I will be still, I will be still.

AVROM. Now wash yourself and then put on your shoes.

The Sabbath is arriving. What a Sabbath!

GOLEM. Go away!

AVROM. Didn't you hear about the great miracle?

GOLEM. What miracle? What miracle? Go away!

(*Stretches out on the bench, facedown.*)

AVROM. He's truly crazy! (*Opens door to leave.*)

GOLEM (*calls*). Send the rabbi here.

AVROM. Stand up and come into the synagogue.

Just wash your face.

GOLEM. When he arrives, I'll then

Get up and wash my face. When he arrives.

AVROM. Why, have you ever heard the likes before?

GOLEM. I've been here for a week now, and he hasn't

Come by to see me even once already.

AVROM. He is supposed to come to visit you?

GOLEM. He's tossed me, tossed me totally aside.

He's put me here, and now he doesn't come.

I begged him; Please don't take me from this cave,

And please don't take me from this utter darkness.

AVROM. What cave?

GOLEM. You really do not know? That cave!

AVROM. I just don't know what you're talking about.

GOLEM. I'm not allowed to tell. I must be mute.

Just go! I cannot tell. I must be mute.

(*AVROM steals away into the synagogue. Leaves door open. Men poke in their heads, peer around, and vanish. TALL MAN and REDHEAD enter and stand by the door.*)

TALL MAN. I tell you he's the one. I tell you! Yosl!

REDHEAD. Quiet! You mustn't mention him by name!

TALL MAN. No matter! Look! He doesn't even stir!

REDHEAD. Do you remember how he hounded us

Whenever we did mention him by name?

TALL MAN. Do I remember? Certainly I do!

REDHEAD. Is he asleep? He might decide to pounce
On us!

TALL MAN. They say he sleeps whole days and nights at once.

REDHEAD. You mark my words, there's something strange
afoot!

Again I say, a mystery, a secret.

TALL MAN. A mystery? He's just a man, a golem.

REDHEAD. Do you remember the two wandering beggars?

TALL MAN. Of course! And how they were afraid of him?

REDHEAD. The instant they set eyes on him, they ran
Without a word; they ran like men possessed.

TALL MAN. Well, who can say? The rabbi ordered them
To leave. He must have known them from before.
He didn't want them to remain in Prague.

REDHEAD. Do you know what I want to tell you now?
He is the man who hit and beat Tadeush!

TALL MAN. He is? But he left the Fifth Tower with us.

REDHEAD. If I say he's the man, then he's the man..

TALL MAN. How do you know?

REDHEAD. I know. For that night opened
My eyes, though who and what I cannot say.
I only know that something odd occurred
In Prague the night that we were driven out
From the Fifth Tower our bundles on our backs.
We mutely slogged along—do you remember?—
From street to street and didn't know whose door
To knock on, he behind us, huge and heavy,
With empty hands, with dangling arms, with feet
Like hammers. . . . In my heart I felt each step
He trudged. And when we suddenly peered around,
We saw him still behind us, standing in

The middle of the street, not even stirring.
Remember that?
TALL MAN. Good thing that he fell back.
REDHEAD. And no one even thought of calling him.
I can still see him standing in the middle
Of the street, with his arms still dangling,
And heard and saw that something was afoot
In Prague.
TALL MAN. Oh, what a night! Oh, what a night!
REDHEAD. And he went back to the Fifth Tower and stayed
there.
Did you know?
TALL MAN. Yes, I heard that he was back.
AVROM (*enters*). Prayers are about to start; the rabbi's here.
GOLEM (*after lying with his face to the wall, he now leaps up*).
He has arrived? He has arrived? He's here?
AVROM. He's here! Why do you ask?
TALL MAN (*scared*). He's not the same,
He's altogether different—different now.
REDHEAD. How scrawny and how scraggy, but he doesn't
See us. Or doesn't recognize us either?
GOLEM. I must get dressed—I must! Quickly! My shoes!
(*Finds shoe, starts putting it on, then flings it away.*)
Let him come here, and then I'll put it on.
Just send the rabbi here, and I'll be waiting.
AVROM. Why, have you ever heard such madness here?
REDHEAD. Perhaps he needs him. Who can really say?
GOLEM. I want to see the rabbi.
REDHEAD. Are you scared
To step inside the synagogue yourself?
GOLEM. He told me to remain here all the time.
He's locked me up, and he won't come at all. (*Sits with head drooping.*)

TALL MAN. You must have done some wrong to him—some wrong.

(*GOLEM bellows.*)

REDHEAD. Should I hand you your shoe?

GOLEM. Just go away.

REDHEAD. We're in the synagogue, not in the tower.

GOLEM (*stands up, his eyes focusing on the REDHEAD*). The tower?

TALL MAN. The same eyes, don't you see? Just come away.

REDHEAD. He stands once more as he stood in the street.

His arms hang limp; he stands and listens there

To something happening right now in Prague. . . .

AVROM. Why do you tease him?

REDHEAD. I'm not teasing him!

I only want to tell him that the tower

Is empty now.

GOLEM. Empty?

REDHEAD. And all the doors

And windows are now fully boarded up.

GOLEM. Then I'll just go and tear the boards all off!

REDHEAD. And somebody will board them up again.

Besides, nobody sleeps there anymore.

GOLEM. I'm heading back. I will not stay here now!

REDHEAD. Who's stopping you?

GOLEM. The rabbi's stopping me.

(*Hollers.*) Go get the rabbi! (*Bangs on the wall.*) Get the rabbi now!

What do you want here? Tell me, who are you? (*Surprised.*)

You've come from there? You boarded up the doors

And left? And the Fifth Tower is all alone?

Alone? And he who sits there, waiting for me,

Can never leave and never come to meet me?

REDHEAD. Who is it who's been waiting there for you?

GOLEM. What do you mean, who?

If I am here, then he is there alone.
And all along I've heard him calling me,
Calling me in a choking, strangling voice,
As if someone were suffocating him.
Now I know why. The doors are boarded up.
Away from me, just get away from me!
(*He hurls himself into their midst with flying fists, just as RABBI enters.*)
    RABBI. Don't raise your hand!
    GOLEM (*recoils. Senses RABBI's eyes upon him and bows his head.*
Suddenly he joyously shouts). Oh, Rabbi!
    RABBI. Against whom do you raise your hand?
    GOLEM (*stammering*). Forgive me, Rabbi.
    RABBI (*to the assembled Jews*). Enter the synagogue.
(*Jews step into the synagogue.*)
    The beadle says that you would like to see me.
(*GOLEM remains silent.*)
    Why are you silent? Speak. What do you want?
    GOLEM. What should I want?
    RABBI. You called me, didn't you?
    Your feet are bare.
    GOLEM. Rabbi, should I get dressed?
    RABBI. Get dressed?
    GOLEM. But you abandoned me.
    RABBI. So shabby, so unkempt, and unwashed too.
    The beadle says you lie awake all night.
    GOLEM. I cannot sleep. I'm scared.
    RABBI. You're scared of whom?
    GOLEM. All of last night I lay awake in dread
    Of my right shoulder.
    RABBI. Why of your right shoulder?
    GOLEM. Rabbi, I just don't know. I turned to look
    With both eyes at my left hand. All at once,
    I saw my right eye rising in the air,

And growing big, it crept to the other side.
I fell upon the ground with my face down
And hid my eyes and lay and heard somebody
Force me to see my shoulder once again.
RABBI. And after that?
GOLEM. I saw I couldn't hide.
My shoulder suddenly ripped off and turned
Into an arm that stretched up to the tower.
The fingers bent and curled around my neck
As if someone were trying to embrace me,
To kiss me, and I yelled and cried and hollered,
And then my arm stretched out to beckon to me,
And all my fingers winked and cracked and twisted,
And all of them began to weep and wail.
The moaning reached all the way to the tower.
RABBI. Yet you wanted to stay there all the same.
GOLEM. Because you wanted to be far from me.
RABBI. How do you know?
GOLEM. You don't need me anymore.
RABBI. How do you know?
GOLEM. I've carried out your missions.
RABBI. How do you know there are no further missions?
GOLEM. You never come or call me anymore.
Stay here with me.
RABBI. I *am* with you. I'm here.
GOLEM. Remain with me forever, never join them.
RABBI. Do you quite know just what your lips are saying?
GOLEM (*jumps up*). I know.
RABBI. Why are you jumping? Please stand still.
GOLEM. Why do you torture me?
RABBI. I set you free.
I told you, go wherever you desire.
GOLEM. You fettered me.

RABBI. I let you go; you stayed.
GOLEM. And where should I have gone?
You hold me tight!
RABBI. How do you know?
GOLEM. I now know everything.
Your hand lies over me, but you're not with me.
RABBI. You know, and what you know confuses you,
Bewilders you instead of pleasing you.
How should I be with you?
GOLEM. Stay here with me
Forever in this anteroom—forever.
I'll let you have my sleeping bench. I'll lie
Upon the floor, and I'll be at your feet.
RABBI. So much distress and hatred in your heart!
So much dark passion and so much cold fury
And helplessness flow in your veins! How can
It ever be your fault? No mother's breath
Did ever hover over you in childhood.
No angel's wing did ever graze your cradle. . . .
And I was sure you'd save yourself, find peace,
And start to live as everybody lives,
Just as Jews live—
GOLEM. Oh, Rabbi, Rabbi, you
Can't free yourself of any helplessness.
Nor can you transcend any obstacle,
Least of all you yourself. What does it matter
That you perceived a dim glimpse, a faint glimmer,
If everything revealed to you did not
Refine your life or calm your nervousness
Or let a smile be born upon your lips?
You ask me to desert the world, discard it,
And stay with you. Now, what if I do stay?
GOLEM. My restlessness will leave me then.

RABBI. But it's
Your fate; you fashioned it all on your own
When you first looked upon God's world. Nor did
You smile. Is it enough for you to trudge
And drag about half barefoot and half shod
While Jews are praying? Isn't that enough?
(*GOLEM stands covering his face.*)
RABBI. You're miserable, I know. But once or twice
Try going to the synagogue with all
The worshipers and try to understand.
I told you to keep still, to stand aside,
But not be alienated. And once you
Appeared among the people there, you took
So strange a stance and looked so s-so
That all those people scattered in their terror.
How everyone and everything would warm
To you if only you smiled once, just once.
(*GOLEM, stands very sad.*)
RABBI. Why hold your tongue?
GOLEM. Don't leave me, please don't leave me.
RABBI. The congregation is waiting to pray
With me. Should I just sit and wait for you?
GOLEM. Then let me go back now to the Fifth Tower.
RABBI. The tower is closed.
GOLEM. Forever?
RABBI. Yes, forever! (*He walks toward the synagogue door.*)
GOLEM. Don't leave me now, don't leave me! (*GOLEM seizes RABBI's arm.*)
RABBI. Shush! Enough!
GOLEM (*demanding*). I said, remain!
RABBI. So you're in charge?
GOLEM. I am!
RABBI. Are your lips speaking now?

GOLEM. My lips are speaking.

RABBI. Really? Your lips?

GOLEM. Yes, mine! You see this hand?

It's also mine!

(*GOLEM holds his fists menacingly over RABBI's head. RABBI doesn't flinch. His eyes pierce GOLEM, who remains poised with his fist in the air as if frozen.*)

RABBI. Why do you stand without stirring? Lower your arm.

(*He steps into the synagogue, shutting the door behind him. GOLEM collapses, throwing his arms around his head. Starts to tear his hair and his clothes. He stretches out, facedown, and looses his breath in a long moan. Hush. The prayers ushering in the Sabbath are heard through the door. The candles on the reading stand in the anteroom flicker and splutter. GOLEM gets up on all fours, crawls over to sleeping bench, and throws himself upon it. Door opens now and then; heads peer in and vanish again. GOLEM stands up, tries to put on his shoe, but his hands shake. He finds pieces of bread and takes a few bites, grimacing as he chews. He drinks some water and sprinkles it over his face.*

Suddenly he takes an ax out from under his pillow, the ax he used for chopping wood. He stands by the door, opens it gradually, and looks into the synagogue, then shuts the door. He is obviously mulling over a dreadful idea. He swings the ax very high. All at once he runs from the door to the window, shatters the pane with his ax, and jumps through the window and into the street.

The cantor's every word is now heard sharply. He starts to recite, "The song of the day of Sabbath." The worshipers follow him when suddenly shrieks of terror and the wailing of women and children are heard from the street, then the crash of shattering glass and collapsing walls. The congregation is heard stampeding toward the door of the anteroom. The door bursts open, and people flood in. No one knows what's happening. They all rush into the street.)

RABBI (*dashes in, deathly pale, claps his hands together*). He's gone! He's gone! (*He tries to run out but encounters the returning throng of* men, women, children, all wringing their hands, moaning.) What's happened?

ALL. The servant! GOLEM! With his ax!

There are two men with bloodied heads out there!

He's destroying Prague!

He's wrecking houses!

(All follow RABBI out; the doors are open, scuffles and shouting!)

TANKHEM. My head, my head! Who'll save us? Who?

(He dashes into the synagogue. The hubbub in the street draws nearer and nearer. RABBI leads GOLEM by the hands, GOLEM clutching a bloodied hand. The throng bursts in and presses toward GOLEM. Women moan. With one hand, RABBI holds back GOLEM; with other hand, RABBI shields GOLEM against throng.)

RABBI. I order all of you: Into the synagogue!

THRONG. He has shed blood!

Jewish blood!

Stone him!

RABBI. I order all of you into the synagogue!

(Throng steps inside synagogue. RABBI shuts both doors. GOLEM stands in the center of the room; the ax descends slowly as if frozen in his hand.)

RABBI. What have you done? Do you know what? Tell me!

GOLEM. I have shed blood!

RABBI. And do you know whose blood?

GOLEM. Jewish blood!

RABBI (buries his face on the reading stand, where Sabbath candles are burning).

The blood falls on my head, falls on my head!

He came to save us, yet he spilled our blood.

Oh, Lord, are we now punished for our joy?

Are we chastised for trying now to save

Ourselves? And didn't you grant your approval?

Wasn't this done for you? Why must we suffer? (Hush.)

Or did you only want to test me now?

Did you reveal to me the Superhuman?
Allow me to create, produce, command?
Only that I might finally review
My insignificance, my dreadful sin?
And more than that, my sin against all Jews?
In my despair, in my intolerance,
I wished to turn my back on all those ways
Of all your people, ways that are eternal,
Ways that are silent, patient, full of faith?
My sin in wanting what the foe lays claim to?
The enemy demanded what was his.
The blood that I desired to save I spilled! (*Pause.*)
I totally forgot about the ax.
Why stand there? Speak. You found the ax so useful.
Now let me bow my head, let it split me.
Let the ax have a taste of my blood too.

GOLEM. Rabbi.

RABBI. Quiet! Do you still say Rabbi? You Golem!

GOLEM. Rabbi.

RABBI. How grand and just, God, is your punishment.
And he—he can't even feel guilty now.
He's got two massive fists, and if he lifts them. . . .
You opened up my eyes to see that I
Totally lack all power over fists.
And now? What now?

GOLEM. Rabbi, you'll stay with me.

RABBI. Golem, the captive of your giant fists.

GOLEM. You'll stay with me.

RABBI. Inside a net of blood and unpurged madness.
And if I leave you?

GOLEM. Then I will once more—

RABBI. You've reckoned it, you've reckoned very well.

GOLEM. For yearning.

RABBI. Really? For yearning? You have taken me.
And now you hold me prisoner for all
The Jews, for all the Jews and all the world.
Without you I won't take a single step.
I'll sit and sleep here—a resourceful plan!
GOLEM (*joyfully*). You'll stay with me forever, never leave?
Why do you glare at me so furiously?
How have I harmed or hurt you? Sit down, Rabbi.
Or would you rather rest? You're very weary.
No one will come inside us here—no one!
RABBI. No one will come inside us here. And there
The worshipers are standing and are waiting.
(*RABBI sits down on bench and wearily rests his head on his arm.*
GOLEM, thankful and satisfied, stands next to him.)
GOLEM. You will not leave, Rabbi, not ever leave?
RABBI. With you, with you, I will not—will not leave.
I'll stay here. And I'll sleep here, and I'll eat here.
With one shoe on and with my face unwashed.
And there the throng will stand, and it will wait
To sing the psalm that ushers in the Sabbath.
And I won't stand before the worshipers.
GOLEM. What are you saying, Rabbi? Careful now!
You are about to fall, Rabbi. What's wrong?
RABBI. They'll weary soon of waiting, and they'll finish
Their prayers without me, and they'll head for home.
While I'll be staying here with you—just you.
The candles will soon sputter and die out.
Darkness will reign, darkness unlike the Sabbath.
What do you say, Yosl? What do you say?
GOLEM. I'm silent, Rabbi.
RABBI. Silent? I thought you spoke.
It will be dark, and we will sit together.
As we do now, you with your blood-stained ax

And I—

(*He sinks down, breaking off. A hubbub resounds from the synagogue. Someone is struggling to reach the door. It bursts open, and Deborah rushes in. Someone inside shuts the door again.*)

DEBORAH (*Weeps*). Grandfather, Grandfather!

GOLEM (*joyful*). Oh, Rabbi, look! It's Deborah!

RABBI (*barely lifting his head*). What is it, dear?

DEBORAH. I'm frightened, Grandfather. Come out from there.

Grandmother's crying, everyone is crying.

Come, tell us, Grandfather, tell us what's wrong.

GOLEM: The rabbi's staying with me. Please don't cry.

You've come here too, Deborah, you've come here too?

DEBORAH. What is he saying, Grandfather? Talk to me.

RABBI. Don't cry, my child!

GOLEM. Why don't you come to me,

Deborah? Are you afraid—afraid of me?

DEBORAH. What is he saying, Grandfather? Talk to me.

(*She throws her arms around RABBI.*)

RABBI. I'm tired and I'm resting. . . . Please don't cry. . . .

DEBORAH (*charges at GOLEM*). You murderer!

(*GOLEM grabs her arm.*)

GOLEM. Don't shout! Don't be afraid. The rabbi's resting!

Do not awaken him, and do not cry.

I will not hurt or harm you—will you stay?

DEBORAH (*struggles against GOLEM*).

Don't touch me! Get away from me! Away!

GOLEM. Don't shout! The rabbi doesn't shout at all!

And I'm delighted, I'm so overjoyed. . . . (*He moves nearer.*)

How fragrant is your hair, how sweet the scent.

How warm your hands—why do you run away?

I hold you tight, Deborah. You are mine!

You are all mine, Deborah, you've come to me!

DEBORAH. Grandfather, why are you silent? Look at him!

(*RABBI sits there, totally dejected.*)

GOLEM. Yes, you're all mine, all mine. And you are good!
Where have you been till now? Oh, Deborah!
(*Hugs her tight. Deborah's crying is stifled by the embrace.*)
RABBI (*stands up, wringing his hands*).

Is she your prisoner too? (*With greater energy.*) Yosl! You, Golem!
(*GOLEM releases DEBORAH. She flings her arms around RABBI.*)

DEBORAH. Hide me! Hide me! Take me away from here.
RABBI (*firmly*). Go tell the worshipers that I'll be coming.
DEBORAH. Come now! I'm scared!
RABBI. I did tell you to leave.

Calm down, my child. Calm down. It's time you left!
(*DEBORAH leaves, terrified.*)

GOLEM. Where is she going to? Where to? And why?
RABBI. No one must witness the fulfillment of
Your missions.
GOLEM. Missions? What missions? Haven't I performed
Your every mission, every single mission?
RABBI. The final mission—look! The candles are
All dying down. A single light, the last
Is flickering and guttering. Soon it too
Will fade. You have to hurry, Golem, hurry!
GOLEM. Where should I hurry to, where hurry to?
RABBI. Desert the darkness. The remaining moments
Are few, a very few. When everything
Is dark, the moment of your final labor
Will have worn by! I tell you, you must hurry!
GOLEM. What should I do?
RABBI. Don't ask, don't ask! All things
Are locked and sealed; all is forgiven now.
I'm rested.
GOLEM. I obey! Call me, I'll go!
RABBI. You needn't leave. You will perform the final

Mission before my eyes. Lie on the ground.

GOLEM. To press my ear and listen to the earth?

RABBI. You will hear nothing now. The earth is mute.
It rests. It is the Sabbath. You'll rest too.

GOLEM. I've rested now already. Rested well.

RABBI. You heard me! I will give you Sabbath peace.
Your whole life yearns for rest. Lie on the ground.

GOLEM (*lies down on the floor*). I'm lying, Rabbi.

RABBI. Stretch out your legs.

GOLEM. I *have* stretched out my legs.

RABBI. Stretch out your arms!

GOLEM (*sits up, trembling*).
What will you do to me?

RABBI. Don't ask!

GOLEM (*stretches his arms to RABBI, pleading*).
Do not command me to lie down.
What will you do to me?

RABBI. There's no reply!
Stretch out, stretch out again—a second time!

GOLEM. I'm stretched full length, Rabbi. I'm stretched full
length.
You will not leave me, will you?

RABBI. Shut your eyes.

GOLEM. They are already shut, Rabbi, already!
You'll stay with me forever, won't you, Rabbi?

RABBI. I issue you this decree: Let arms and legs
And let the head and flesh and limbs and sinews
Return to their last rest, their final peace—
Breathe out, breathe out your final breath. Amen!

(*GOLEM is motionless. The flickering candle dies out. RABBI stands over
dead GOLEM for a long time. Finally RABBI stirs. He goes over to synagogue door, opens it, and calls in.*)

RABBI. Go get the beadle.

(AVROM comes to the door.)

RABBI *(to AVROM).*

No one's to enter here till after Sabbath.

And now call everyone to sing and croon

Again the psalm—the psalm of Sabbath praise. *(RABBI leaves, shutting the door firmly.)*

Alternate Ending.

INVISIBLE FORCE.

Now the Fifth Tower is open once again. . . .

Perhaps because this is the final moment

All locks are opening and calling, "Come!"

I'm calling now. I would call anyhow,

Even if all the locks were locked so tight.

(Bends over the dead GOLEM.)

Meanwhile my life is pouring, pouring through me,

Pouring me through that solitary moment,

Grateful now for that salvaged moment here,

For now that moment melts. . . .

(Collapses on the dead GOLEM.)

New York, 1917–1920